GG

483
331
24
22
580 382 280 22 Co S rky 18₅ 18₅ Rep (1988) 16₅ 20 258 33
Co S
459 29₅ 18₅ Northeast Rock 7₅ 7₅ East Brother 9 rky
PA 18₅ (4) Obstr (2) rky 14₅
Great Issac Rep (1977) 9
11 (12) PA West Brother 7₅ 18₅
649 534 225 11 8 16₅ PA 7₅ 7₅ 7₅ 5 rky
600 216 13 (PA) Hen and Chickens 10 Little Issac
467 5 Obstr Rep (1978) 8 (2) 5
618 487 20 3₅ 5 8 7980 W + 10 D Middle Issac
12 13 8 7980 W + 17 N East Issac
609 512 190 Eldorado Shoal Cr S 8 7₅ 7980 X + 14 D GS −39.8 (3) Awas
675 29₅ 9 5 6 7₅ 7980 X + 23 N GS −56 N
Moselle Bank (4) North Rock (2) 6 6 6₅ 6₅
507 16₅ Fl 3s 12m 8M. 1 Wk GREAT 5
697 14₅ (2) 6 6₅
659 200 North Bimini 3₅ (2) 5
BIMINI ISLANDS 227 F 6m 5M AERO Mo (B) R 20s 86m 23M 6₅ Co S
748 R Bn 3 4₅
212 South Bimini 2 Cr Co S
681 Turtle Rocks (5) 18₅
Barnett Harbor Bn Picquet Rock Larks Two Fathoms Bridge
810 22 (4) Holm Cay (3) 13 (With numerous patches of 3 meters)
Gun Cay (8)
670 Fl 10s 24m 23M North
856 Fl 2s 3m 5M Cat Cay (19)
807 13 South
Rabbit Rock Cat Cay (10) Sylvia Beacon
Wedge Rock Fl 5s 10m 8M Less Wat
845 673 Co S Victory Cays (4) 3₅
Sand bores
Ocean Cay 4₅ 3
845 712 (4) Wd
Browns Cay E L B
860 (4)
Browns Channel Beach Cay B A N
776 (4)
712 Low Rock
845 37 Barren Rocks (3)
829 Square Rock
862 858 783 Riding Rocks (4) (bushes) 4₅
South Riding Castle Rock

TO THE ABACO

TO ELEUTHERA ISLAND

NORTHEAST

BERRY ISLANDS

Slaughter Harbor
Great Stirrup Cay
Little Stirrup Cay
Great Harbour
Great Harbour Cay
Lignum Vitae Cay
Cistern Cay
(26)
Bullocks Harbor
Petit Cay
Hawks Nest
Hines Bluff
Hines Cay
Bamboo Cay
Anderson Cay
Abner Cay
Market Fish Cays
Ambergris Cays
Hoffman Cay
Devils Cay
Sand bores
Little Harbour Cay
Comfort Cay
High Cay
Alder Cay
Sand bores uncovering at Low Water
Sand bores
PA
Rocky heads
Cormorant Cays
Samphire Cays
Bonds Cay
Fish Cays
Sisters Rocks
Cockroach Cay
Little Whale Cay
Blackwood Bush
Green Bush
Bushes
Rum Cay
Sand bores
South Stirrup Cay
Crab Cay
Frazers Hog Cay
Cat Cay
Whale Cay
Airstrip
Bird Cay
Chub Point
Whale Point
Uncovers at Water Springs
Mangrove swamp covers at high tide
Joulters Cays
Sheep Cay
Long Cay
Golding Cays
Money Point
Lowe Sound
CHANNEL
WHITE
RED
VAR 3°41'W(1980) VAR

THE TEN KINGS OF THE SEA
THE SALVAGE OF SANTA ISABELLA'S TREASURE

JACQUES
MAYOL

PIERRE
MAYOL

THE TEN KINGS OF THE SEA
THE SALVAGE OF SANTA ISABELLA'S TREASURE

English translation by
CARLA SHERMAN

IDELSON-GNOCCHI

THE TEN KINGS OF THE SEA

by Jacques Mayol and Pierre Mayol

Requests for permission to make copies of any part of the work should be mailed to:
Permission Department
Idelson-Gnocchi Publishers Ltd.,
12255 N.W. Hwy 225-A, Reddick, FL. 32686 USA.
www.idelson-gnocchi.com
www.thejacquesmayol.com

This is a translation of LES DIX ROIS DE LA MER revised and updated by the author.

Library of Congress Cataloging-in-Publication Data
[The Ten Kings of the Sea – The Salvage of Santa Isabella 's Treasure]
Translated from the French by Carla Sherman
ISBN 1-928649246

Edited by Michael Lawrence, a highly regarded marine photojournalist and author of several dive publications. Michael has written and illustrated well over 400 articles for many dive international publications. He is also author of several books on diving.

Jacques Mayol — writer, world-famous diver, and holder of a dozen world records, he was acclaimed for his pioneering work in the field of deep breath hold diving. He was the first man to dive 100 meters (330 feet) in 1976.

A Frenchman born in China in 1927, Jacques Mayol spent most of his life in Italy, in the West Indies on the island of South Caicos, and in Japan. He died in Italy on December 2001.

He pursued his life-long passion for diving and being one with nature and the sea. He also collaborated in the writing and production of many documentary films. He improved his physical performance with yoga and he also had an intimate knowledge of Oriental Philosophies.

Jacques Mayol's life was the subject of Luc Besson's film *The Big Blue* (*Le Grand Bleu*). In that film, actor Jean-Marc Barr's character was based on Jacques.

His most recent book in English "*Homo Delphinus, The Dolphin Within Man*" is considered to be the Bible for all breath-hold divers.

Pierre Mayol, Jacques' older brother, was born on April 22, 1924. Both were Frenchmen born in Shanghai, China. After moving to Marseille, France, they pursued their interest, and acquired complete proficiency of underwater techniques.

During World War II, Pierre joined the 7th US army in July 1944 as an interpreter with a Bomb Disposal Squad.

In 1948, Pierre and Jacques went to Scandinavia, and they traveled together in Norway, Sweden and Finland. The two brothers emigrated to Canada together in 1950. In 1952, Pierre moved back to Europe and Jacques went to live in the United States.

Pierre studied philosophy, logics, metaphysics, and specialized in what is called "proto-history". In France he published many articles in marine magazines. Among his published books are *Les Dix Rois de la Mer*, *Le Grand Doute* and *Les Hommes de Pierre*.

Today Pierre is retired and continues to write books.

Carla Sherman is an independent literary translator, residing in Ojai, California. Mrs. Sherman obtained a Master of Arts Degree in Romance Languages and a Bachelor of Arts Degree in French & Portuguese, both from UFRJ, Brazil. She taught French Literature at UERJ, Brazil. She is an Active Member of the American Translators Association.

Since January 2002, Mrs. Sherman is editor-in-chief at SilentHeart Press, the publishing arm of The River Ganga Foundation, a 501(c)(3) non-profit spiritual organization with offices in Ojai.

She is married to John Sherman, an American spiritual teacher in the lineage of Ramana Maharshi, Poonjaji and Gangaji.

Wyland, the world's premier undersea artist. In 1998 Wyland was proclaimed by the United Nations the official artist for the "International Year of the Ocean" and issued a commemorative stamp in his honor. Today his art is found in museums, galleries, public walls and in many public and private collections throughout the world.

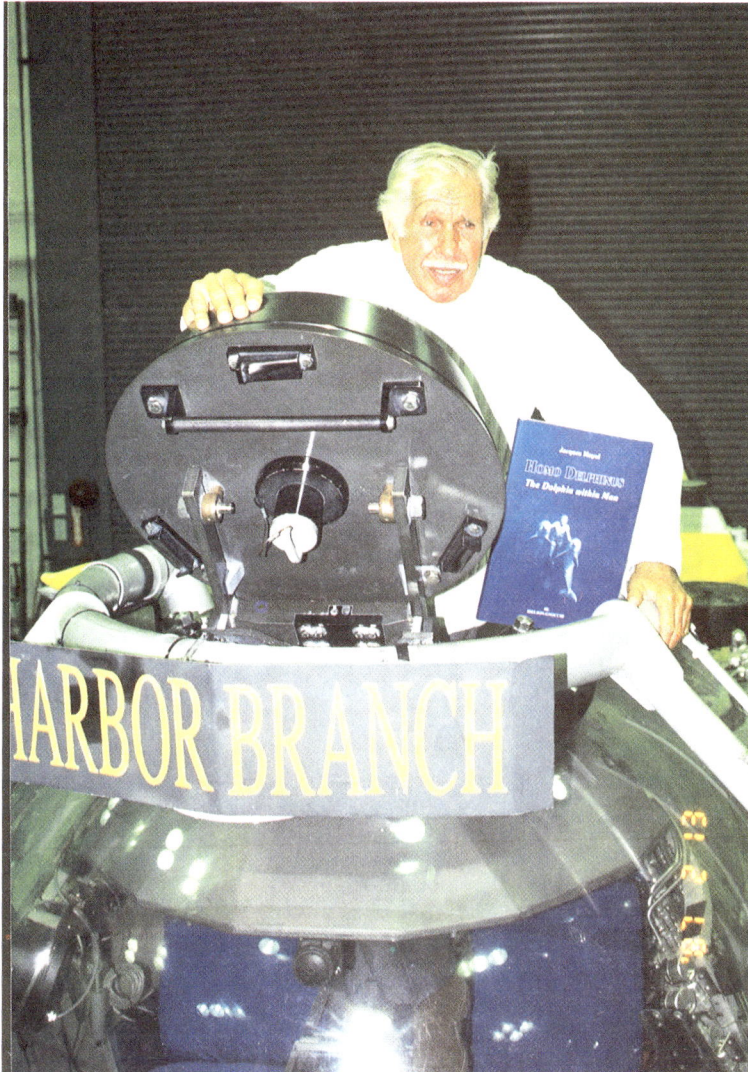

In memory of Jacques Mayol, father of the concept of *Homo-Delphinus* and author of the book which is considered to be the Bible for divers. He who was the first man to dive to 330 feet holding his breath as dolphins do; and opened the doors to a new generation of free divers to new depths.

Special thanks to Wyland and to his collaborators, Julie Edwards and Gino Beltran from Wyland Creative Development.

Also special thanks to Carla Sherman, to Steve McCulloch the Division Director Dolphin Research and Conservation Program Harbor Branch Oceanographic Institution[*], to Pierre Mayol and finally to Dr. Guido Gnocchi, owner of Idelson Gnocchi Publishers Ltd.

MAURIZIO CANDOTTI RUSSO
Editor-in-Chief

[*] HARBOR BRANCH Oceanographic Institution, Inc., is one of the world's leading non profit oceanographic research organization dedicated to exploration of the earth's oceans, estuaries and coastal regions for the benefit of humankind.

PROLOGUE

The Ten Kings of the Sea is a fictional story but it is based on the experiences and underwater discoveries that Jacques and Pierre Mayol both shared together. The book was a success in Italy, France, and recently in Japan. The interest in Atlantis is not recent. While Jacques Cousteau was searching unsuccessfully in the Pacific, Jacques and Pierre were looking in the Atlantic and they made interesting discoveries along the reef of Bimini in the Bahama Islands. Jacques found a shipwreck in the Turks & Caicos Island, and that became part of the book.

In this novel, Pierre and Jacques have attempted to open a new window into the mystery of the sea, and to the mythological links between man and the sea that have always intrigued us. More and more men and women are becoming interested in Atlantis and in the "aquatic prowess".

"The real world and the world revealed by our senses are not different things, but different aspects of the same thing."

(A Zen thought)

FOREWORD

This account of adventures is not entirely the fruit of our imagination. It's based on certain real events, and it takes place in existent geographical sites, and brings back to life characters that we have met and known. As for me, I relocated to Miami in 1956, and a few years later I became friends with Professor Manson Valentine. This friendship endured to his death. Professor Manson Valentine, from the Miami Museum of Science, was a biologist, paleontologist, zoologist and a Mayan and pre-Mayan culture specialist who aroused my curiosity about the vestiges of what he called "a pre-cataclysmic civilization" in the region of the Bahamas, the Turks & Caicos Islands, where I now live, and throughout the Caribbean.

The worldwide media has spoken, often skeptically, of his innumerable discoveries, so many adventures in which I took part. Their true origins remain unknown and my dear Manson, who is gone now, refused to connect them with the mythical Atlantis.

Nevertheless, he continued to dream about it, as we and so many other divers do. It was thinking of him and of all the dreamers that my brother and I wrote this book.

It's our wish that you will find in it a certain resonance of the Big Blue…

This world has always belonged and will always belong to the true dreamers. We dedicate *The Ten Kings of the Sea* to Manson Valentine and all those who, like him, have the courage to see beyond the 'established things'.

Jacques Mayol
Belle Sound
South Caicos
West Indies

When my brother Jacques informed me about the extraordinary discoveries they had made, together with Professor Manson Valentine, of submarine vestiges in the Bimini island area, concerning what could be called a pre-cataclysmic civilization, I immediately linked them with my own years of researches about the true western-Atlantic origin — and in no case eastern or African — of mankind, scientifically known as "homo sapiens sapiens".

In order to develop these facts for a greater number of readers and to interest them in a pleasant and un-dogmatic way, my brother and I decided to write a novel under a more or less fiction form, but based on facts using the Greek philosopher Plato's astonishing description 2600 years ago in the *Timaeus* of the Atlantic ocean, the island of Atlantis, the Caribbean islands and the existence of the American continent!

One of the heroes comes directly out of the Greek mythology, but, let us dream a little, couldn't it be that demigods really existed?

We wish to dedicate the *Ten Kings of the Sea*, as Jacques says, to all those that have the courage to see beyond the "established things".

PIERRE MAYOL
La Bouilladisse Provence
France

"Many and great wonderful are the deeds recorded of your city that are written in our histories and that strike people with wonder. But one of them exceeds all the rest in greatness and valor.

For these histories tell of how great a power your city once stopped, which, in its insolence, was advancing against all of Europe together with Asia, having set out from somewhere far out in the Atlantic Ocean. For at that time the Atlantic could be crossed, since there was an island situated in front of the straits which are by you called the Pillars of Hercules. The island was larger than Libya and Asia put together, and from it there was access to the other islands for those traveling at that time, and from these to the entire opposing continent that surrounds that true ocean.

For this sea which is within the Straits of Hercules is only a harbor, having a narrow entrance, while that other is genuinely a real ocean, and the land surrounding it may be in perfect truth called a continent. Now on this very island of Atlantis there was gathered a great and wondrous power of Kings, which mastered the entire island and several others, and even parts of the continent; and, in addition to these, the men of Atlantis further ruled over the lands of Libya as far as Egypt, and of Europe as far as the Tyrrhenian."*

From Timaeus (24E, 25B) - by Plato c. 427-347 BC

PART ONE
Marseilles, January 21, 1943

CHAPTER 1

"Here we are."

Kurt stopped the other two with a gesture.

They remained motionless for a timeless moment in the night.

It had been a very long day for the young and ambitious Kriegs-marine Korvettenkapitän, Kurt Müller.

During all that afternoon, in the dilapidated quarters of the Old Port, he had felt the hostility that his presence and, most of all, that of his two companions members of the S.D.* had awakened in their passage. In spite of their civilian clothes, the officer and his two bodyguards had not passed unnoticed in the maze of old streets, sometimes swarming, sometimes deserted.

Kurt now became aware that their attempt to integrate into that colorfully dressed crowd had been nothing but a failure. The long gray leather overcoats of his escorts and his own blue Marine raincoat, although lacking insignia, his blond crew-cut hair and the all too characteristic bearing of the other two had betrayed them.

With their turned-up collars and the soft brims of their hats turned down, they waited in the night in front of the car, parking lights off, facing the sea. Then Kurt, the only one who did not wear a hat, led the way. They crossed the Quay and by way of Martegales Street, passed through the first curtain of houses, towards Lenche Square and the Accoules.

There they should find their goal, which they had partially located during the day. They slowed down, quite imperceptibly.

A little bit higher in front of them, stairs cut through the narrow alley, the round-edged steps worn down over the centuries by the many feet that had trod upon them. In the subdued center of the stairs,

---

* S.D.: Sicherheitsdienst: German Security Police (Intelligence Service)

a thin trickle of water oozed following the slope. A cold and humid draft blew down from the top of the hill bringing noises to their expert ears, sounds other than the murmur of the night.

It was a war night, sad and dead.

In the silence, the water rustled. Dirty as it was, it still mirrored in the darkness. The creaking of a flapping shutter made them look up.

Sheets, freshly laundered shirts and pants hung across the street, waving in the darkness. There was no light behind the closed shutters. The inhabitants of that neighborhood, so turbulent during the day, must be afraid of curfew penalties. Or maybe it was simply boredom and wartime deprivations that made them go to bed early.

Silently, they walked towards a gate located a little higher on their left. A finely worked cornice surmounted the dark opening. A big crown was flanked by two dolphins. In the center, a barbed and crowned god with a fish tail and armed with a trident seemed to triumph. "Poseidon," whispered Kurt. "Poseidon."

This was much more than a simple coincidence. Pensive, he stopped. "What are we waiting for?" One of the guards was becoming impatient.

A thought crossed the mind of the young officer. He had more ties in common with those who must have lived here once than with his two companions.

"Nothing. Let's go."

They entered the passage carefully.

The rough walls were whitewashed and they sensed their pale contours in the dark. Sometimes, the dilapidated floor tiles cracked under their feet, the sound immobilizing them instantly. They came out into a backyard, opening directly towards the sky. In the diffuse light, the old house seemed to want to crush them with its weight. They were gripped by a strong saline smell. Dark patches of potbellied nets and ropes coiled up in piles stood out in the half-light. In a corner, the arms of a cart stood up like the two antennas of some night creature.

Kurt's attention was suddenly attracted by a metallic reflection. He stood still, and was imitated by the other two. Hanging on a portico, on top of a rubber diving suit with dangling arms and legs, a copper and brass diving helmet reflected a faint ray of light that came in through the shutter of a window in the entresol. The man was there, that's for sure. They started climbing the stairs, cautiously placing their feet on the timeworn, irregular steps.

***

The officer's head was buzzing with images. It would soon be two years since May 1941. In successive waves, the tri-motor Junkers of the Luftwaffe released over Crete a swarm of paratroopers in the first airborne invasion in History. At the same time, Kurt disembarked from a submarine somewhere on the shore of the island. As the leader of an elite commando team, his precise mission was to contact and coerce a local sponge fisherman, a man whose importance did not seem so evident to him at the time.

It was a very beautiful spring morning and the contrast between the weeks of confinement in the narrow steel spindle-shaped vessel and the purity and luminosity of the sky had impressed the young submarine war specialist. The first ochre and golden streaks of the sun illuminated the steep cliffs of the shore, which the two inflatable rafts reached without difficulty. A tiny fishing port snuggled up deep inside a little inlet. The ancient palace of Knossos must be located right above, on the cliffs.

Kurt was wondering if there was a relationship between this and their goal. He could not find out at that time.

When the commando bolted into the house where their 'prey' should be sleeping, they found no person there. Standing in front of the whitewashed walls that shone in the first rays of the sun and the heavy open overseas blue door with almost transparent reflections, he felt a bit frustrated.

It was evident that in spite of the strict surveillance, the man had escaped.

***

Luckily, things would not be the same this time. For months, Kurt had woven his net patiently, thanks to countless pieces of information, sometimes quite incredible. This man with a disconcerting reputation could not escape him anymore.

In the huge silence, the three men stood still on the stone landing. Kurt lit a powerful torch and directed the beam to the door. The door was also painted with this curious overseas blue, which under the intense lighting acquired the dark and moving transparency of the ocean.

Intrigued, Kurt moved the circle of light on its surface and stopped over a business card pinned to the door.

GIORGIOS MARKANTAKIS
Deep-sea diver

He hesitated for a moment. Then, with a sharp movement, he lowered the latch. The door was not locked. When he pushed down the latch, the door opened completely and the officer rushed into the room, his Luger in his hand. The other two men followed him.

Behind the long table that served as his desk, a man got up. Books, documents and rolls of navigation maps were piled up hodgepodge on the table.

"Don't move," shouted the officer in Greek. "We don't want to harm you."

"I have been waiting for you for a long time, Kapitän Müller. Your visit is not a surprise for me." The fisherman answered in German.

They looked into each other's eyes and Kurt felt an unpleasant sensation. He had just called him by his name. In this game of cat and mouse, he was not sure that he was playing the role of the cat anymore. The presence of the two bodyguards helped him overcome this first moment of confusion.

Kurt observed the man closely. He was big and powerful. An intense sense of restrained vitality emanated from him. His face had regular features hardened by two deep groves in his cheeks. It was surrounded by an untidy red beard. Thick and curly hair covered the high forehead; his cold light-colored eyes, overhung by deep eyebrows watched closely.

The blue and white striped knitted fabric, the disparate objects from the ocean depths spread out in a jumble on the table or scattered around, all evoked in Kurt the image of a Neptune who had escaped from his underwater kingdom.

Responding to a gesture from the officer, the two guards holstered their guns and positioned themselves each to one side of the door.

"Are you Giorgios Markantakis, deep-sea diver by profession?"

Met with silence, he added curtly, "I'm sorry, but you are my prisoner."

"Prisoner! This is a very big word. In reality, my dear Müller, the elements that have determined our encounter escape you. Besides, we either talk freely or it's useless to go any further."

Slightly disconcerted, the German saw his mistake.

"Don't be mistaken about my intentions. Don't forget that Germany is at war and I am forced to take some precautions."

Still and quiet, the man stared at him.

For Kurt, the matter seemed now to be much more complex than he had anticipated. In the beginning, all the measures surrounding his mission had seemed excessive. It was, after all, just the capture of a simple sponge fisherman. Later on, at the Central Command, in the face of his precise instructions, he had to admit to the importance of the mission. During the time of his investigation, while he was tracking the man, amazement and skepticism alternated in his mind. In that moment, still in a confused way, he could sense that this man represented much more than the simple business card pinned to his door indicated. That day spent last summer at the Obersalzberg came back to his mind now, and it all became more understandable.

In the company of the guests of the day, he had climbed the wide stairs that led to the entrance, under the arcades of the Berghof, the villa that the Führer of the Third Reich had built in the Bavarian Alps.

While he waited, he admired the varnished paneling of the ceiling in the big hall. Then, the secretary came to get him — a man with a round, cunning face and a stocky silhouette.

The Führer was standing next to a big world map globe, accompanied by a high dignitary of the Wehrmacht, who stepped aside in order to leave the two men alone. Behind the panes of the immense picture window, the eternal snow of the Untersberg displayed its immaculate splendor.

"I'm not going to need you, Martin."

The man's look, bourgeois and commonplace, had surprised the strict Marine officer that he was. His singing Austrian accent had even sounded vulgar to his Northern German ears. Only the gray and piercing look gave up the ferocity of his personality.

The brief conversation was forever etched in his memory.

"My dear Müller... I hear many great things about you... brilliant, efficient and athletic. These are three qualities that are rarely found in the same individual. I love men like you. It's these men who, reversing the decadent course of History, will forge our Great Reich. You have a role to play, and it might well reveal itself to be essential in this implacable fight that we find ourselves in. I have chosen you as an underwater world specialist. The Oberkommando of the Kriegsmarine has informed you about what they expect from you. Nevertheless, in many aspects, your mission will seem strange. But I count exactly on your power of reasoning, power described to me as being exceptional, to bring to a practical reality the facts and the information that may seem to pertain to the realm of dreams. Regarding all that seems to go beyond the scope of this war mission, I want you to speak only and directly with me — your Führer."

Suddenly, without further ado, he turned towards his secretary, who was coming back accompanied by another guest.

***

From the change in Markantakis' attitude, Kurt felt that the man was going to start speaking. Psychologically, he would gain a first point over his adversary. But his task was complex. It would be necessary to convince this giant to give him the whole set of unbelievable information — information to which he alone held the key — the existence of a range of giant underwater caves under the continental plateau of the Bahamas. Completely invisible from the surface, they would be converted into operational bases for the pack of Kriegsmarine U-Boats, in the heart of the economic and financial system of the United States. These caves would represent a terrible weapon, a decisive asset in this merciless combat that would lead them to victory.

CHAPTER 2

"Kapitän Müller, even if you cannot for the moment see the connection, I agreed to meet with you because you are originally from
Heligoland."

The officer was visibly affected. This simple sponge fisherman was
in fact very well informed. Too much so.

Again he experienced the same sense of insecurity and he turned to
his two bodyguards. Their impassive presence reassured him. "I see," he
spoke with feigned indifference. "We are both island people. This should
make our dialogue easier. I have noticed that those who are born on
islands, whatever their latitude, have many things in common."

"It's true, but this is not what I meant." The Cretan man smiled.

He deliberately turned his back on the German men. He walked
toward the breadbox hanging on the wall. He picked up two glasses
and a bottle covered with plaited raffia.

"What about some rum? It's true rum. It comes directly from
Jamaica."

"From Jamaica? You're not going to convince me that you have direct
connections with the Caribbean. Right now, in the middle of the war."

"Believe what you will." He raised his glass.

"In these grayish times, a little of the warmth of the tropical sun
that you know so well will do us good."

In order to gain some time to pull himself together, Kurt took off
his raincoat. In spite of all his precautions, this strange fisherman was
fully informed about him. He took the glass and smelled the aroma,
sweet and strong at the same time.

"It's true," he finally spoke. "I navigated the Caribbean and the
Antilles on a small oceanographic research boat for four years, before
the war started. I know every corner of the area between Trinidad and
the Bahamas... the good places too."

He gave a hint of a smile.

The Cretan man put down his glass and stared at the German.

"The Peter Kreuter II," he said, after a moment. "I know. Our paths have crossed more than once."

Kurt pretended to be focused on his rum. He was trying to understand. He had to understand. There seemed to be nothing from his past that this man didn't know. In the Caribbean, he had accomplished a secret mission under an assumed name. Troubled, he could only respond:

"You too easily resort to mystery, Mr. Markantakis."

"Mystery exists only for those who don't have the answer."

With a sudden movement, he picked up the bottle and filled both glasses to the brim.

"Come on, relax. Tonight there won't be any more mysteries. Let's drink; let's drink to the good old times of buccaneering and the Brotherhood of the Coast. I was a different man at that time... Believe me, Kapitän Müller."

Kurt was astonished. He examined the Cretan man's light-colored eyes, looking for some sign of craziness but there was nothing in this man that gave any hint of mental disorder. He was very likely just trying to throw him off balance with these absurd remarks. He should let him come closer, to win his trust.

The Cretan man bore his scrutiny with patience. Very relaxed at the other side of the table, he mastered the situation with his huge size. His hands leafed through an atlas lying flat on the table. Kurt guessed immediately that the giant was preparing another maneuver to confuse him even further. He was not mistaken. Markantakis stopped suddenly and, with a pompous gesture, he pointed to the chosen page with his index finger.

"It was here," he said, "12,000 years ago, in the beginning of the Age of the Lion, in the middle of the Bronze Age, that an immense kingdom that you call by the name of Atlantis disappeared under the surface of the ocean."

The conviction with which he pronounced these words did not fail to produce in Kurt the desired effect.

The Cretan man laughed again, triumphantly. His thick beard surrounded the white teeth.

"I see, Müller, that all this seems fantastic to you. Nevertheless, all that I have just told you is based on tangible evidence. You can verify this whenever you like". He stopped for a moment. "But at your own risk."

Kurt noted the threat, although couldn't know what was being threatened.

"Excuse me. I don't really see what you're trying to get at," he said. "I've read Plato, like everybody else, and I'm ready to admit that he gave an amazing description of Atlantis, of the archipelagos and even of the American continent. And he did all that 2,000 years before Christopher Columbus. But the rest is nothing but wild imaginings, or if you prefer, the work of a philosopher and poet. Which are the same for me."

"You seem to appreciate neither philosophers nor poets."

"No. Especially when they try to turn into reality something that is nothing but fiction."

"Ah! Müller, Müller…" The Cretan man sighed deeply, shrugging his powerful shoulders. "You men of today, with all your rationalism, you are nothing but kids. Too bad for you if you cannot read between the lines."

He swallowed his rum in one gulp. Suddenly, with a strong, almost aggressive voice, he started on a curious narrative. Legends and historical facts were tightly mingled in it. But he spoke of them as if he himself had lived them all. At least that's how it seemed to the young officer. Kurt was being quietly conquered by this powerfully convincing flow of words. He finally shook himself out of his torpor and came awake with difficulty. His eyes wandered around the room. How much time had passed? In the dim light, he noticed for the first time, hanging on the walls, different weapons from various times and places. What they all had in common were signs of having spent long periods underwater. In a corner, three amphorae, covered with marine concretions, stood up on their pointed bottoms. A little bit further along, there were two huge rounded vases decorated with marine animals. 'Those are priceless Minoan pithos, if they're authentic,' he thought.

In Kurt's eyes, the room seemed to be a personal sanctuary. In any case, this accumulation of art objects and antiques salvaged from the sea, contributed to create a disturbing atmosphere around this man who certainly couldn't be a simple sponge fisherman.

A voice marked by irony brought him back from his thoughts.

"I have a feeling that you are dreaming."

"I'm afraid I must have lost the habit of the Caribbean and their rum."

Kurt had answered with a certain humor, but he was not happy at having been surprised like that.

"All you have to do is get in the habit again."

"Oh, yes! And what for?"

Instead of responding, the Cretan man came out from behind the table.

"You seem interested in my little museum, if I may call it so."

Kurt got up in order to follow him. He came closer to the big vases. He caressed the round and smooth side of one of them. It was magnificently decorated with an ochre octopus. The tentacles seemed almost to be really moving.

"Minos, second period. The Cretan art was at its peak," murmured the officer.

"I'm going to surprise you." The Cretan man was amused. "This is at least six thousand years older."

"This is impossible! The octopus, the inverse double spiral motif... They are characteristic..."

"Yes, evidently. The symbolism is the same. It has its roots in the dawn of time. This is one of the distinctive features of this kingdom of the sea, and Crete was just its last distant offspring."

Kurt shook his head in silence. This myth was reappearing a second time. This was absurd. He would not be fooled by this little game.

"It's certainly an extremely valuable object," he said finally, looking for the other man's eye. "Like everything else in here. How have you been able to recover such vast treasures?"

The big Cretan man laughed.

"Oh, this is not very much. I am... a collector. A little special, I have to admit. Besides, you would not understand. In any case, all this is only temporary."

"Temporary?"

He evaded the question with a movement of his hand.

"This is one of my passions. One of my functions too. It's the justification of my existence in a certain way. Salvaging is my business."

"Salvaging? On whose behalf?"

"My own... Why not? The ocean is my domain and I believe that everything I find belongs to me."

He moved away and bent down. Standing back up, the muscles of his arms tightened, he showed Kurt a heavy round shield. The polished metal reflected the light, highlighting the concentric circles that decorated it.

"Tell me, Kapitän Müller, according to you, this object belongs to what period?"

"In my opinion, it's similar in every aspect to those that were used in Europe during the Bronze Age... I would say Hallstatt."

"Bravo! Perfectly correct. I found this shield with these swords that you can see here, in the delta of the Nile. I did a series of dives there in the thirties. In the exact place where, 1,200 years before Christ, a gigantic naval combat between the Peoples of the Sea and the fleet of Pharaoh Ramses III took place."

The two men were sitting down again.

While he spoke, the Cretan man leaned back and laid his long legs on the table. Kurt was surprised by this gesture that could only be made by an American or by a man who had spent a great part of his life among Americans.

"Whether Classical History likes it or not, Kapitän Müller, your ancestors had been established in Northern Europe for millennia, on the islands off the present Frisian territory." He crossed his hands and, cracking the knuckles of his huge fingers with a sharp noise, he put them behind the nape of his neck. Swinging his chair on its back feet, he stretched his whole body.

"The islands were vast, because the level of the Northern Sea was way under what it is nowadays. From that land, they controlled an immense maritime empire... Southern Scandinavia, the Baltic Sea, the Northern Sea, all the Atlantic shore and part of the Maghreb. Protected by the immense forest that covered all of Western Europe, they formed a separate world. A thalassocracy proudly and completely turned toward the sea. Lost in their northern territory, saturated with a legendary reputation, feared for their warrior power and their science of metals, they lived like sea divinities, separated from other peoples that they despised.

"They considered themselves the distant descendants of the powerful kingdom of Poseidon, swallowed forever under the waves."

Kurt was perplexed. He stared at the big Cretan man's face. He seemed gloomy and serious. What was he really trying to get at? This was the third time he made a direct remark about this myth, about which the young officer had heard much speculation in the salons of Berlin. They always described the myth in the haziest manner.

"Suddenly, towards the end of the 13th century B.C., some signs announcing a cataclysm would force this people to break their isolation and throw themselves into the southern islands. It was a fantastic and cruel epic, Kapitän Müller, of such dimension that humanity had never known before and will never know again. Under the command of the Ten Kings of the Sea, the coalition united the distant descendants of the people of Atlantis. Defying their fate like their ancestors had done before them, they started their march towards the coveted regions.

"Preceding the long columns of two-wheel carts carrying women, children and the elderly, a gigantic invasion force would surge into the Mediterranean shores, by land and by sea. While the main body of the forces penetrated directly through the Elbe and the Danube, across the continent, the rest took over the opulent and powerful civilizations of the Mediterranean basin from the rear, with the implacable movement of a pincer.

"In Greece, in spite of their colossal fortification, the proud cities collapsed one after the other. In the crash of the weapons, the clashing of the long swords, the muffled noise of the clashing shields, Mikonos, Troy and Tyre disappeared forever, drowned in this tide that had come from hell. Crete itself, the rich city, with its sumptuous palaces, would be razed by fire and iron."

Intrigued by this original reconstitution of historical facts perfectly known by him, Kurt did not stop looking into the other man's eyes. For a moment, he had the voice inflexions and the gestures of a Chief of Staff commenting on the tough campaign he had just taken part in.

"In the Mediterranean, the Balearics, Malta, Corsica, Sardinia, Sicily, all the islands were conquered and ravaged by those invaders who came from the sea. During that period, in the East, the second prong of the pincer separated itself, penetrating into Asia Minor.

"Under the blows struck by the Peoples of the Sea, the powerful Hittite Empire collapsed in its turn, definitively scratched out of History. The route to Egypt was finally open. In 1,200 B.C., the final assault was launched. Through Western Libya, a coalition army advanced towards the Delta. The Egyptians, who were accustomed to desert war, would smash it to pieces. In the East, where the borders of Syria are located nowadays, Ramses III himself destroyed the greatest part of the forces of the Peoples of the Sea. But it was on the water that the disaster was the most humiliating. The Ten Kings of the Sea decided to make their final assault toward the Delta of the Nile.

"A fleet too huge to be counted advanced to spread death and destruction in the heart of the Empire of the Pharaohs. Everything had been anticipated, except the absolute lack of wind. The big sailing boats — the ancestors of the Viking longships — were attacked by the Egyptian galleys."

The Cretan man took his long legs off the table and got up in all his height. He took the shield in his hands again and resumed his narrative.

"Regardless of freeboards protected by shields like this one, the very thin arrows shot by expert archers hit their mark. It was a slaughter. By the thousands, the men perished. One by one, the boats were capsized and the survivors drowned. Thus finished in disaster the great adventure of the Peoples of the Sea. Under the command of their Ten Kings, they returned to the place they had come from in the dawn of time, the depths of immense underwater caves in the western part of the Atlantic."

CHAPTER 3

A grenade exploding suddenly in the room would not have had a more powerful effect on the German officer.

Since the beginning, the ambiguity of the Cretan man's words had masked their real importance. Throughout that fantastic and sometimes absurd narrative, what Kurt was looking for was finally surfacing. For the first time, the caves, which were the goal of his mission, were finally in sight.

But he must be careful. He must keep all his lucidity so as not to fall into the trap of hasty conclusions. The confidence with which the man spoke, and his erudition, were the essential elements he should take into account. If he was not a mythomaniac, the existence of those caves had all chances of being real, and he knew the site well. The difficulty would be to separate what was true from what was nothing but pure fiction.

His orders were very simple. He should negotiate, whatever the method or the price. Kurt decided that the moment had come to throw his cards on the table.

"Personally, it's hard for me to follow you. All this seems to pertain to a fantastic realm."

"It's possible." The eyes of the Cretan watched him closely from behind the deep arches of his eyebrows. "And I understand very well that the existence of a universe of gigantic caves in the Caribbean might seem hardly credible to you."

"Not really. I've always suspected they existed. Don't forget the four years I spent aboard the Peter Kreuter II. It's the rest of the story that bothers me, Mr. Markantakis."

"What rest? The History lesson that I've just given you? All that I have just revealed to you is true. I simply wanted to highlight the irreducible opposition that exists between the peoples of the land and the children of the sea, like you and me. It's precisely those peoples of the land that are responsible for this silent conspiracy about the reality of this kingdom of the sea. Look: heaven has never existed elsewhere but on the islands! Even nowadays, scattered on the surface of the oceans, the vast majority of them still reflect remnants of the balance maintained by the presence of the sea. Look at what happened to my dear Crete. The continental Mikonos took hold of an island worn out by earthquakes and the superb cities of Knossos, Haghia Triada and all the others saw their palaces transformed into barbarian fortresses and the low walls of their paradisiacal gardens changed into fortified enclosures! But not even that kept them from crumbling later on, under the vengeful attacks of the Peoples of the Sea."

With a strong voice, he continued.

"The man of the continent is a slave who can and must only be managed with a cudgel, a herd animal whose power derives simply and solely from quantity... History is the witness. Be it in Europe, in Asia, in America — let's not talk about Africa — all the great civilizations have enclosed the individual in the double ferocious yoke of religion and hierarchy. And it's still the same today, just like it has always been. On the other hand, the sea cherishes the free man. It has put him on the island, which is the expression of individuality on the geographical level."

The image of the rude and peaceful life in the small fishing port at the foothills of the high and white cliffs of Heligoland, perpetually lashed by the snarling waves of the Northern Sea resurfaced in Kurt's memory. Higgledy-piggledy, a current of impressions were blending into it; euphoric memories of far away islands, intoxicating smells of tropical shores, echoes of joyful music, women's laughter, burning embraces, bright sunshine and cheerful waves.

He regained self-control. We are fighting a war; there is no more room for emotions.

"No, Mr. Markantakis," his voice was firm and curt. "It's not the caves, nor the presumed History of my ancestors that bother me, but the game that you apparently want to play. Nature has given me a critical and pragmatic mind. Like everybody else, I have a little corner for dreams, but it's only reason that guides me. Like every scientist who deserves his name, I can only believe in demonstrable and controllable facts."

He stopped to look at the man, who remained impassive.

"Since the beginning of this evening, I've been admiring your erudition and your knowledge of the sea, which I suspect is even larger than what you show. But too many hours have passed by. It's time for me to enlighten you on the exact purpose of my mission."

The German officer got up from his chair, and without being aware of it, regained his inherent stiffness.

"I've been sent here by my government to start and complete in a successful manner negotiations regarding those caves you were just telling me about. Our country is at war with merciless enemies. By land, the weight of the Barbarian hordes of the East with which our brothers of Anglo-Saxon blood have associated themselves, to their future misfortune, threaten to get the better of the quality and the heroism of the German people by the simple play of the relationship between the masses. On the other hand, our underwater fleet proves terribly effective and is spreading devastation and terror on the vital supply lines of the enemy.

"The creation of a network of impregnable and indestructible bases where our U-Boats would have the possibility of being put into port in total safety is the main condition of the success of the gigantic combat that we are fighting on and under the seas. We have an imperative need to approach the North American territory, wherefrom a continuous fleet of weapons and supplies leaves for their fronts in Europe. Thanks to your caves, which according to the little amount of information that has reached our hands must be located in that vicinity, we would be able to cut that umbilical cord definitively. Our Führer has given me the honor of receiving me to talk about this matter. For reasons that escape me, but that I'm beginning to guess, he seemed to believe that you would agree. He is ready to give you anything you ask for, honor, power and wealth. As far as I'm concerned, I'm convinced that after the Victory, only our Grand Reich will offer the ideal conditions of development and expression to a personality such as yours."

A long silence followed. Outside, coming from some distant farmyard, a rooster could be heard crowing faintly. Nostalgic and triumphant at the same time, the notes chimed out in the distance. The big Cretan was the first one to speak again.

"Your request, Kapitän Müller, is too important for me to respond immediately. I have a suggestion to make. Why don't we see each other again tomorrow evening?"

The officer agreed without further discussion. He would not be able to get anything else from this man today. In any case, the ground had been cleared and sowed. He would harvest the fruits very soon. Naturally, he would put him under tight surveillance. He didn't want the man to escape him.

"It's a deal," he said simply. "We'll return tomorrow at the same time."

When he started descending the steps of the stairs, followed by the two other men, he heard clearly the sound of the latch of the heavy door being locked.

'Perfect,' he thought. 'He's locking himself up in his den.'

CHAPTER 4

When the German patrol boat approached, the men aboard the small boat from Marseilles resumed their usual fishing movements.

A group on the front part of the boat hauled in the *gangui**, with its big green glass float balls banging against each other, its fish nets piled up on the pointed floor of the prow, imprisoning a swarm of multicolored fishes. The big brown and patched triangular lateen sail slowly started climbing up the stocky mast.

Hidden under the deckhouse, the man who had taken refuge there after a series of breath-hold dives was quickly getting dressed, the sea water still dripping from his body. He took pleasure in putting on the warm, dry clothes that awaited him. Then he contemplated the two objects he had just brought up from 80 feet deep. The triangular object, with two holes in it, covered with marine concretions was certainly a primitive anchor. The other one, more important, was a conglomerate resembling scoria resulting from the fusion of some metallic ore.

"Giorgios will be happy… he was right," he murmured.

It was made of copper and its manufacture in that area, when the sea level was much lower than it is today, about 15 or 20 thousand years ago, seemed unbelievable.

He put everything away quickly, together with the fins and the small goggles he had made himself. He hid them under the fish-traps and wicker baskets, so that nobody would be able to notice them. Then he came out into the fresh air.

The eastern breeze was beginning to get stronger. He looked at the German patrol boat with relief, while it moved away, apparently reassured, with its powerful engines emitting a muffled and regular sound.

* Gangui: fishing net in Marseilles

Pressing one of his nostrils, then the other, he expelled the remainder of seawater that had accumulated in his sinuses, in spite of his nose clip.

On the stern, firmly established on his two legs, wrapped up in his old and wet oilskin, the captain of the fishing boat greeted him in a jovial manner, with a thundering voice.

"Well, Zé, did you see them, those ghosts from another time?"

He could not help but smile. He loved that Marseilles accent, which in his ears seemed to reflect an optimistic view of life, an instinctive wish to smile at it at all moments, through all its good times and bad times. Being a Greek man, deeply and atavistically impregnated with the sense of tragedy, he could feel all its simultaneously bright and solid charm — but from a distance, as a foreigner, as if that mentality were out of reach for him.

'Nevertheless, we're both children of the same Mediterranean', he thought.

"Yes, I could verify all that I wanted."

By contrast to the captain's, the sound of his own voice seemed affected to him.

"Well, then it's because everything is going the way you want it to go."

Respectful of the silence into which the diver usually sank, the man at the helm preferred to conclude with an encouraging note.

Silently, the man who had been called Zé leaned against the housing of the engine in order to get warm. He placed his hands, frozen by the cold seawater, with his palms wide open, in front of the opening of an exhaust pipe from which escaped the hot gases.

He still had in front of his eyes the vision of that strange site off the coast of Marseilles, known by the fishermen as the Veyron, over which he had just spent almost two hours diving in apnea. He had gone from discovery to discovery in that labyrinth of caves, galleries and intersecting corridors, sometimes at right angles. He had come across what seemed to be a real shipyard, full of these primitive anchors, cut out of dark and hard rock. The scoria too sometimes appearing in an actual flow seemed to be witnesses to the manufacture of metals from an extremely distant time. He regretted that he wasn't fitted with a full hard hat diving suit with lead weighted boots as when he found that mound full of holes like a Gruyere round. If the top was about 40 feet from the surface, its slopes sank more than 160 feet deep!! It was simply too deep for a diver in apnea, especially in those freezing winter waters!

During his last dive, having well reconnoitered the environment, he grew bolder and, swam to the extremity of one of those horizontal corridors that pierced the western flank, emerging into a real chamber. Raising his head towards the vault, he noticed the sparkling mirror of the surface at the end of a chimney about 5 feet wide. He hesitated but a second before entering it. Stroking the water with the palms of his hands, he let himself be lifted upwards, passing through 20 feet past an immense inner wall before emerging into the open water.

'Yes, intelligent men lived and worked there, a long time ago,' he thought, 'but how could it be that Giorgios, that sorcerer, knew about this site, and above all, knew its exact location?'

***

That afternoon, in late January 1943, the weather was gloomy and gray. Heavy dark clouds passed by quickly, low above the lead colored sea. On the horizon, the grayness was lit by a wide and sparkling strip shining on the surface of the water, the brilliant reflex of the sun, which hid itself obstinately. Its rays had managed to pierce through well under the low ceiling of the clouds.

In that silvery scintillation, the pointed up-turned outlines of the flat-bottomed *bettes** and the fishing boats that had just recently regained permission to fish stood against the sky. Closer to him, Planier and its lighthouse marked the limits of the zone authorized by the Kommandantur for fishing. The outline of the German patrol boat could be seen against the sky.

Pushed by the wind, the sailboat headed quickly for the Lacydon, leaving behind it the torn naked cliffs of Maïre and Marseilleveyre, which wore the long cottony and almost black streaks of the bad weather mists.

On the starboard side well on top of the hill, the Good Mother,

* Bette: fishing boat typical of the Mediterranean Sea. Its prow is decorated with a phallic symbol.

perched upon the summit of the tower of the Church of Notre-Dame de la Garde, watched over a town numbed by the winter on that sad and gray day of the war.

Between the Chateau d'If and the Pointe des Catalans, the wind broke down and the wheezy but regular panting of the old Diesel engine brought the boat past the high, elegant and powerful tower of the Fort Saint-Jean, made of square rosy bricks, under the tall steel structures of the transporter bridge and into the Old Port.

He slowed down by the old round church tower of Saint Lawrence's Church, a parish of fishermen and people of the sea. Beginning a turn to portside, accompanied by the intermittent chug-chug of the engine and the incessant squawking of the seagulls, he carefully slipped between the multitude of hulls, boats and trawlers of all kinds. He docked in front of an elegant Majorcan scale, very close to the fish market, parallel to the quay.

Without delay, Ze' jumped off the boat. In the cold grayness of the afternoon, the usual crowd strolled about along the quay. It certainly wasn't the colorful and cosmopolitan swarming of the time before the war. The clothes and the look of the walkers already reflected the tiredness and the hardships of what would soon be three years of defeat, occupation and humiliation.

He avoided stepping on the long nets spread out on the thick irregular cobblestones, picked his way through the piled up crates, the empty wicker fish-traps and the piles of wooden barrels, and walked into the old quarters through Radeau Street.

Like every time he returned to the ground, the strong smells surprised him. The smell of fried food dominated an indefinable mixture of smells. The pleasant smells of the countless pieces of washed clothes hanging on the windows and the spices mixed with the stench of the garbage and filth accumulating on the narrow sidewalks.

On the other hand, the perfume of Bouterie Street, through which he forced his way shoulder to shoulder with the crowd, did not displease him. It was the perfume of the countless women of all races and colors, young girls hardly nubile or matrons harrowed with age, all of whom earned their living from the commerce of their charms. In those times of boredom, they offered a pleasure spiced up with all sorts of sauces, according to the taste and the possibilities of the client.

Since they knew him there, he escaped the usual trap of the hat stolen with a nimble hand, which then had to be recovered deep inside a pleasure den. He grazed the countless bars, small pubs, pizzerias, dives, and girls' boxes, all with their tired signs.

In front of the Athena Bar, he stopped.

A big dark-haired woman was well planted there. She had her two hands tucked away into the pockets of a fur-lined cloak half-open to her generous figure, around which a garish dress fit closely. She smiled at him, with a mocking look in her eyes.

"The guys are here." In order to leave him some space to pass through, she stepped aside with a movement that was meant to be provocative.

"You don't ever miss an occasion, Rosette", he grumbled, as he entered into the narrow corridor.

He opened a little door to his right and entered into a smoky back room thick with the strong smell of anise. Around the two tables, some men — visibly fishermen — were playing tavli. They spoke Greek and drank ouzo manufactured in the underground. A man, standing alone moved toward him, with an extended hand and a worried look.

"Zé… I'm very happy to see you again. Much has happened since you left for the sea. There was an attack yesterday and the Fritz are furious. They cornered the Cretan in his house and interrogated him until dawn. They're probably going to do the same again tonight. The curfew is being enforced again."

"Oh… I understand now why the patrol boat lurked around us all day today. This means that we won't be allowed to go to the sea either. I need to inform the others."

Before leaving, Zé stopped in front of a notice framed in red and black, hanging on the dirty wall. It was written in German on one side and in French on the other:

BEKANNTMACHUNG — NOTICE

FOLLOWING A NEW CRIMINAL ATTACK, THE CURFEW IS AGAIN FIXED AT EIGHT PM.
ALL CIRCULATION IS PROHIBITED AFTER THAT TIME TO THOSE PERSONS NOT POSSESSING
AN AUTHORIZATION TO TRAVEL AT NIGHT.

MARSEILLES, JANUARY 22, 1943. THE FORTRESS COMMANDER:
MAJOR GENERAL MYLO

***

The long howling of the siren announcing the end of the alert finished with a sinister decrescendo.

Very quickly, activity resumed, feverishly but methodically, inside the immense concrete bunker. Its brand new mass occupied a vast area on the Mourepiane terreplein. In that gigantic serpent nest, protected from the biggest bombs, three submarines, back from their deadly mission, had their wounds dressed by the service and repair teams of the Kriegsmarine. Through the glass panels of his office, which overlooked the entirety of the giant hangar, Kurt watched the daily show absentmindedly. Hosts of mechanics in their white overalls congregated around the long steel-hulled submarines. Kurt noticed for the first time how the intense lighting of the spotlights in the artificial cave gave the scene a ghostly aspect, a character of unreality.

A concert of sounds, coming from underneath him and deformed by the echoes against the thick concrete vaults reached his ears: calls and guttural orders, the rumbling sound of the steamrollers, steel sheets resonating under the blows, the crackling of the blowtorches, and from time to time, suddenly dominating the hubbub, the shrill cry of a horn.

He took a look at his watch. It was 8:50 pm. He would soon meet Markantakis again.

He was surprised by his own impatience. He needed to reflect, and to breathe some fresh air.

Outside, the wind was blowing violently.

He took a few steps, hands in his pockets, the collar of his jacket turned up. Next to a shed that must have served as a shelter for the workers, a few marine guards were stamping their feet around an improvised wood fire.

For a moment, the smell of the smoke took him back to his childhood, to his home in Heligoland, where the same brutal wind ruled. With a taste of sorrow, he could see himself there, marveling at the tales and legends that the old people loved to tell, the exploits of the Nordic heroes.

In fact, this mysterious Cretan was also, in his own way, an extraordinary storyteller...

The gusts of wind were blowing twice as hard now, forcing him to struggle step by step as he walked.

He went back to the giant bunker, looking for shelter. Looking at the immense concrete vault, he suddenly thought of his caves. How many bunkers like this one could fit into one of them? All this was very likely nothing but a myth, a huge bluff. But he was not the small boy anymore, who would let himself be told anything, with open-mouthed credulity.

Thinking of the imminent second interview, he decided that it would be the last one, no matter what might be said. He would use force, if need be. Back in his office, he found a typed note that had been left on his desk blotter. The note said that the diver Markantakis had not moved from his house all day. The report made by the lieutenant commanding the patrol boat in charge of watching over his associates was there too. Kurt shook his head with a half-smile. The report was positive: the men aboard had engaged in activities that had nothing to do with fishing.

CHAPTER 5

He had not moved. The three German men found themselves entering the same room, with the same scenery of marine odds and ends, the same fortunes spread out, in the same diffuse and slightly unsettling luminosity. It seemed as if it was still the same evening.

Only the tension had disappeared. The two S.D. detectives took their indifferent guard next to the door and the conversation was resumed smoothly.

Kurt and the Cretan kept themselves in politely neutral ground. For a long time, they discussed the underwater war as technicians and ocean specialists.

It was the giant who mentioned again the caves. Kurt caught a very subtle shift in the Cretan's behavior and deduced that he had done it deliberately. The game went on, but now it was time to finish it.

"I'm sorry, Mr. Markantakis," he said suddenly and abruptly, "we have bowed and scraped enough." He got up and, without being aware of it, resumed his uptight stance. "You must make a decision. We would like to have precise information about those caves. I've already told you: we will accept all your conditions."

As usual, the Cretan took his time before responding. He sunk into his armchair. His hands played with a short dagger, setting it out and back into its cover. He must use it as a paper knife.

"My very dear Kapitän Müller, will you please sit down?" he said finally, in a deep voice. "Once again, the seaman you are has let himself be manipulated by the men of the land. What I sensed in the beginning has been confirmed. You have not been told the real goal of your mission. These caves are just a pretext. They're sort of a gesture of strictness. Much beyond them is the alliance with our own power that is looked for."

The officer was visibly affected and it took all his will power to maintain his cold-blooded attitude. For a brief moment, he asked himself how he had been so able simply to reject the hypothesis that he was dealing with a mythomaniac. He had already rubbed shoulders with others, not the least in the mysteries and mythology of the Nazi Party. They were all certainly as brilliant as this Cretan man.

"I hope you realize the import of your words," he said laconically.

"I'm not used to speaking thoughtlessly. You're still young, Kapitän Müller, young and indoctrinated. Moreover, doubly indoctrinated by politics and science. It's exactly in the name of their doctrine that the people of your government have persuaded themselves that we could save them from the disaster that is lying in wait for them."

"What do you mean?" asked the officer abruptly.

"The business is too long and secret for me to explain everything now. Simply know that, contrary to all your information and all appearances, history is never made on the surface. The more a political fact seems evident, the less it's likely to be real. The big currents of the human epic are always hidden."

He seemed to hesitate, and then continued.

"Bits of certain fundamental truths that should never have reappeared in this Dark Age have reached the ears of some of your people in authority. Believing themselves to be initiated, they want to reverse the inexorable course of History. This undertaking, which is as big as their ignorance, is bound to fail."

Kurt tensed up. It all seemed to him to be nothing more than a flimsy tissue of extravagance.

"Frankly, in other circumstances, Mr. Markantakis, I would have burst out in laughter. I'm more and more convinced that you make fun of the world."

He broke off suddenly. The light in the room seemed to be more and more blue-shaded. In spite of him, the memory of certain crystal-clear waters arose from his subconscious. He began to feel the fatigue of the hours spent in that climate of tension. Like the day before, he had a hard time getting rid of the drowsiness that overcame him.

"You're right, Kapitän Müller. It's getting late and it's time to finish." The quiet and soft voice came to him from a distance. "Nevertheless, listen to me until I have finished. I'm going to appeal to your scientific objectivity, if not to your reason; I do this for you, because I've known you for a long time. We come from the same lineage. The same salt of marine depths runs in our veins. This that I'm going to tell you will collide with your logic and your convictions. But nevertheless, weigh carefully my words. Your conclusion will depend on your understanding of them." He kept quiet for an instant. "And your destiny."

Without responding, Kurt turned slightly toward his bodyguards. They seemed tired too, but at a small sign made by him, they instantly recovered their vigilance.

"In spite of appearances, I have a certain admiration for the sages of your Third Reich." The Cretan's voice was clear and precise again. " Their progress in the military domain is considerable and it reflects well the particular genius of the old German tribes. In the underwater sector, the weapon that Germany has forged for itself is, in a certain sense, worthy of the Peoples of the Sea. Nevertheless, your most perfected submarines are blind and they trail along just about 60 or 80 feet under the surface."

"And you certainly have something better to offer us…"

The Cretan burst out in laughter.

"Your formidable U-Boats don't impress me more than the rowing boats in an outing on the waters of the Spree in Berlin. You're nothing but kids, I already told you. Your science has no idea of the forces at our disposal. They pertain to the spirit and not to what you call the matter. They totally escape your contemporary mentality, convinced as it is that everything comes from matter. No matter what uncultivated shaman from the islands, any sorcerer from our old countryside or from our beautiful Caribbean islands knows certain aspects of it and is able to control them. There are levels in the mastery of these energies. It was up to my people, as the depository of this science, to make profane, skeptical and ignorant people like you reach a level of inconceivable perfection."

"And all this in your caves!" Kurt was full of a bitter disappointment.

The other man got up without responding. His mass was really impressive. Under the striped sweater, Kurt could make out his powerful muscles, more accustomed to hard physical effort, instead of sterile intellectual games and philosophical banter. The man picked up a roll of ocean charts and opened it out on one side of the long table.

"Come and see!"

Kurt left his seat reluctantly. He passed slowly to the other side of the table and bent over too.

It was a chart represented the Atlantic.

On both sides of the blue ocean, marks and annotations in different colors covered a part of the coastlines. To his surprise, it did not take him long to spot the familiar pattern. It showed the location of all the Kriegsmarine underwater bases. They were all there. The known bases as well as the most secret ones, such as the one in Tierra del Fuego or the one at the mouth of the Río de la Plata. His gaze returned to the Cretan, who smiled at him.

"You see, I'm well informed. And all this information has been obtained neither from your opponents nor from those on your side. There's nothing that happens underwater that I'm not aware of. By principle and by vigilance."

Ideas were rushing into the officer's mind. By what kind of magic could this man have gained access to such secret data? There was only one possible explanation: a leak in the very high ranks of the Oberkommando. He would need to discover its source immediately, before any further action. He was getting ready to interrogate the Cretan but he held back. The man had just placed his finger on an area surrounded by a particular blue that he recognized: it was the same blue on the doors. He didn't have time to be surprised.

"These caves, or rather this gigantic submarine complex, are located in this area here, somewhere under the Bahamas continental plateau. Unfortunately for those who have sent you here, it's out of reach for them. Out of reach for anybody, by the way."

"Yes? Why"

"Let's see, Kapitän Müller. I thought I had said enough for you to guess that."

Kurt looked at him for a moment, hesitating about what attitude he should take. He resumed with an abrupt tone.

"I'm sick and tired of your little games, Mr. Markantakis. Let's put an end to them. What exactly do you demand in exchange for your information? By the way, I'm afraid you don't have a choice here, except that of answering my question."

The two guards had gotten up and placed themselves one on each side of the officer.

The giant kept his calm.

"Today, this area is the refuge of our people. There's nothing visible left of the immense kingdom of the sea. There are innumerable forms of existence. Your matter is just the grossest form. The entity formed by us represents a tremendous concentration of energy, a quantum of forces completely concentrated in this territory. But it's located in a universe that excludes all possibility of interface with your universe.

"Kapitän Müller, I've followed you for years. I've also watched your education with deep interest. So I could see what they meant to accomplish. Paradoxically, they have made you my envoy. I am the one who is going to give you your mission. You're going to go back to those who have sent you here. You will tell them there is no possible negotiation. We don't have anything in common. I have just…"

"Enough! Enough!" Kurt slammed his fist on the table. "Who do you think you are to give me orders like this? One word from me and you don't exist anymore. I don't claim to have known you for long, but I guarantee that your delusions of grandeur can be treated very well in psychiatric hospitals. Your mind spews out nothing but baseless assertions. Never the least beginning of some proof."

The two men confronted each other with their eyes.

Slowly, without ceasing to look at the officer, the Cretan opened a drawer under the table.

"Here it is, your proof." He handed him a tiny box. Opening the lid, he took out a small flat piece of metal shining with strange brightness.

After a slight moment of hesitation, Kurt picked it up.

"What is this now?" he asked while examining the piece.

It was very beautiful in its simplicity. On one side, there was a very finely engraved double spiral. The other side was decorated with a series of concentric circles. In the center, two dolphins were standing head to tail.

"What is this?" he repeated mechanically.

"It's a piece of the diadem worn by a venerable and very ancient queen of the kingdom of Poseidon."

He lifted his eyes. Pensive for a moment, he thought of the treasure of Troy, brought back by Schliemann from the Hissarlik excavations. He had had the occasion to study it closely, accompanied by the curator of the Berlin Museum. Indeed, this piece reminded him of certain pendants of royal headdresses. But the material intrigued him. Like all polished metal, it reflected light, but an iridescent light that reflected all the colors of the rainbow.

"It's orichalc," the Cretan said simply.

"Orichalc? The metal of Atlantis. Is this another one of your jokes?"

"I don't make jokes with this kind of thing. By the way, when I give it to you, you'll be able to verify easily that it's not any kind of metal known until now. But this will only happen when you come back, if you decide to join us."

Kurt was exasperated. Before he could speak, a woman screamed nearby. A general hubbub followed. Distant sounds of slamming doors, shutters banging and, right under the window, the muffled but distinct sounds of people taking flight.

Very clearly dominating the rumbling, a guttural command in German reached them.

Surprised, the officer looked at the two hesitating S.D. detectives.

"A roundup!"

The bearded giant took advantage of this short moment of hesitation and, sliding his hand under the table, he brought up a revolver.

A deafening detonation filled the room. Faster than him, one of the bodyguards had shot almost at point-blank range.

Hit in the middle of his chest, the Cretan collapsed. Blood squirted under his white sweater with blue stripes. With a start, on his way down, his arms tried to hang on to the long table. Then, the heavy body continued to fall, bringing down with him the books and chart rolls that were scattered on the floor.

"Idiot!" shouted the killer. "He tried to trick us!"

"You are the idiot! You should never have done that. We needed him alive!"

In a crazy rage, Kurt became aware of the disaster. Leaning over the body, he held one of his wrists and lifting the arms, he tried to find the pulse.

"He's dead. You're good for nothing, except to torture and kill. We needed him to speak. Let's go, quick! We can't waste a second."

The two detectives searched the body and the desk drawers very quickly, while Kurt put the little box in his pocket and folded three times the chart of the Atlantic that they had just examined. "Nothing. No I.D. papers. But there's a strong possibility that he's an American agent," said one of them, standing up and handing to Kurt a short barreled revolver. "Smith and Wesson. It's one of their favorite guns. They're practically impossible to find here."

Outside, the sidewalks rang with the noise of studded shoe soles.

"Quick, inside." The officer pointed to the old casket at the entrance. He opened the heavy rounded lid, while the other two were dragging the Cretan's body by his feet, leaving bloodstains on the floor. They coiled him up with difficulty, inside the casket. Kurt put the lid down and he had to use both his hands to force the huge rusty key in the lock.

"He has exactly the coffin that suits him," said one of the bodyguards.

Both men burst out in laughter under the furious gaze of the officer. He felt guilty. The Cretan had treated him with friendliness. He was just like him, a child of the Sea.

When they opened the blue door, they found themselves face to face with a small group of men on their way in. They were French policemen and Germans in uniform. One of the bodyguards quickly took out of his pocket a card marked with the eagle of the Third Reich and extended it to the officer who obviously commanded the group.

"Kapitän Helmut Reiner of the Sicherheitsdienst," he said. "This is Detective Schumacher and…" He hesitated for a moment while pointing to Kurt. Detective Braun, my colleagues… Special Security Service mission. What's happening here, lieutenant?"

"Under the orders of the Führer and of the French authorities, the immediate evacuation and destruction of the Old Port district."

"There's nobody here. We have just searched everything."

The lieutenant gave the card back after scrutinizing it carefully, clacked his heels and lifted his arm.

"Heil Hitler!"

"Heil Hitler!"

While the patrol climbed the steps of the big stairs toward the upper floors, Kurt and the two men quietly went down towards the central courtyard. The first rays of dawn gave an even more sinister aspect to the array of fishing and diving objects. Kurt noticed the diver's equipment, always at its place, and he felt a pang of anguish.

Outside, on the narrow streets, people were dazed or crying. They got together in front of the doorsteps, having in front of them bundles of quickly gathered personal belongings that they were allowed to take with them.

In the frozen dawn air, the lines converged towards the gathering places on the Old Port.

Like a giant anthill stricken by surprise, the old district, nested for millennia on its hill, disgorged its life through all its pores. Mostly simple people or specimens of an illicit underworld, those inhabitants gathered together on the sidewalks of the quay, under the strict surveillance of the policemen. Without understanding, they were subjected to the events of this Sunday morning, a Sunday that could have been like any other Sunday.

Quickening their steps, the three German men passed through the cordons of the Feldgendarmerie and the French police force.

In front of the City Hall, beyond the lines of trucks, Kurt turned back once more. The first prisoners were beginning to be crammed together on their way to the camps from which many would never return. Superimposed over the roofs and facades of the old houses, the sarcastic image of the bearded craggy face reappeared in front of him. A long shiver ran thought his body.

"One could say he was Poseidon, the God, in person," he murmured.

PART TWO
Miami, September 1973

CHAPTER 6

It was the third time he saw her this week.

She had a very special way, almost childish, of leaning against the guardrail of the small footbridge over the shark tank. With her face resting on her long hands, she seemed fascinated by the goings-on underneath.

A slight breeze, still fresh because it was morning, was blowing at times from Biscayne Bay through the Miami Seaquarium, lifting the wild locks of her flaming red hair.

Jonathan was surprised at first when he saw her alone like that, before opening time, but he quickly established the link between the woman and the presence, these last days, of a restless and noisy television team that was filming at the MGM studios and tanks nearby.

She was always barefoot, just like him. But their clothing had nothing else in common. The old, faded and patched blue jeans and the white T-shirt with scattered holes that covered his athletic torso didn't show any signs of affectation. They reflected exactly his financial situation.

On the other hand, she always dressed with discreet elegance. The turquoise shantung set she wore today confirmed her taste and her easy familiarity with expensive things. At least that's what Jonathan thought, while he approached her quickly. A girl used to dough, but also a quite a girl!

If the first aspect could be seen as an obstacle, the second justified all audacities. As a confirmed womanizer, and an authentic descendant of a famous French buccaneer of the halcyon years who, in times past, had lost his way in Louisiana, he decided on an immediate approach.

She saw him coming toward her. Her knowledge of men, along with her intuition, allowed her to size him up instantaneously as a young wolf or rather a young shark. His place should be there, with the other sharks, in the tank... unless he had just escaped.

The idea made her smile.

Jonathan Larue was dazzled. He had always had a soft spot for tall redheads, maybe because they were rare. Until now they had always escaped him.

Her naughty nose and her fresh face peppered with freckles promised a playful and spontaneous character, tempered by the clear, slightly disillusioned look of her big green eyes.

"You know," he said with a light-hearted tone, "you shouldn't lean over too much. It would be a bad idea to fall into that. They're hungry and their lunchtime is a long way off. I'm the one who feeds them."

"And they haven't yet munched you?"

Her response pleased him. This young person had a sense of humor nevertheless.

"Do you know," he resumed, "that sharks don't eat one another unless they're injured?"

Her small and mocking laugh titillated him.

I need her, he thought, all the while looking for the right words. He did not find any. He had never been good at saying nice things to girls. On the other hand, he knew perfectly well how to thrill them. In his opinion, this was the main thing.

"Are you from around here?" she asked.

She had resumed her straight face, but a mocking spark was still shining in her eyes.

"If you wish. I've been working here for the last ten days… as a diver."

"Yes! So it's you that I see, with that huge orange helmet, feeding all those big animals. Aren't you afraid?"

That was a typically feminine remark, he thought. She pouted in a pretty and fearful way when she said that. He could have eaten her on the spot.

Since ages ago he did not fear the inhabitants of the underwater world. In fact, he didn't remember having ever experienced the least fear. He had always felt at home underwater. Its inhabitants inspired in him deference, curiosity, sympathy or admiration — but under no circumstances fear.

He explained this to her. As he became animated describing to her the beauty and the wild power of the white shark, the great Carcharodon carcharias, when it attacked its prey, she surprised herself being overcome by his ardor. The fascinating mixture of insolent strength and the healthy body of this young adventurer, a person shaped by the sea, disturbed her.

The habit of frequenting the silver-plated but tainted milieu in which she moved about since her marriage, a marriage which had made her abandon the cheap night clubs where she claimed to be a singer, had made her forget what a true male was.

"And you, what do you do here every morning, or almost every morning?"

He had asked the question for the sake of form, since he already knew the answer.

"I'm bored. Or else it's because I get bored somewhere else that I come here to dream."

Jonathan noticed her wedding ring. If she was married, her husband was certainly part of this world in which she was bored. He leaned against the guardrail beside her and became aware of the sophisticated fragrance of her perfume. He loathed all kinds of artificial smells, but refrained from saying so.

Right beneath them, under the shimmering surface of the water, a dark and imposing form glided along quietly.

"Maybe you prefer the company of the sharks?" he asked.

"Oh, there are sharks everywhere, you know."

They both burst out in laughter.

"I'm very bad company too. Look at this, I'm already very close to you."

She replied quickly.

"All my life has been nothing but a long train of bad company."

Her good humor finally melted away the last obstacles that could still oppose a mutual attraction.

"What about a good cup of coffee before the rush starts?" he asked abruptly.

"Well, I won't say no to that."

He held her hand deliberately in order to test her, but she quickly withdrew it.

"Be careful, my husband is not far away."

She smiled at him and this gave him the certainty that it was a done deal, only postponed just a little.

Side by side, they walked slowly to the cafeteria. A hot and humid smell emanated from the thick tropical lawn and from the immense flowerbeds of the Seaquarium, recently watered. Along the cemented path, already burning under the sunshine, tiny water puddles evaporated after the big morning wash. They waded through the pathway like two big children.

When they got under the cafeteria's awning, they were grateful for the shaded freshness.

A feverish activity began to reign on the other side of the big zinc counter, with the characteristic hubbub of banging, jingling and other various noises typical of a kitchen that is waking up. The mouth-watering aroma of bacon and eggs sizzling on the hot griddle tickled their nostrils.

"Could we have two cups of coffee, Mac?" Jonathan asked the young black man on the other side of the counter. He was spotlessly clean in his short sleeve shirt and his immaculate, freshly starched white chef's hat.

"Of course, Frenchy."

He took the two cups and joined the young woman. She was sitting at a table, after having cleared the chairs.

"Did he call you Frenchy?" A spark of amusement shone in her big green eyes.

"Yes. I'm half French, half Cajun. I'm originally from Louisiana. Jonathan Larue, at your service."

He put the two burning cups on the table and slowly took hold of the young woman's right hand, covering it with his own.

This time she did not withdraw.

"You work really fast," she said simply, displaying a falsely candid expression that excited him enormously."

I'm Linda Klein, an O'Reilly and Irish by birth."

He let go of the captive hand to prove to her that it was him who kept the initiative.

"It's a very long story... and a little complicated," he said.

He didn't like to speak about it, but curiously this girl inspired trust. Suddenly he had the desire to explain to her.

"My father met my mother in France, during the war, when he was a G.I. He was an explosives expert in a Bomb Disposal Squad. One day, what could not have happened, happened, unfortunately... in Germany. The war was finally over. As he was removing the primer from a charge, it exploded right in his face and killed him on the spot. I was born a few months later. Since the marriage proposal file had already been sent to Washington, I was legally recognized as the son of an American man.

"Nevertheless, my mother decided to remain in France, where I grew up and lived until I was 16 years old. She died in a road accident. At that time, I landed on American soil for the first time. I was penniless. My father's brothers took me in. We lived in the old family farmhouse, in the Louisiana Bayou.

"It was comprised of a couple of ruins and a wooden house. They worked their asses off in the middle of that stinking swamp, surrounded by their big black pigs!"

Jonathan was in fine form. He was not a literary type but he had the instinct for words. His descriptions hit the mark. Sometimes the gorgeous redhead burst out in laughter, losing the sophisticated varnish she had taken so much time and trouble building up. By association, images of her own poverty-stricken adolescence in the Irish ghetto at the Bowery, New York, where her father ruled as a broke tyrant over his large offspring, came to her mind. For the first time, she saw them in an almost comic light.

"At eighteen, I joined the Navy. I couldn't take it anymore… I had only one idea in my mind: escape that shithole. I was not made for slave work. My ancestors had brought in enough blacks from Africa, so that I wouldn't have to do that kind of work in their place."

She approved him, because in her own way, she had done exactly the same.

Their refusal to grow up in the poverty-stricken rut that had been the lot assigned to them by those fierce or malicious gods that govern men's destiny revealed an identical fortitude.

"I had the good luck to be trained as a Navy S.E.A.L. diver. That was a revelation. All the latent tendencies inherited from my pirate ancestors that lay dormant in my genes exploded. Even better than my ancestors and under official blessings, I learned to become a dangerous being. Not only on the water but underwater too… a real shark!"

He broke up in laughter under the young woman's admiring gaze.

"Have you really killed men?"

"I had no choice."

She remained silent for a moment. Then, looking at his hand, she asked:

"What about this scar next to your thumb?"

"It's the result of a deadly hand-to-hand combat in the middle of the Vietnamese jungle. I had no weapons. But I at least managed to get rid of my aggressor forever."

"With your bare hands?"

"Of course! The karate they taught us in the free corps is very different from the Japanese martial arts. A human hand can become a deadly weapon."

He stopped suddenly and looked at the electric clock close to the entrance.

"Let's be serious. I have to take care of my animals. When can we see each other again, Linda? I'm going to finish early today, it's a half-day, you know."

In any other situation, she would have sidestepped, she would have been difficult, but she was strongly attracted to this young man, dragged along in his turbulent wake. For once her feminine soul didn't urge her to pretend indifference; she felt no need here to protect herself from the unknown. She thought about David, her husband. He was probably flitting amidst his court of starlets. Those girls would do anything in exchange for a short scene in a TV movie or even in a TV commercial.

"Where you want, when you want," she found herself saying to him.

He looked at her — she was certainly not an easy girl, though.

He was confused. He could feel that this was more than a simple hit.

She probably understood it or rather she could sense it, with this intuition that women possess and which had always surprised him. He could feel it as a warm wave of sympathy. He got up suddenly and stole a quick kiss from her lips.

"Two o'clock in front of the souvenir store next to the entrance," he yelled at her while he went away quickly.

He turned his face to look at her. She had also gotten up and smiled at him in a playful way. A smile that looked to him to be complicit.

He watched her as she disappeared behind the flowering hedges surrounding the TV's dolphin lagoon. He went in the opposite direction, toward the isolated shack, the fish house where he was supposed to cut up the frozen fish with which he was to feed the sharks four times a day.

***

He prepared some gorgeous pieces, whistling all the while. Big tuna or grouper heads, big chunks of ray that he hung at the end of a chain and then swung over the famished mouths of the shark channel guests.

The shark channel was an immense tank shaped like a wheel, where sharks of all kinds ceaselessly circled, clockwise. It was ten feet wide and six and a half feet deep and it was the center of attraction for tourists thirsting for thrills.

Jon had much more fun watching the facial expressions of the crowd than teasing as long as possible (so that the show would last) the unfortunate and starving sharks, who in their frenzied efforts, some- times managed to propel themselves almost completely out of the water. They could almost reach the small wooden boardwalk where he stood to feed them.

He even experienced a certain eroticism while he watched the reactions of some female spectators in the face of the fury of these bloodthirsty creatures.

But today he was in a hurry; he had better things to do.

The sun was blazing when he walked towards the exit, heading for the gift shop. For the first time in a long time he felt alive again. He had managed to get 20 dollars from Herby, his team member, and also the keys to his old Mustang. Life had become beautiful again. It remained to be seen if Linda would really be there.

He spotted her from afar, as he climbed down the covered path and his heart started pounding slightly, exactly like right before a deep dive.

For the first time, he noticed the alluring scents that filled the humid and burning air, originating from the countless flower groves in the long central flowerbed he walked along.

She wasn't barefoot anymore. The high heel shoes she wore emphasized the small of the back, enhancing her pleasant curves with feminine charms to which Jonathan could not remain indifferent. She still had that half-smile on her lips.

"Where are you going to take me?"

A hiss and a creaking noise made them lift their heads.

"I'm going to take you on a monorail ride."

"No, thanks. I prefer the deep sea to the risks of the space."

They looked at the small streamlined blue and cream-colored car, full of mirthful and happy faces, and laughed. The monorail glided slowly, hung on its rail, between the sky and the ground, until it reached its nearby stop. They braved a rising rainbow-colored wave of visitors that poured in and headed for their cars parked in the huge parking lot.

"You need a change of atmosphere." Jonathan joked, while he opened the aging Mustang's door. He held it open courteously as she slid into the sagging, somewhat ragged seat.

"This car belongs to you?"

"Yes," he heard himself lying to her. "Why? Does it bother you?"

"No, it's not the car that bothers me," she smiled, "but what it suggests."

"Maybe you mean that I look broke? Well, you're totally right. I'm flat broke. I told you a lot of stories… this car doesn't even belong to me!"

He sat down in his turn. With his hand on the ignition key, he turned in her direction and looked her straight in the eyes, waiting for her reaction.

"I prefer you a thousand times like this because…" She could not finish.

He embraced her with his powerful arms and crushed her lips with his. Her instinctive impulse was to resist him. But she yielded to the burning wave that overwhelmed her.

He started the car suddenly. In the rumbling sound of the engine with an exhaust badly tuned, the car leaped forward, throwing the young woman against the back of her seat.

He paused at the stop sign and then turned onto Rickenbacker Causeway, the magnificent avenue bordered by palm and coconut trees that connects Key Biscayne Island, where the Seaquarium is located, to the Miami seashore.

He hesitated for a second. If he turned right, he would drive through the sumptuous forest of pines, palms and giant coconut trees across Crandon Park. This would lead them to the tip of the island and a fantastic view of the Atlantic. There, they would be able to wander around the old romantic lighthouse. They could wade through the shallow waters between the golden sand beach and the long bank that appears when the tide is out, a little oblong island parallel to the shore, about 200 yards from the coast. They could fuck there in the open air.

They could end the evening under the stars on the old blanket that Herby kept in his rattletrap.

Suddenly he thought about the sand and the mosquitoes and turned left abruptly, heading for Miami.

He knew by heart this not so verdant section of the Rickenbacker Causeway, but he never got tired of it. For him, it was a kind of path to the open sea and adventure, like his new job a diver-trainer at the Seaquarium.

He accelerated.

With her red mane floating in the wind, Linda looked delighted. She was enjoying the landscape too. To the left, they could see the yellowish bay. It was magnificent, in spite of the growing pollution of its waters.

On a clear day such as this, they could see Soldier Key and Elliot Key and even make out the long string of islands stretching lazily all the way down to Key West, 150 miles southwest.

From the long bridge to the toll plaza, there was a magnificent view of the emerald blue sea. The air here was invigorating, as always. Concentrating on what he was doing, Jon breathed slowly and deeply. Linda examined him on the sly.

'How old could he be? Not more than thirty.' She was at least five years older than him.

Her eyes lingered on his broad powerful neck.

She smiled to herself.

He must have unconsciously sensed that she was observing him, for he turned his face to her briefly.

"What are you thinking?"

She could sense the impact of his bright eyes moving all over her and she was flustered for a moment. Then she smiled.

"Better not tell you."

They reached dry land and, passing through the city, came to Southwest 8th Street.

Twenty years ago, this was just another aging neighborhood. Now it was alive with movement and color, flooded with thousands of Cuban refugees who had escaped Castro's regime. The Mustang now was running on what could have been any common artery in any South-American city. Signs made of paint and signs made of light telling of bodegas, panaderias, farmacias and ferreterias crowded one another on the walls of the low painted brick buildings. The buildings revealed

the power and the dynamism of these new conquistadors who, ironically enough, now came from the new world.

At the moment, the long straight avenue, overwhelmed by the sun,
lay dormant in the drowsiness of the hot early afternoon. The only ani-
mation was the comings and goings of customers in the cafés, drug-
stores and restaurants, where menus with big letters, stuck on the windows, offered arroz con pollo and moros y cristianos instead of the
endless hot dogs and cheeseburgers.

Little Havana sank into the siesta hour.

"I hope this is not the place where you plan to give me a change
of atmosphere. Is it?"

The half-ironic, half-alarmed tone with which Linda had just broken the silence made him burst out laughing.

"I see what you mean... but this is not it. We're going further."

"Because," she insisted, "David and I have a huge number of Cuban
friends."

"I'm taking you to my buddy's place. It's different, you'll see."

The wide straight US 41, the Tamiami Trail, quickly opened itself in
front of them.

Leaving behind the elegant residential districts, the Mustang accelerated. The houses became more and more sparse along with the vegetation. Soon, the Everglades spread the monotony of their ponds and
quagmires on both sides of the overheated asphalt strip.

Curiously enough — was it the effect of the scorching heat? — he
maintained an absolute silence. She respected it. Every once in a while,
he would turn his head in her direction and smile at her. He finally told
her, as if to excuse his behavior,

"Linda, it's for me an absolute rule that I have to concentrate on
what I'm doing, even if it's something as simple as eating, drinking or
driving. This is the key to effectiveness. That's what my old Master Taka-
hashi taught me in Japan."

"Did you live there for a long time?"

"Enough time to learn the arts of Budo."

"Budo?"

"Yes. The martial arts: kendo, aikido, karate..."

"Budo. The Japanese language is so charming! Hey, Jon, speak to me
in Japanese, will you? How do they say, for instance, I love you?"

"Anata o aishiteru."

"That's very complicated!"

"Yes, but it's fun to learn. For instance, do you know how they answer the phone?"

"No."

"That's simple. Moshi-moshi. It's pretty, isn't it?"

Linda laughed like a child.

When the highway and the canal were about to start a wide curve towards the right, he slowed the car and stopped at the junction of a broad dirt road.

"At this point, we leave the rotten civilization for a while. I'm taking you to one of the last islands of resistance, where there are still real men."

Jonathan seemed particularly happy.

Leaning toward Linda, he pressed his lips languidly on hers. She reacted with sudden passion. The heat of the long kiss sealed their pact definitively.

"You have to focus on what you do," he said jokingly.

"Yes, now I know what you mean." A mischievous spark shone deep inside her green eyes.

"Let's go."

Very soon, the landscape changed. Passing through a fringe of tall cypress trees, they entered dense woods. After many miles on a bumpy dirt road, the wheels tossing up a cloud of dust, they made a turn into a clearing facing a group of broken-down wooden houses. Together with the trailers scattered around them, they formed a lost small town.

"This is Pinecrest, Linda. It had its moments of glory in Prohibition times. Al Capone built a hotel here. According to the rumors, more than one union big shot came here on holiday and disappeared without a trace... thrown to the alligators.

"Even nowadays, Pinecrest escapes the law. On the administrative level, it's detached from the rest of the county. It's an excellent place for hiding A hundred people live here, gladly refusing the benefits of our consumer society. Although everybody is armed, there's less crime here than in all the rest of the country."

They stopped at an old gas station. While Jonathan was getting gas, Linda went to the restroom to fix her hair and her light makeup a little.

She could hear bits and pieces of Jonathan's conversation with the attendant.

"You're not in trouble, are you Frenchy?"

"No… I came here just to visit Tony. He's still here, isn't he?"

"Yep. He's still hanging out in his trailer."

When they started making comments about her, she came back out quickly.

Both men stopped talking and Jonathan came toward her.

She didn't know quite why, but Jonathan seemed to fit well in that kind of crazy 1930's scene with his young, tall, well-muscled body. He moved lazily, displaying a winning smile. Instinctively, she could feel how in harmony he was with this free and uncultivated environment.

He took her hand.

"Come, let's go see my buddy."

"Oh, yes… Tony!"

"How do you know?" He was downright surprised.

"Feminine intuition."

"You always have to make fun of me… but I adore you."

He held her by the waistline and kissed her on the lips, passionately and violently.

"Well, then… you don't pull your punches," she said, thinking of the fresh lipstick she had just put on.

Together, they walked toward one of the two taverns. Together with the only grocery store and the gas station, they formed the commercial center of the hamlet.

'At the Alligator's Lodge', said the sign hanging over their heads, a representation of the gracious animal.

They climbed the worm-eaten wooden step and entered the big room. It felt fresh, when compared to the outside. In the dimly lit room, they leaned against the long varnished counter and Jonathan ordered a beer for himself and a coke for her. "I have to explain to you who Tony is."

As they waited, Jonathan drew her a quick picture: they had met in Vietnam. They both served with the United States Marine S.E.A.L. unit. They reveled in the impossible missions, the suicidal underwater raids behind enemy lines, the fears and enthusiasms they had in common. As he became excited by the rising flood of intense memories, she suddenly envied him. She had pretended to be steady for too long. She was tired of the quick embraces, too simplified and more and more rare with her husband. The bastard must be happy with that.

Jonathan stopped suddenly, in the middle of a sentence.

"Well, I didn't come here to tell you my life story."

He looked at her. An unusual glow was shining in her pupils. Could it be the heat? A thin layer of perspiration covered her skin with moisture and this excited him.

His left hand tapped nervously on the wooden counter. He squeezed her and was surprised to see that her skin was burning hot.

As she turned to him, he told her straight out:

"Tony is going to let us use his bedroom."

She was surprised at her own reaction. This day was definitely not like the others and Jonathan wasn't either. Instead of slapping him in the face, as it was fitting for a young woman of her new social rank, she cuddled up against him and searched for his lips.

"Well, my children, you don't worry."

A big sprightly 40-year-old man with very short blond hair, wearing a pair of clear Army pants and a short sleeve rainbow-colored shirt, his arms covered with tattoos, had just appeared behind them.

"Linda, this is Tony Anderson, the greatest fighter and also the greatest bluffer of all time."

"Frenchy, I can see that you still have a ready tongue."

"When will be the next treasure hunt?"

"No. For me, that kind of small game… it's over. I devote myself to breeding alligators now. I'm never going to get rich, but it's more reliable."

"Unless you're crunched by one of them."

They burst out in laughter.

"The sharks never got me and these little lizards are not going to have me either."

Friendly, he eyed Jonathan up and down.

"And you, Frenchy, how have you been doing ever since?"

"Bad on the financial plane and very well on the sentimental plane. As the French say, unlucky in cards, lucky in love."

"In any case, congratulations."

Jokingly, Tony turned toward Linda and added:

"My dear Linda, you could not be more unlucky."

Without getting upset, Jonathan interrupted him and explained it all quickly to the young woman. Since coming back from Vietnam, where Tony had been seriously hurt, they had done several expeditions in the Bahamas and in the Caribbean waters, searching for hypothetical treasures. By then, the small bonuses received when they left the SEALS had been spent. All their adventures ended in failure.

The last one was the most disastrous. There was an unpredicted hurricane and all the expensive dive and salvage equipment, unfortunately bought on credit, joined the gold ingots, silver bars and many other treasures destined to be held in their hands. It all ended up on the bottom of the deep blue sea.

The wounds had healed with time and Tony and Jonathan now roared with laughter at the memory of their final, dismal failure.

"Linda, if you had seen us desperately clutching a small coral reef for 48 hours. The rented cruiser had sunk. The compressor, the water dredge, the tanks... All our equipment was taken by the storm... just when we were certain we had found a nice little nest egg. Tony, you made such a face when the Coast Guard came to get us!

"Okay... Okay:" Tony was slightly mortified.

"You know, Linda," Tony said, "the hardest part is that he's telling the truth. Jon is capable of the worst damn-fool things, just for the beauty of the gesture."

Tony said that prudently, suddenly realizing that his friend had not come there just to get off with a girl. He knew from personal experience that Jon always managed to combine business with pleasure.

"What are you up to now?"

"I plan to give all that back to you."

"But you're crazy! With what money? In any case, without me this time, I already told you."

"We'll find the dough. You have to come, Tony."

"No, old buddy, don't count on me anymore; this time I'm done with the sea. I don't want to hear anybody speak about that anymore. I've become a landlubber and I like this place. Also, who would feed my alligators?"

As he got ready to insist, Jonathan realized that Tony's decision was irrevocable. Even the toughest ones, sooner or later, must desire to get settled down.

"It's a pity," he said, suddenly becoming serious. "I'm planning a fantastic blow. It's the richest treasure of all time and it's totally within our reach. All we have to do is to collect it."

"Is that true?"

Tony looked impressed by the quiet certainty of his friend, whose slightest reactions he knew by heart.

"Can we know where it is?"

"Warderick Wells Cay. Do you know it?"

"No."

"Well, you'll hear about it."

CHAPTER 7

"Do you really intend to leave again?"

They were lying down, both naked, on the big bed in the trailer. She said this with a soft voice that surprised him, after the sheer ferocity of their coupling.

He turned over on one side and leaned on one elbow. With his free hand, he drew imaginary arabesques gently sliding his index finger on Linda's skin, moist with perspiration. Her breasts were a little heavy, her belly flat and the hair of her mons veneris was an incredible golden color.

"Why? This would bother you?"

He was experiencing a new feeling for this young woman. He was not in love with her — he didn't believe in love — but he admitted the attachment a struggling man could feel for a woman who understands him, and the value of that feeling. He was on the verge of asking her if she would like to accompany him, but he held back. Let's not mix sex with business, that's what Tony always said. And basically, he was right. He changed his sentence completely.

"I'll come back very rich, you know, and I could take care of you completely."

"You're deluding yourself, Frenchy." She called him Frenchy, almost tenderly, instead of Jon or Jonathan. "We could never live together, we're too much alike; two small wildcats with very long teeth, who have learned to survive and then conquer so they could live better in the jungle of our modern society. We'll end up tearing each other apart. It's much better if we sharpen our claws and our fangs on others, each on their side."

He was impressed by her lucidity. She was really a purebred. She made love with the passion and the ardor of a lioness in heat and she possessed a cunning and clear-sighted intelligence.

One more time, a warm surge of fellow feeling passed through him.

He thought he would like to hold her tenderly, but he was not used to that attitude. He wanted to explain to her how rare this was for him and how that proved the admiration he had for her. But the words did not come.

"You're right. You are totally right." He contented himself with whispering that.

He started caressing her again. This led to another rude test of the mattress springs.

"I'm hungry."

"Me too."

"But what can we eat in a place like this?" she asked, as she got up in one bound.

He admired the full curves of her body, and, vain and satisfied, beholding her boundless freckles, he could not but think with a smile that he had just accomplished a first: he had finally made love to a real red-head.

"Jon, what can we eat?" she repeated. "I'm starving."

"You'll be surprised. Frog legs are the great specialty of the Big Cypress Swamp."

She jumped back as she worked with her arms behind her back, trying to fasten her bra.

"You're half French, and you're just pulling my leg. That's horrible!"

"Absolutely not. They're very good, you'll see."

"Never!"

"I'll make you eat them by force."

They had fun squabbling like children, reveling in the joy of this exceptional moment of happiness.

He opened the window, and through it came the lively distant sounds of a fiddle playing country music.

They came out of the trailer quickly. The sun was already beginning to set. The surrounding undergrowth reeked with the heavy fragrances of wet soil, pierced by the fugitive exhalations of the peppery scents of tropical night flowers as they opened their petals and offered themselves to the darkness.

The Saturday folks had just begun to arrive. Tony waited for them at a table in the big rustic room, sitting alone looking at a fresh bottle of beer. Three more empty bottles stood as proof that he had been there for quite a while already.

"Oh! Here are the lovebirds," he said when he saw them come in.

"He seems pleased to see us," Linda began to say gently.

Laughing, Jonathan interrupted her.

"He was just really fed up with waiting for us."

Tony called Linda to witness:

"You see how little importance he attaches to a real friendship? This is just like Jon."

"She's hungry, stupid. And I see you haven't ordered anything yet."

Faced with the actuality of a huge portion of fried frog legs, Linda forgot her initial hesitation and started to eat with great appetite.

While the two men talked as they ate, she let herself be distracted by a nice voice accompanied by typical chords. The melody was vivid and nostalgic. For an instant, Linda was very far away, completely alone with the music. She suddenly felt her arm being pulled by someone.

"Excuse me," she said to Jonathan and his friend. "This is something I haven't seen for a long time. It's a big change from the phony nightclubs where my husband usually takes me."

She applied herself to listening to them. Jon was still trying to convince Tony to take part in the new expedition he wanted to organize. Little by little, Linda let herself be taken by the extraordinary perfume of adventure, which breathed from that fascinating conversation, although it all seemed very commonplace to them.

They were of the kind that lives in the margin of an always more stifling society. The notion of time and space seemed non-existent to them and tomorrow was mixed up with today and yesterday.

She shivered listening to the report of the dangers they had faced, but the contempt for danger and the material and physical risks they took revealed to her their perfect indifference to the fate of others.

It was however their attitude towards the so-called day-to-day realities that really stunned her. Jonathan had confided to her that he was still living at the shelter and eating the leftovers and bits of sandwiches thrown by satiated tourists in the trashcans of the Miami beaches.

Right now, he was speaking of pieces of eight, golden doubloons, ingots, fortunes in jewels and pearls lying at the bottom of the ocean in the Caribbean coral reefs, as if that treasure was already his, reserved for him for all time by the providence that watched over his destiny.

She stared at Jon with attention, envying his fortitude and the inner fire that would sooner or later allow him to bite with gusto into the huge cake that is the riches of the world, she was sure of that. In her own way, she too had accomplished her difficult ascension by the sweat of her brow. But she was more than 30 years old now, and she had reached her summit. Disillusioned, she could see that she would go no further. Frenchy had appeared right in time to shake her a little bit. With that day, he had brought to her a new desire for life.

"No, nothing will stop me this time; I will find the money. Nothing has been left to chance. I've checked all the tips given by the old man at Cockburn Harbor against what I could gather in the Seville and Cadiz archives."

She experienced a sudden surge of tenderness. Jonathan was really beautiful when he got excited like that!

But he circulated in a selfish universe, indifferent to all that didn't satisfy his young and wild animal instincts, and she knew that she meant nothing more to him than a simple passing fancy.

She reached impulsively for his arm, touching his muscled biceps. He turned to her and smiled mechanically.

Suddenly, in spite of all that, she decided she would do anything to help him.

***

As if escaped from a cartoon, grotesque and clumsy, two large turtles were trying very hard to nibble at the scraps of steel wool hanging between the weight belt and the neoprene wetsuit wore by Jonathan, floating just below the surface of the water in the main pool of the Seaquarium.

Breathing through a hookah, he was clinging as well as he could to the edge of one of the windows while cleaning it. Today was a drudgery day. He still had exactly 24 underwater windows to clean. He had already finished the portholes of the upper floor of the huge aquarium in which dolphins, turtles, sharks, tarpons, jewfishes, cobias, groupers of all sizes, sawfishes, queen angelfishes, rays, moray eels and other smaller fishes in all forms and colors ran alongside one another, seemingly living in harmony.

It was not as glorious and amusing as training dolphins, or catching sharks and resuscitating them by walking with them in the shallow waters of the basin built specially for that purpose, until the water circulating in their gills made them regain consciousness. After the shark channel, he thought, this is the show that makes the girls most excited!

With the steel wool in his hand, he scrubbed the window mechanically, thinking about everything and nothing at the same time, amusing himself making faces at the kids and making sheep's eyes at the local beauties.

In the shade of the corridor, he noticed again the outline of a man who had been observing him for some time already. What the hell did he want?

When his work was done, he climbed up the ladder, followed by turtles and dolphins still wanting to play, and ran soaking wet toward the divers' square to change.

***

"Linda told me that you're an expert in all that concerns diving."

Jonathan sat on the bench in the Seaquarium dressing room, peeling off the bottom of his wetsuit, still dripping with basin water. He recognized the man that had just spoken with him as the man standing up at the basin.

So this is the husband, he thought to himself.

The man was over 40, corpulent without being obese, the top of his head widely bald. He radiated affluence in his light blue alpaca pants that cost 100 dollars at Max Bros, his harmoniously matched navy blue, short sleeve polo shirt and his soft Italian moccasins.

"She tells me that you're the key to all my problems," he said, while chewing on the rest of his fine, hand-rolled Havana cigar, its fragrance spreading around him, both strong and sweet at the same time. I'm a film producer and I need an expert like you for my underwater sequences. The guys around me can hardly swim. They came this close to being surprised to see that seawater is salty.

Jon looked at him with an ironic smile.

"You know what they say here; an expert is anybody who comes from somewhere else."

"Ha! Ha! Bravo! I love your frankness, but I'm all the same sure that you are able."

His direct and clear laugh pleased Jonathan.

"I'd really like to help you, but…" said Jonathan.

The man didn't give him time to finish.

"Everything is arranged. I talked to the Seaquarium director. He is a pal, he can't refuse me anything. From now on, you're at my service. If you want to, of course."

Feeling upset for having been treated like simple merchandise, Jonathan was on the verge of refusing, but the expeditiousness with which all had been arranged impressed him despite himself. On the other hand, he had always felt close to those who go straight to the point, like him.

"When do I begin?" he asked lazily. "What do I have to do?"

"Listen, my friend, you'll be my technical advisor. You'll be kept on the Seaquarium pay list and I'll give you 100 dollars cash every week. Does that suit you?"

"$150," said Jon, just for the sake of form and to see the man's reaction.

"As you wish, I'm not in the habit of splitting hairs. Meet me tomorrow at 8:30 a.m. sharp, in front of the studio basin."

***

The cooperation between the two men immediately proved profitable. They were both precise and brought their professional seriousness, their care and their know-how to the execution of whatever they chose to undertake, each one in their own unique personal manner.

Soon, David swore only by his new assistant and, although he was not inclined to sympathize with those he disdainfully called landlubbers, Jonathan learned very quickly to appreciate David Klein's effective down-to-earth and efficient behavior. He kept an eye on everything. He was always in good humor, but he tolerated no mistakes or incompetence.

"I hate when somebody bluffs me," he told Jonathan, "and I hate even more to waste time."

Moreover, he had an innate sense of the market price of everything around him: the objects, and also the animals and the people. Jonathan played the game with him. They often amused themselves calculating the price in dollars of whatever came in front of their eyes: Kendall, the second cameraman, not more than 5,000 dollars. The blue shark that was fed by Jonathan, 2,000 dollars. The new female assistant of the script girl, with her short and bleached hair... not even the price of admission!

When Jonathan asked him what amount he represented according to him, David suddenly became serious. He took his cigar out of his mouth and spat a piece of tobacco that had remained stuck to his tongue and looked at Jonathan.

"Do you really want to know?" he asked after a brief moment of silence. "It's the oracle that speaks through my mouth. According to where the wind blows from... not more than a piece of shit or a million dollars in ingots and golden coins."

He immediately burst out laughing, slamming a big slap on Jonathan's back. The young man was stunned by what, for him, sounded like a prophecy.

Every now and then, he noticed Linda's long silhouette. She had joined them at the shooting set many times, but always accompanied by her husband. He could see she was still sentimental about him. He would catch a smile or a look outside David's field of vision. But as soon as he suggested the possibility of seeing her again, she became distant. He could hardly understand her game, but had decided not to give it any importance. He really didn't want to arouse any suspicions in David, who was starting to show him real friendship.

Jonathan had initiated him in diving with scuba tanks one day and David's sudden passion for the underwater world had made him even more likable.

"You know, Jon," he said one day. "If I could begin again, and if I was 20 years younger, I would do exactly like you. I would choose the underwater adventure. The life that I live is really damn stupid."

"It's never too late," replied Jonathan.

He couldn't foresee how this small sentence would dangerously worm its way into David Klein's subconscious mind.

***

He had finally rejoined Linda. The orchestra languorously prolonged the slow tune and, on the other end of the long dance floor, protected from indiscreet eyes, she was lovingly coiled up to him.

"I don't understand you anymore," Jonathan said to her. "I have practically not seen you during the whole week. I thought we were already over."

"How could you believe such a thing? I'm working for you, darling, and you don't even notice that. David is infatuated with your way of seeing life."

She threw her head backwards, shaking her long hair, and laughed.

"He can help you. If you know how to maneuver him, he can be your springboard to fortune. And then, I'll be yours completely."

She squeezed her body against his and Jon could feel her naked breasts under the evening gown against his chest. The memory of the unforgettable time they spent together in Pinecrest reappeared in his mind. A sudden surge of desire welled up inside him. His hand flattened in the hollow of her back, and slid down and over the bottom.

"Are you crazy?" Linda moved away from him.

The piece of music was over and they went back to their places, as if nothing had happened. To celebrate the end of the shooting, David had organized a soiree at the Flamenco Supper Club. It was one of the most select clubs in Miami and it was run by Cubans. The evening promised to be lively.

Shirley, the heroine of the TV series they had just finished shooting, was a splendid dark-haired blue-eyed woman, whose siren body and aquatic feats were just beginning to burst onto the small screen. She held David tightly, under the stiff and reproving eyes of the small bleached blonde. She leaned against David, with her bodice widely open revealing her perfect breasts, perfectly naked, and tried very hard to cover both sides of his head with her hands, covering the last hairs, so she could see if baldness suited him.

"Dave," she chuckled "you'll be even more handsome and impressive like that."

David pushed her away, laughing.

"Watch out, here come Linda and Jon. Hey, Frenchy! Come sit down next to us."

Linda, suddenly turned icy, sat down and Jonathan grabbed an empty chair in front of him and sat down nonchalantly next to her. David said:

"Shirley, this is the guy for you. He is a real fish, just like you. You would make a splendid aquatic couple. I can already see you in a fantastic series that we could do together; a new Tarzan, but underwater. You would then get married and would have many little fishes."

He burst out laughing, happy with this idea.

The lights went down in the room and then off. The spotlights lit up the dance floor. A group of pretty young women, dressed as Spanish gypsies entered the room undulating and smiling, accompanied by the clatter of castanets.

Jonathan loathed the phony, tainted atmosphere of nightclubs. He was caught by surprise by the fresh cheerfulness and good humor that reigned here.

A sudden nostalgia for the Caribbean shores took hold of him. He remembered what Linda had just told him. After all, why not? David was nice. He had money and he seemed to trust him completely.

When he least expected it, the right moment presented itself, and it was David himself who offered the opening. They were alone for the first time at the table, face to face. All the others were dancing.

"Jon," David muttered as he lit up the huge Havana he had just bought from the cigarette girl, "Jon, what are you going to do now? Don't tell me you're going to keep diving in that bathtub, playing the asshole in front of all those voyeurs at the Seaquarium, who are only waiting for the moment when you will be eaten by the sharks." He laughed again. "But I don't think they're wrong, see, I do exactly the same. One must get what one pays for." He was chuckling with pleasure, delighted with his own cynicism.

Jonathan was curious to see what he was trying to get at, so he let him speak. He could not yet dare to believe that the gods might again be on his side.

"Listen," resumed David, "I've decided to rest a little. I don't know if I told you or not, but I own a magnificent 45-foot cruiser. It was one of Linda's extravagances. It sleeps at the marina, it costs me a fortune to maintain, and I almost never use it."

He stopped, staring at Jonathan with shrewd eyes, watching out for his reaction. But Jonathan maintained a frozen attitude, a smile on his lips.

"You've opened new horizons to me with your diving," David said, "so here's what I propose to you."

He stopped for a brief moment, so he could impress even more.

"I'll take you for a 15-day cruise in the Caribbean, all expenses paid, salary to be discussed. We'll take Lindy and Shirley with us, the four of us… but beware! There'll be absolutely no orgy."

Shaking the ash off his cigar on the carpet, he guffawed in his habitual way.

Jonathan also took some time to respond. He was thanking Linda inwardly. David was trapped.

"I have something better to offer," he said. "And there'll certainly be no orgy on the boat, because there will be no women on board."

David was puzzled.

"Yes," said Jonathan, "how would you like to make a fortune at the same time?"

"Are you serious, Frenchy?"

"I couldn't be more serious."

"But it's not any criminal venture, is it?"

"Absolutely not."

Jonathan's face lit up with is best smile.

"It's the salvaging of a fabulous treasure, a Spanish galley that sunk over three hundred years ago. It was crammed full of gold, silver and jewelry looted from the Incas. I'm the only one who knows its exact location and I tell you right away: shipwrecks are my specialty."

Literally chewing on his cigar, David looked at Jonathan with new eyes, saying nothing. Until then, he had taken him for a young puppy. He was certainly skillful in his field, amusing in his carefree attitude, but he had never dreamed of attaching to him any importance whatsoever. Only his way of moving around Linda without ever seeming to touch her had sometimes disturbed him.

The music had just stopped. In the general hubbub and the noise of chairs and tables, the dancers were coming back to the table. Leaning over to Jonathan, he whispered hastily:

"Come see me at the boat tomorrow, shortly before noon at the Coconut Grove Marina. The trawler's name is Barracuda — pier 27, slip 103. Don't say a word to anybody."

David had made up his mind in a flash of lucidity. If Jonathan were lying, he would not lose anything. He would have had a good outing. But if it was true… He could already see all the possibilities and the consequences, professionally and otherwise.

Linda came back to her seat. A little change in their attitude suggested that something important had just happened between the two men. Her eyes crossed Jonathan's. He smiled at her with an expression of intense inner joy that she had never seen in him before. His head made an imperceptible movement up and down, meant for her eyes only. It's in the bag!

CHAPTER 8

To celebrate their agreement, Jonathan decided to grant himself a free morning. He called the Seaquarium and told them he was sick.

But he did not stay very long in the sinister dorm at the shelter where he was still spending his nights, this in spite of the relative afflu-ence his new job with the TV crew allowed him. He put on a pair of shorts, an old white T-shirt turned yellow, and left. Outside, he smelled the moist city air and walked quickly to the Coffee Shop on the corner of 22nd St. and North Biscayne Boulevard. It was not the best place in the world, but the coffee at least had nothing to do with the boiled brown water served at the refectory. He quickly drank a cup of burning hot coffee and ate two doughnuts and then took the bus.

The bus was packed with a heterogeneous crowd. They're all broke, just like me, he thought. They can't even afford a secondhand clunker.

As usual, he looked at the buildings passing by, blocks of all sizes, arranged like cubes one after the other. Bordering the wide avenue, some thin palm and coconut trees, themselves also prisoners of man's madness, gave a splash of greenery to that desert of reinforced con-crete. This time, he consoled himself with the thought that very soon his eyes would rest on the infinite blue of the sea, far from all that hor-ror.

He got off the bus on Flagler Street and entered into a maze of nar-row streets. He had always had a soft spot for Little Havana with its vitality, its smells and colors.

He got on a second bus that took him to the corner of South Bay Shore Drive and 27th Avenue. Then he walked up to Coconut Grove and the Marina.

From a distance, Jonathan could sense more than he could see the Barracuda. The rustic outline of the trawler stood out clearly against what, in his opinion, were the far too fragile lines of the cruisers of all sizes. By what miracle could a man like David, so little informed about the things of the sea, have chosen a boat so suitable to their projects? Jonathan saw in that destiny's reassuring sign.

Closer to the boat, he experienced a feeling close to euphoria. He admired the straight and solid stem, the cabin's rustic cubic form surmounted by the flying bridge, the quarterdeck wide and clear.

He noticed a silhouette behind a windowpane. 'Certainly David,' he thought.

With one leap, he crossed the thin gangway connecting the boat to the quay. The teak boards of the freshly washed deck smelled good. Walking along the deck on the port side, he passed through the sliding door into a vast and luxurious wardroom.

Nestled in the hidden recess of a comfortable seat with a glass in his hand and a smile lighting up his business-man-who-was-finally-relaxed-because-he-was-resting face, David was waiting for him.

"Welcome aboard," he said jovially, still very happy with his own choice of words. "Well, Frenchy, what do you think? Surprised, huh?"

Jonathan wanted to have a laugh at his expense.

"Not too bad at first sight. But tell me, David, how were you able to choose so well?"

"You should know, Jon, that when I decide to do something, I always do it well."

"That's true, that's true, I can't deny that… But without realizing it, when you bought this boat, you won the big prize."

"Well, that's great!" Since the compliment came from Jonathan, David could not have felt more flattered.

"Will you have a drink now or do you want to see the boat first?"

"I would rather see right away what it has in its belly."

They lifted a trap door and went down.

The twin Diesel engines with 250 HP each seemed to be in perfect shape.

As Jon admired their tidiness, David gave him the details.

"I have an excellent mechanic. He asks nothing more than to join us."

"No," Jonathan replied dryly. "Just as we'll pass without women, we'll pass without a mechanic."

As he admired the luxury of the interior design, he was mentally calculating the changes that would have to be made. They would need a lot of space to store the diving, prospecting and salvage equipment. The back cabin would be perfect for that.

Made to confront all kinds of sea, well equipped and self-sufficient, the boat was spacious but also capable of being handled by a small crew. It was the ideal partner for a discreet, fast and effective operation.

It was exactly the boat they needed! Now he had to tell David about his responsibilities.

When the visit was finished, they sat down next to the coffee table. A pleasant breeze entered the vast cabin, bringing with it the freshness of the open sea and all the confused hubbubs of the Marina. The short curtain of the picture window right behind him was flapping in the breeze, now and then caressing the nape of Jonathan's neck.

"Don't expect a pleasure trip, David. It's not because we have this boat that everything is taken care of. Very frankly, the only reason I told you about all this is because you have the money. What I bring is an exceptional business, and I'll prove that to you very soon. People would talk about it for a long time in the treasure hunters' brotherhood, if I wanted to shout it from the rooftops to the rest of the world... But everything will have to be done in the most secret way. There'll be no sharing this with anybody whatsoever. I couldn't care less about fame and even less about patrimony or heritage."

He started laughing.

"You know, David, to do this business effectively, you have to put yourself in the place of the Spanish conquerors. No pity, no sentimentality! The gold belongs to the strongest. Misfortune to the defeated, as the Romans said. And they knew all about that."

"Vae victis!" David interrupted him, lifting his glass.

"Do you speak Latin now?" Jonathan seemed really surprised.

"Well, no, you idiot. I've just taken part in the shooting of a sequence about the first Christian martyrs."

They guffawed noisily and Jonathan thought that with David on board he would not ever be bored.

"You're right, boy," David continued. "I too am in the habit of putting the dots on the i's with my future associates. Go on, I'm interested."

"Well, since we must be frank, I hesitated even in spite of your dough, because you don't seem to be suited for excessive physical labor."

"You don't upset me, absolutely not, Frenchy. I just wonder which one of us works the most in this fucking life! How much is what we can salvage worth in your opinion?"   David continued, bringing his glass of whisky to his lips.

Jonathan took some time to answer the question. "Three years ago, Kip Wagner, who I already told you about, cashed a check for $228,000 after the New York auction of just a part of his discovery. And this is just a small example. For what concerns our treasure, I prefer not to speak in terms of numbers. The Santa Isabella, besides its usual load of thousands of silver and gold coins embossed in place, transported an extremely mysterious cargo. According to the page of the manuscript that I could examine at the Archivo General de España, in Seville, she's listed on the loading manifestos under the denomination Venerable Treasure of the Ten Kings of the Sea."

"Are you telling the truth, Frenchy?"

"Yeah, but even more strange is the way in which the Santa Isabella disappeared. I read with my own eyes the confession of the Admiral in charge of the protection squadron during his trial, archived by the Casa de Contratación.

"According to him, the Santa Isabella literally vanished into thin air. In a moment it was there, in the thickest mist, surrounded by its guard dogs and then, suddenly, when the mist lifted, it was not there anymore. Not only there was no storm, but also they had been becalmed for five days off an island in the Bahamas, a disturbing dead calm."

David swallowed his whisky in one gulp and then said, a glint of irony in his voice,

"I see very well what you're trying to say. It was the first disappearance in the so-called Bermuda Triangle! Well, I tell you right away, Frenchy, I absolutely don't believe in this kind of twaddle and I'd be very disappointed to see a guy like you believe in it."

"Me! I believe in everything and nothing." Jonathan got worked up. "Our universe is nothing but hot air. It's all put on anyway."

"Maybe, but when you're in deep shit, that doesn't stop it from smelling bad."

David's remark relieved the atmosphere.

"But how can you know where the wreck is located if there never was a wreck?"

"Some have seen it."

"Some have seen it… And they have never touched it?"

"No. They were local lobster fishermen whom I taught how to dive with scuba gear."

"Oh, yeah?"

"Will you let me finish? They never touched it because for them — and this is disturbing nevertheless — the corner is damned, haunted. It's frequented by zombies, chickshawnees* and other ghosts from the past."

"I see… I see."

Jonathan noticed his future partner's hesitation and he acknowledged it.

"For reasons that you must understand, I'll only be able to tell you its precise location after we reach a perfect agreement."

Jonathan smiled.

David started speaking slowly, weighing all his words.

"A lot of things bother me in your story. A ship that wrecked without wrecking, a haunted island, a cargo unlike any other… I've never been a shipwreck hunter, Frenchy, but I have some notion of reality anyway. Nobody, especially not me, would ever dream of taking on the expenses and the amount of effort that an enterprise such as this must require based on such wacky evidence. I hope at least that you don't take me for a clown."

"Another drink?" Jon had taken the bottle of whisky and was pointing the neck towards David.

David agreed with a movement of his head.

"David, I'm going to tell you the whole story. Then you can consider it and make your decision. I've been involved in this business for two years now. In the beginning, it seemed to be nothing but a rumor. I was on another wreck site with a pal of mine, Tony Anderson, a sensational guy, an expert in the matter. I haven't yet given up on the idea of making him join us. Well, we were at Cockburn Harbor, on the Turks and Caicos Islands, in ransit to the Silver Bank. A group of us treasure hunters had gathered together at a local inn.

"There was also an old Spanish professor present, an ethnologist

---

* Chickshawnees: legendary bad omen birds, with a human face, part of the Bahamas folklore.

who had come to do some research on the old Arawak Indians and also to study the landing places of Christopher Columbus. The conversation went on about all the mysterious disappearances that had happened in that area — total instantaneous disappearances — without leaving any tracks. Each one of us told a little story or gave his opinion, until the old man told us this one about the Santa Isabella. He did not say the ship's name, though. For the audience, it was just one case among many others."

Jonathan stared at David, who did not say a word.

David had just lit one of his endless Havanas. Almost strangling the cigar, he sat deeper in his seat. Behind the dark sunglasses, his eyes had the kind of fixed expression that Jonathan had learned to recognize.

He went on.

"Be it intuition or the reflex of a well-informed hunter, it all rang a bell for me. I didn't say anything, but I did all I could to make them change the subject of the conversation. He admitted to me that he had found that story by chance, when he was consulting the archives in Spain. Unfortunately, he couldn't remember which archives, the name of the ship or the location. He couldn't even say if it was in Cadiz, in Simancas, at the Archivo General de España, or in Seville, at the Archivo de Indias. So I landed a contract with a firm that specializes in offshore work in the North Sea and left for Europe. I stayed there for six months and after that, I decided to go for the sun and the good life in Southern Spain, where I played the tourist. I started out in Cadiz, the last place where the headquarters of the Casa de Contratación were located."

"What's that?"

"It was a State organization created by the Kings of Spain in the 1500s, so that they could give an official cover to the looting of the riches of the New World. It was the Casa de Contratación that prepared in the slightest details each one of the expeditions of the Flotas, which were armies of merchant ships escorted by war galleys. The big books at the Casa, as well as those at the Seville Archives and other places, have become bibles for treasure hunters."

"Why is that? Anybody can consult them?" David sounded intrigued.

"Yes, provided that they're willing to take the trouble, that they know old and modern Spanish, that they can decipher the handwriting of the time, and that they have many months available and a lot of patience."

"In fact, it's an open secret, if I understood it well."

"Well, actually no, and you didn't understand anything at all," said Jon, happy to laugh at David's expense. "Luckily for us, people of our kind who frequent those places are very rare."

At Jonathan's remark, David smiled again.

"The vast majority of library rats are there for their studies or to do their research."

"Go on, Jon, you're doing well, you're beginning to interest me."

Jonathan continued his story, trying hard to remain as sober and explicit as possible. Step by step, he described the long path he had traveled to the final certainty. ·

After a stupid brawl one evening with some representatives of the Spanish police in Santa Cruz, he spent a few months in a jail in Seville. Repatriated by the American Consulate, Jonathan arrived in Florida completely broke and with his morale well below zero. Between small jobs and plunders, often times passing the hat, he survived in that fauna of beach-combers and bums of all kinds who drag their idleness and their weariness along the sands of the beaches and the boards of the Marinas from Haulover Beach to Pier One.

One day, freshly shaved and wearing a new pair of jeans pinched the day before from the display at an Army and Navy store, he landed a job aboard a big rental cruiser — what unexpected luck!

From charter to charter, he traveled up and down all the islands and islets of the Bahamas, from Great Abaco to the Turks and Caicos Islands. He sobered up and recovered a civilized veneer.

The months passed by.

He dived every time it was possible. But one probe after the other brought only disillusion. He seemed to be jinxed. And then, all of a sudden, without warning, there came a revelation!

As he was searching in vain the bottom of the sea in the Exuma Sound, he came upon a small crayfish fishing boat. After a few glasses of whisky, the fishermen revealed to him the existence of a most strange site, an island renowned for being haunted. A very old shipwreck rested on the bottom close by.

"My heart leaped in the air, Dave. We were cruising off the coast of the island, and I identified some of the details described by the admiral.

My Bahamian friends obstinately refused to land on the island. I had agreed to a day of fishing with them. They loved that because when I was with them, their catch was multiplied by five. In spite of everything, with the help of the rum, I learned many strange facts that only reinforced my conviction. A whole ensemble of superstitions and legends crowded the corner. The best and also the most impressive one, because it corresponded to the fantastic aspect of the disappearance of the Santa Isabella, was that the island had become haunted after the sinking, a long time ago, of an immense sailboat that had been struck by the wrath of the Gods of the Ocean. This because the vessel transported in its holds — hold onto yourself — the sacred treasure of their first ten kings. A similar coincidence can't be made up. What do you think?"

"And in certain full moon nights, you can hear very clearly the souls of all those damned people who come back to the island to moan and whine," said David with a deep voice.

Surprised, Jonathan looked at him.

"It's exactly like that. How did you guess?"

"It's not difficult. It's always like that in legends. Didn't your mother ever read fairy tales to you?"

"Well, okay, I get it. Clearly, I haven't been able to convince you."

"Absolutely not, you fool. I just want to warn you against the danger of illusion."

"They're not illusions. I went back there."

"Oh, yeah?"

"A few months ago, I went aboard a boat just like yours, as a diving instructor. My Cuban employers apparently had a lot of time to waste. I took them over there and took advantage of the opportunity to search all the bottom of the sea and also every little nook and cranny of the island. In one of the countless caves near the surface of the water, I found traces of a shipwreck covered by the sand. I immediately searched the area and it didn't take long for me to notice a protuberance that distinguished itself neatly from the abundant surrounding corals. I extracted it with my dive knife. After I got it out of the water and broke the limestone coating, I found a piece of eight, just as I had often seen, but always in somebody else's hand."

Jonathan looked at David, who was not flinching.

"I was almost out of air so I went back on board," he continued. "By one of those sudden setbacks of destiny that seem to character-ize my life, my employers had decided to get under way immediate-ly to a precise point right in the middle of the bay. After a mysteri-ous appointment with a big Chris-Craft, they would head back to Miami."

"I think I already guessed what comes next," David interrupted him. He seemed to be enjoying himself.

"Yes," said Jon, "you laugh, but it was not as funny as that. We were intercepted 3 miles off the shore by a Coast Guard patrol boat and some Narcotics Bureau agents. My employers had just received an enor-mous amount of pure heroin, almost 500 pounds, arriving from Mar-seilles, I think. Needless to say, I found myself in jail for the second time. I have just now come out; with my name completely cleared and I can hardly wait to take my revenge."

David finally had the reaction that Jonathan was not expecting any-more.

"Bravo, Frenchy! You're the kind of guy that doesn't let himself be beaten down by events. I told you, sometimes I'd rather be like you."

He crushed his cigar on the ashtray and continued joyfully.

"Whether you're bluffing or not, I've decided that I couldn't care less. The local old bags are beginning to tire me. I need some of the fresh flesh of the islands. I'm going with you."

He stopped, suddenly pensive.

"Tell me… can you show me that eight reales coin, a piece of eight?"

"No, it was confiscated with everything else," whispered Jonathan, confused by David's reaction.

"Too bad, too bad, it would have pleased me to touch it, especially if it should be the only one," he said with his usual humor.

"Are you joking? If it's really the Santa Isabella — and everything seems to prove that — the record of 30,000 pieces of the famous Lucaya treasure collected by Gary Simmons and his three pals six years ago will be broken wide open."

"At how much was it estimated?"

"Hans Schulman, the numismatist expert, spoke of 2 million dollars at the time and he affirmed that even that was way under its true value."

"I see…" David whispered, pensive. "What is the part of the State in all this?" he asked.

"Twenty-five percent, but each declaration regarding the demand for the exploitation license of a shipwreck gives place to different dealings. The law approved by the government of the Bahamas is relatively recent, from 1962 or 1963. It was created after many discoveries and its aim was only to touch a piece of the cake. It's the development of autonomous diving that has caused all that… It's the price, the ransom of progress, in a certain way."

"Ransom is a very convenient term, Frenchy."

"Now you see why I said in the beginning that this wouldn't be a pleasure trip," said Jon. "We'll have to be extremely discreet if we don't want to give a quarter, if not half, of the fruit of our work and our ingenuity to a bunch of parasite anonymous government officials. I think you agree with me, don't you, David?"

David shook his head affirmatively many times, with a smile on his face.

"I'm always against needless sharing. If it's possible, naturally."

"Okay! It's more than fair that those who take the risks also take the profit without having to give any explanations to anybody!"

The two friends enjoyed a short digression. They shared the same point of view. There was always on one side, people like them, who were constantly leading on the edge, opening the way, and on the other side, a crowd heavy with inertia, envious profiteers that followed them passively.

"But I decided to take up the challenge," continued Jonathan. "I'm not going to last very long, I know, but during the time that's left, I'm going to live as I please."

"You don't deny your blood, you're a true descendant of your buccaneer ancestors. Deep down inside, you're a romantic man, Jon, kind of a poet."

He suddenly became serious again and added,

"But let's talk business. I bring in the boat and I'll finance all the operations. I just had a wonderful idea! The production of a new series for my TV company! The world of coral and its richness! And, by the way, I can enter a big part of the cost of our venture as general expenses. What do you think?"

"Not bad, except for the title. This would justify our presence in the area with the local authorities as well with the curious crowd."

The first hours of the afternoon passed very quickly. They went over the main lines of the project and could not find any major obstacle. The only shadow, and a really big one, was that they needed a third man. With only two men the expedition would not be possible.

"What about your pal, Tony? Are you sure he would not join us?"

David was finishing his third sandwich.

"Nevertheless, one quarter of the money is a big amount."

"A quarter? Why a quarter?"

In his surprise, Jon dropped a knife. He picked it up slowly, staring David in the eyes.

"It's time to lay my cards on the table. I will go 50/50. Those you might bring with you, that's your business."

Jonathan's silence revealed a bad spark in his already hard look. David hastened to add:

"Think fast and well, Frenchy, I think it's perfectly fair. It's I who take all the financial risks and I'm also throwing my reputation and my career into this project."

"I see," said Jonathan, "I have no choice. In principle, I agree, but we'll see. After all, neither you nor I know what might be the conditions of our third partner."

"Maybe you're right, but it's a matter of principle for me too. I'm sorry to insist, but I think it's better to make up your mind right away. Again, I'll cough up all that's needed, including the most sophisticated equipment that you think is required."

After a brief silence, Jonathan's fixed and hard expression turned into a wide smile. He held out his hand. David held it and shook it vigorously, as he looked right into Jonathan's eyes.

"Perfect," he said, "from now on you're at home here. Make yourself comfortable on board. The Barracuda is now our headquarters."

Both men got up and David accompanied Jonathan up to the little rear gangway. The moment Jonathan set foot on the ground he turned back.

"David," he called.

"What?"

"Don't say a word to anybody."

***

It was almost 6 pm when he arrived at the shelter, after having strolled through Northeast 21st Street. He had spent quite some time in the ship chandler stores, making an initial list of the things they would need.

From time to time, his hand held tightly the wad of dollars in his jeans pocket — a total of 200 dollars in small denominations — that David had given to him in a burst of generosity or clever calculation.

A vague smell, acrid and persistent, of chemical disinfectant merged with the more human and appetizing odor of the kitchen as Jon passed through the big gate. He collided with the bums, wanderers and broke guys of all kinds that frequented the place. It was the rush hour of the 'boarders' who, for a modest amount, had meals and a bed every night.

Leaning against the front desk counter, as he waited for his turn to settle his bill, he examined the faces passing by, trying to find out each time what was the main reason of the decay of the poor wretch. Despite the common assumption, alcohol was not the main cause; it was just the second-degree executioner. All of them, one moment or another in their fucking lives had been, for one reason or another, hit in their quickworks and they lacked the necessary strength to right the helm in the midst of their personal storm. He was different from them.

A voice brought him back from his thoughts. It was the receptionist.

"Are you leaving us, Larue?"

"Yeah, I found work. Room and board and my laundry done."

"You owe us $15.75," said the employee with a neutral voice.

Jonathan ostentatiously took the wad of money out of his pocket and gave him a 20-dollar bill.

"Keep the change."

He got a suspicious look.

"I didn't steal it, it's an advance. I formed a partnership with a millionaire."

"I didn't say anything." The employee remained undisturbed.

Jonathan regretted his own change of mood. For him, it's just a parade of bums just like me all day long. That made him smile.

For an instant, he thought of getting in line at the refectory as a goodbye gesture but when he saw how long it was, he gave up. I'm becoming sentimental; this is not good, he thought.

He went up to the second floor in the big dorm number 5. His bed was under a window, a place of choice from which he could catch the fresh air coming in.

He didn't have much, just a few things that he quickly put in his sailor bag. He removed his personal padlock that he used to lock up the small locker over the head of the bed. He gathered some papers and a file folder labeled W.W. Cay in which were gathered all his notes regarding the wreck. In the bottom of the shelf there stood a little yellowish photo in a leather frame. Jonathan took the photo and, in a pensive mood, contemplated his mother's face."

"So you're really leaving, Frenchy?"

Jon was startled.

"What are you doing here, Jerry?"

"Bill, the reception guy, told me that you had just paid your bill and that you're leaving. I came to say goodbye."

"That's very nice of you. Yes, I'm out of here."

"Looks like you're loaded."

"It's unbelievable! You can't hide anything here."

Jonathan was joking, but deep down inside he was impressed with the speed with which the news had spread.

'As long as the same thing does not happen with the expedition,' he thought.

Jerry was not a wreck like all the others. It was impossible to determine his age. Between sixty and seventy maybe. Just like the others, he seemed to have been shaken a lot in the course of his life. He was originally from Germany and he looked a little bit like Rommel, but emaciated and aged after a succession of defeats.

They had often talked and drank a lot of beers at Chez Harry, the local inn that was the branch of the Mission for all the bums in the area. His erudition had left Jonathan flabbergasted and they had gotten along well together around a love in common: the sea.

A sudden impulse that he could not explain moved Jonathan.

"Put on a shirt, a clean pair of pants and shave yourself, Jerry. I'm taking you out to a big meal."

CHAPTER 9

If Jonathan had done well — Chez Pierre was one of the most sought-after restaurants in Miami Beach — old Jerry had more than risen to the occasion. He took a shower and shaved closely and carefully. His white hair, still thick for his age, was shampooed, and gave his craggy buccaneer's face a certain air of dignity. The weariness that was evident in his spruced up countenance took on the semblance of sophisticated disenchantment.

The open collar of his very proletarian but fashionable sky blue dungaree shirt revealed a shiny luxurious silk head square by Dior, a gift from Linda to Jon.

They had managed to pass by the bad-tempered doorkeeper in his richly brocaded uniform without difficulty. Jerry seemed to be what he was not, an affluent yacht owner — and Jonathan looked exactly what he was — a young ocean shark to whom no one tried to show their superiority anymore…

Together they formed the classic pair of the yachtsman and his skipper, usual customers at restaurants and bars in marinas.

The two men were sitting at a discreet table in the big room, facing Biscayne Bay. The room was decorated in a rustic manner, with braids of garlic, big red peppers and onions scattered here and there. A few oil paintings with violent colors hanging on the picture rail projected the image of enlightened patronage on the two brothers from Marseilles who owned the joint.

"Order whatever you want, I'll have what you have," said Jonathan.

The old man examined the menu. Then, speaking quietly in French, he ordered fish soup for starters, then a lamb shoulder accompanied by a white Cassis and a red Bandol, both from the South of France.

"These wines acclimatize better to Florida, don't they?" he asked the sommelier, who looked surprised to see an expert customer who was clearly a sailor and looked somewhat neglected.

"You speak French now?"

Jonathan didn't try to hide his bewilderment. The contrast with the hiccupping Jerry of the interminable drinking sessions at Harry's was very big.

"Why? Is that really so rare? You know, I wasn't always this that I apparently have become... just apparently."

"I suspected as much. We're all in the same boat. By the way, there were several rumors at the Mission about you. They said that you had been part of the flower of thinking heads at Cape Canaveral."

Jerry did not respond.

"You're German, aren't you?"

"I'm an American citizen and proudly so."

"But you were German before that?"

"Listen, Jon, if you invited me here so that you could bore me with these questions, you could well have done that at the shelter. The past is past. Let's forget it. This is the only advantage left for us in this continent."

"You're right, Jerry, I'm sorry. With all the respect due to your advanced age, I beg you, please forgive me."

"Don't laugh at me on top of everything else. I could prove my superiority in terms of physical endurance to many young fellows of your age."

"And of resistance to alcohol too."

To Jon's surprise, the old man did not take offense.

"I'm forced to penalize you," he said simply, "and it is I who will ask the questions now."

"That's straight enough. Go on, we'll see."

"First of all, what happened to you? Did you win the lottery?"

Jonathan almost replied with another one of the verbal pirouettes that were his specialty, but moved by a sudden impulse, maybe the same one that had moved him to invite the old man to the restaurant, he told him about his meeting with David Klein.

He refrained from telling him about the treasure, but explained to him that the purpose of the expedition was to do a systematic search of the coral depths of the Bahamas and shoot sequences for an important TV series.

"What are you searching for exactly?" asked an attentive Jerry.

"Well, everything and nothing," answered Jonathan, carelessly. "In fact, David wants to take a three-week rest… but since this is a guy who knows how to join pleasure and work, we will pretend to be working. But he's always on the lookout for the sensational and would not be displeased if he ran into something fantastic by accident."

Jerry lifted his stemmed glass to the height of his eyes.

"There is no accident; there is never accident," he whispered, pensive.

"His wife is a hell of a size," said Jonathan to change the subject.

"Women on board are always dangerous."

"Precisely, old man. I decided there'll be no women on board."

Jerry suddenly woke up from his daydreaming.

"What did you say, Jon? You… and no women! The trip must be much more important than what you seem to want to tell me."

"It's David. In terms of work, he's a real stickler for principles," said Jonathan, a little too hastily.

"Oh, yes!" said Jerry, who didn't seem the least convinced.

The lamb shoulder arrived just in time to change the course of the conversation. It lived up to the restaurant's reputation. Once again, Jonathan was flabbergasted by the old man's know-how.

He had insisted on tasting the wine himself before it was served, and watched by the impassive wine steward, he indulged in the usual ceremony.

"It has endured the trip superbly and has aged very well," he said as a form of conclusion, after having drunk the small amount of wine he worked religiously with his tongue and his palate, his eyes half-closed.

The old man had a hell of a past. That was certain. The more he thought of it, the more the young man wondered if he was not in fact dealing with one of those brainiacs who, starting in 1945, were recruited without false shame from the enemy ranks, in the name of science. Their names were cleared immediately and some of them, even before the war was over, had become full American citizens very quickly. In any case, much more easily than the unfortunate ordinary immigrant from Europe or other places, people who sweated over the quota of the country's entry lists.

'This was an additional illustration, if necessary, of the sense of equity and the morality of the administration,' he thought, looking at Jerry, who was chewing his food with great concentration.

Jonathan had been very talkative until then. The proximity of a new beginning, the conviction that he was engaging himself — finally with all the means at his disposal — in the path that should inevitably take him to fortune kept him in a state of constant internal over excitation of which he was hardly aware.

He talked extensively about all his diving activity. The sudden revelation of the underwater world that was offered to him in the brief period of time he spent as one of the US Navy S.E.A.L. divers had acted as a catalyst for that which would become a true vocation. After being discharged, he had specialized in that area, becoming a professional diver. Very quickly he limited the geographical sector for his activities to just the Caribbean Sea and most particularly, the Bahamas archipelago. Enthusiastically, almost lyrically, he let filter through his jokes a juvenile passion for that life with no hindrances in an universe of sun, turquoise blue water lagoons and coral reefs swarming with multiform and multicolored wildlife and flora and gigantic rocky slopes opening suddenly toward the dark blue of unfathomable abysses.

He suddenly stopped talking about himself. Jerry intrigued him hugely. His curiosity was awake and the moment had come to uncover the true identity of his friend. To win his trust, he engaged in a conversation about a theme that was dear to both of them — diving. Jerry in fact started making confidences himself. As Jonathan was relating the existence of prodigious and not properly explained abysses called Blue Holes, Jerry suddenly interrupted him.

"I had the opportunity to explore many of them, many years ago."

"You?" Jonathan could not hide his astonishment.

"Yes, son, I told you that as far as I'm concerned, you shouldn't trust appearances. Your underwater universe was mine well before you came into this world."

"Are you telling me that you were a diver?"

"Yes, exactly, and in a way as such you have never been."

He paused momentarily to produce a stronger effect.

"Among other things, I was the commander of a submarine during the war."

There was a brief moment of silence. A smile danced on Jonathan's lips.

"I'm beginning to understand," he said.

"What are you beginning to understand?"

"Many things… your old pirate mug, for instance, and the reason why you were so friendly with me… right away!"

Jonathan stretched his arms over the table and tapped many times on the old man's shoulders.

"A meeting of two sea sharks, an old one and a young one, that deserves a celebration," he said.

He called the headwaiter and ordered champagne. As Jerry protested, Jonathan rebuffed him.

"In this world of fools and bumpkins that will end up completely asphyxiating the planet, it's time for us to recognize one another."

Jerry's furrowed face was illuminated with a smile of contentment.

"Would you like to recreate the Brotherhood of the Coast by any chance?"

"Yes, exactly, why not? But this time we would live under the sea. I know a couple of immense underwater caves with depths I could never reach. They would serve very well."

Jerry's expression changed suddenly. He looked like somebody who was in huge pain.

"What's going on? Did I say something I shouldn't have said?" Jonathan asked, truly disturbed.

"Maybe, but you wouldn't understand anyway. Others have thought about that before you, a long time ago — an underwater residence."

Jerry was almost whispering.

"Yes, I know, the underwater house… I'm not the one who invented it."

"No, not that way. You were thinking of a brotherhood, weren't you, Jon? Of a group that would integrate itself totally into the sea element, our original home."

Jonathan protested, looking at the old bum who seemed very unusual that evening,

"I never said that, or you have misunderstood my words. It was a joke, not even that, it was a figure of speech. I know very well that it's impossible."

"Well, you're wrong, old buddy," Jerry resumed adamantly. "Many strange events in the last years could be explained in this way."

"What do you mean exactly?"

"All those mysterious, instantaneous disappearances, with no trace left of boats or airplanes cannot be just a group of fortuitous circumstances. I'm convinced that they're the result of a calculated intent."

Jonathan looked at him astonished.

"But all of this, it's all put on, this is grandfather talk, you've been outmoded by modern life. This is a vein that has been explored by some writers and their editors. People are so stupid... It's normal that the ones that are more cunning take advantage of them. If I had the talent, I'd do exactly the same. You can make several million dollars in the most simple and most dishonest way possible."

Jonathan burst out laughing at his own witty remark and then he added,

"I spend all year round in the middle of the Bermuda Triangle, if that's what you mean, and I have never disappeared."

"No doubt it was not yet your turn. You're just a young man, Jon. You have many things to learn. One should never make an affirmation without being sure."

"Listen, old bum, you won't get me with that. You've either spoken too much or just not enough. At the point where you are, you have to tell me more."

"Son, it's exactly what I intended to do, and first of all I want to warn you. I didn't start navigating in that area yesterday. Before the war started, I had become an expert in that part of the continental plateau. I was born in Germany. You had guessed right it was not that hard. Our old rulers, may the devil have their souls... they had decided, for reasons that escaped me at the time, to conduct a systematic study of the depths of the ocean in that area.

"It's evident that we didn't have at our disposal the resources that are available today, but the amount of information that was gathered was nevertheless considerable and I was put in charge of studying it. The war started and I was initially put in charge of a U-Boat, and during a few months, anonymous in the pack of submarines, I participated in the extermination of the allied fleets. Your people gave us the nickname 'Sea Wolves'. We had really become wolves."

The old man stopped and his blue eyes stared into space. "We were almost successful."

Usually not very sensitive to other people's stories, Jonathan could sense all the bitterness still present in the German's voice after all those years.

"You see, son, you brag about having pirate ancestors, but I've really been a pirate of the seas. Through the periscope, I vibrated with enthusiasm when I saw the smoke that marked our prey. I've burst with joy with the crew when, having taken a deadly hit by our torpedo, a ship's stem would reach desperately toward the sky before being swallowed up by the sea. I have been in a sweat, my body tight with distress, when our submarine's skeleton shook and squeaked under the impact of the depth charges strewn by the enemy frigates chasing after us."

He stopped suddenly, aware of Jon's silence.

"Basically, you couldn't care less."

"Absolutely not, grandpa, I envy you. But the time for these big emotions is definitely dead and buried and I think you're wandering from the subject at hand."

"You certainly have nerve, Jonathan, but you're right. To make a long story short, when the wind began to turn, I joined a brain trust in charge of organizing the total war effort. I was specifically in charge of its underwater aspect. Everything I did there was top secret. I was very brilliant at the time."

He sighed, and then he inhaled a deep breath of air while he straightened his bony torso.

"I thought I knew everything," he went on, "and I was proud of belonging to the group of people who were at that time my gods. I was proud of being privy to facts and information that were hidden from the majority. Nevertheless, I missed the biggest and most terrible of them without even realizing it."

Through the picture window, he pointed to the thousands of lights of the Marina that shone far away in the quiet summer night.

"You see, son, all those crazy people float over the biggest threat humanity has ever known."

"This isn't right, Jerry, you're talking nonsense! I have a feeling that you've lost the habit of champagne!"

A sudden shiver passed through the old man's body. He suddenly stared at Jonathan. The muscles of his jaw were tense under the old sunburned skin. "Listen, young idiot," he finally said, "and mark my words. From Bimini, straight ahead, up to Puerto Rico, a deadly danger lies in wait for the imprudent: a danger that stems from forces beyond the understanding of modern man. Once they're revealed, they might well destroy all our civilization."

"You're delirious!"

"I know, I know, they also said that at Grumman Aerospace, and they kicked me out as if I were a good-for-nothing. In the face of my persistence, my 'obsession' as they called it, they had me committed to an institution and I was definitively kicked out of the Kennedy Space Center."

Jerry was shaking his head, disenchanted.

"They all thought I was definitely nuts when I found myself on the streets of Coco Beach, sleeping on the curb, looking for food in trash-cans. Nevertheless, against all appearances, I had more time to reflect, a lot of time actually… and in my worst drinking binges I never stopped thinking of it."

"And what was your conclusion?" Jon asked with a bit of irony in his voice.

"I know what you think, son, but by crosschecking, by deduction, I've located a few geographical and underwater proofs of what I'm asserting."

"In what form, Jerry? Don't you realize you've suddenly started speaking like the Sphinx itself?"

"It would be hard to explain, I myself don't know exactly how, but they will cause a stir."

"Well, old man, if David could hear you, he would pay a small fortune for that."

"Exactly, and that's where I count on you."

"Do you mean exactly what I think you mean?"

"Exactly! There are just the two of you and you'll necessarily need somebody, an expert. Neither of you is a sailor and the ocean bottom is treacherous around those small islands and the coral outcrops are as sharp as razors. A small mistake and you will inevitably sink, losing the boat and everything else. I'm not only a skipper by trade, but I know all that area like the palm of my hand — and now you know that it's true. Take me with you."

Jonathan wondered for a moment what was happening to him. It was impossible, but with Tony's failure to show up they were stuck. He trusted the nautical qualities of the old man. Almost against his will, he heard himself responding, "I'll talk to David."

Jerry straightened himself up on his chair.

"You're a man, Jon… I know that… In spite of your young age."

"Careful, grandpa, nothing is decided yet. I'm not the one who decides."

"I can see your hesitation. I wasn't born yesterday, son, and I know very well what you're going to do down there."

As Jonathan opened his mouth to interrupt him, the old man added abruptly, "We don't chase the same prey. I don't need to be a soothsayer to understand that what interests you is gold, you and your David Klein. I don't need it anymore. I've never needed it."

"What do you want then?"

The old man was excited, to the great amusement of his young companion. "I want to finally **know**," he said, stressing the word 'know'.

"Know what?"

"One day I will tell you."

"Attention, Jerry. Curiosity is a worse flaw than lust. Remember Adam and Eve and the tree of knowledge? That's the only thing I can remember from Sunday school. If my memories are exact, it's since that time that man has been in this fucked up situation."

Jerry could not help but smile.

"You're really a funny guy, Jon. You try to be cynical but you're more profound than you think you are. What really interests you in life?"

"Nothing, apart from gold and women."

They burst out in laughter and Jon poured the remainder of the champagne into the two glasses.

"Back to what I was telling you," continued Jerry. "I'm not at all interested in your treasure. Let's say I have my own researches to do. Don't smile. I don't ask for anything, strictly nothing, except for room and board and transportation, evidently. You know, my experience will be indispensable to you. On the other hand, for me, an occasion such as this will never present itself again."

"Ahem… from a certain point of view, that might be of interest to us." Jonathan was thinking especially of the part of the booty that could be saved. It would be fifty-fifty, minus Jerry's expenses. It was very tempting.

"Jerry," he finally said, "if we make a deal, you must make sure your mysterious forces will shut up."

"I'm willing to, but unfortunately they strike without warning."

As he said those words, the old man regained his gloomy and worried look.

CHAPTER 10

Jerry was accepted. After listening carefully while chewing on his cigar, David made an affirmative sign with his head.

"Okay, guys," he said, "no need to go any further. I agree."

He got up, threw his butt through one of the openings and held Jerry by the shoulders.

"Jon trusts you, that's the main thing. From this moment on, you're the captain of the Barracuda. You'll have room, board and your laundry done and also your expenses paid. And on top of that, I'll give you 100 dollars per week. Do you agree, Jon?"

"I'm very grateful, but really, I don't want any money," protested Jerry.

"I insist. I don't want anybody broke around me. That's too bad for my morale."

What had been no more than an idea now became reality. The two following days were spent in intense activity. At Seafarer's Cove, Jonathan chose two magnetometers. A little portable one and a bigger one, much more sophisticated, that would function in the greater depths and could distinguish ferrous from non-ferrous metals. At Crook's they bought a big and powerful water pump still in perfect condition, although it was on sale. Maybe it was somewhat cumbersome, but it was exactly what they would need to power the water dredge on the sandy ground in the bottom of the sea. They also bought everything else they might need — hoses, pipes, ducts, ropes, slings, baskets, etc.

"Deliver all that tomorrow morning as early as possible to this address," Jonathan said, as he gave the salesman a business card.

He looked quickly at David, who was writing a check. He had an inscrutable look on his face. As they were leaving the store, Jon held his arm.

"There will be a small problem."

"If it's a small problem, so much the better," replied David half-humorously. "I have a feeling we are rushing into big problems."

"What's up with you, are you starting to regret it?"

"No, but it's clear that you're not the one who is paying."

"But you said it yourself and I quote, when I set out to do something…"

David stopped walking and patted Jon on the back in a friendly gesture.

"You're right, Frenchy, one must never regret what one sets out to do. What did you want to tell me?"

"Well, I'm afraid the back cabin's hatch cover is too small. We'll have to widen it if the water pump can't pass through."

"Why can't you tie it down outside on the quarterdeck?"

"Because nobody should be able to see it. I intended to stock everything up in the cabin since it has easy access."

"Do everything you have to do, Jon, but save a bunk at least for the old man. That's where we'll stash him away with the rest of the relics."

Again he tapped Jon on the back, pleased with his sarcasm.

Jerry was waiting for them on board. They saw his long silhouette up high on the flying bridge. He was wearing a magnificent captain's cap, with leather peak and turned-up brim.

"He works fast, your German friend," David said to Jon. "Pretty soon I'll have to ask his permission to go on board."

They climbed the small boarding ladder.

Jon spent the rest of the afternoon bringing everything up onto the boat all alone, because the other two had left. David went home and Jerry disappeared until the following day to some mysterious destination that he dared not specify.

He was dead beat. He was almost done when she called his name from the quay. Recognizing Linda's voice, he ran out of the cabin, at the same time furious because of her lack of prudence and titillated with the idea of seeing her again.

"Jon, I came to take you to eat something. Aren't you hungry?"

He would have devoured her all raw just like that, in her gray sweatshirt, jeans and moccasins. Nevertheless, later on, as they ate their cheeseburgers sitting side by side on high stalls at the counter of Charly's, when she enticed him by pressing her body against his, he surprised himself thinking… 'She is not the wife of an unknown man any-more. She is David's wife.'

Linda could see his hesitation.

"Dave went to Fort Lauderdale… to play a poker game with his friends. He'll be there all night long."

As he kissed her on the lips, he decided in spite of himself that this would be their last time.

***

"You're going to be away for how long?"

Appeased, she had huddled up against him, her head resting on his chest. Jonathan had placed his hands behind his head and he was observing the slow progression of a fly on the ceiling.

"David didn't tell you anything?"

"You know I hardly ever see him and when he's with me, he's im-mersed in his scripts or studying stock prices on the financial newspapers."

"But he loves you and he's very attached to you."

"Yes, as much as he loves any of his collection items."

"You're funny. He gives you money, security, affection and even freedom. What else do you want?"

"You!"

Jonathan freed himself and turning back slightly, he leaned on one elbow and looked at her.

"You're sweet, but you're crazy."

"Maybe, but I'm saying that seriously."

There was a very slight threat in her voice but he wasn't fooled.

"What do you mean?"

She hesitated for a moment, visibly weighing her words.

"Jon, you mustn't forget that it was thanks to me that Dave accept-ed you. Your part of the treasure will allow us to live richly together. You said that yourself, I hope you'll remember that."

"Yes, of course, but first we have to pull it off," he said. "For that to happen, David mustn't suspect anything at all."

"Promise me you won't forget your promises."

"Why?"

"Because if you don't promise me right now, I'll go tell him every-thing that goes on between us."

She seemed to be joking but Jonathan knew that she was enough of a gambler to risk losing everything.

"I promise," he said stretching his arm in a fake solemn gesture.

"Now I'm completely reassured."

She got up with one jump, laughing.

"I think it's wise to go home now."

She turned back to pick up her things and Jon admired the fullness of her buttocks stretched by the movement. He experienced a sudden welling up of desire but Linda had already gone into the small shower room.

***

Jonathan was almost falling asleep when the noise of somebody walking on the deck pulled him out of his torpor. He turned the ceiling lamp on. Through the hatch that he had left open so that he could have some fresh air, there appeared a staggering silhouette — David.

"Hi, Frenchy, are you sleeping?"

"Yeah, do you know what time it is? It is almost 2 am!"

David stumbled as he climbed down the two steps.

"I was cleaned out… They took everything," he said.

"I see that you take it very well."

"Yes. It's not a reason to make a drama. I'll recover everything next time."

He stopped and, standing in the little chamber next to the entrance, he smelled the air.

"It smells very much like pussy in here. Did you have a woman visitor?"

"Of course not, why do you say that?"

Jonathan kept his calm, trying to gain some time so he could find an answer.

"I'm not seeing things! It stinks like woman perfume."

"Oh, yes… I see… I broke a bottle of eau de toilette I had just bought."

David continued with a voice suddenly serious. "Lindy came here. It's exactly her perfume. I know it by heart."

"But you're completely nuts!"

Jonathan was desperately looking for an exit.

"Then how do you explain that it's her perfume?"

"Well, I didn't want to tell you right away. When we went shopping, I thought of giving your wife a little departure gift. Since I know the brand of her perfume, I bought her a bottle of eau de toilette that I just broke."

"What brand?" asked David simply.

"Mitsouko."

"Where are the shards?"

"I cleaned up and threw everything overboard."

David collapsed into the seat next to the bunk.

"You're lucky… or you have a quick mind, Frenchy. I'm willing to believe you this time. But be careful. Lindy is my little treasure; she's my personal shipwreck."

He burst out laughing.

"Fifty/fifty is out of question, not even one-third/two-thirds. If you touch her, I'll kill you."

"Don't get all worked up Dave, I'm not in the habit of hunting in my friends' territories."

"Understand me, Jon, I consider you as more than a friend… You're a breath of the open sea that came into my life… I trust you completely."

He stopped and made a vague friendly punch. "I know very well that you're not particularly good… but I'm not either."

They laughed and Jonathan thought it had been a close shave for him.

It was evident that David took the adventure to heart. He needed to reimmerse himself for a moment in that especially exalting atmosphere of preparation that precedes an important trip.

Jonathan Larue was beginning to find David Klein worthy, a full buddy.

***

With the delivery of a brand new Zodiac and its outboard motor that they installed directly under the flying bridge, all the equipment was now on board. The three men decided that the moment had arrived for them to have a little rest. They sat down in the big wardroom, each one with a bottle of beer in their hands. The strong, pleasant smoke of David's cigar filled the air in the room.

"So," said Dave, "is there anything still holding us here?"

"No problem!" responded Jonathan.

"Tomorrow we'll load the provisions and we can leave. What do you think, Captain Jerry?"

"It's perfect for me. I think the moment has come for somebody to tell me precisely what route we're going to follow."

"It's not for lack of trust, my friend," said David, "but I'd much prefer that Jon tells you only when we're on the open sea."

He shook his cigar over the ashtray full of butts.

"Understood. But I'd like to know at least in what direction I must point the Barracuda's bow," replied Jerry.

"Toward Bimini, old man, that place that you love so much."

Jonathan had a mocking expression on his face when he said that.

"Exactly," said David. "Jon already told me your strange ideas about that place."

"They're not just ideas," replied Jerry with tiredness in his voice. "Things really happen over there."

"All right! You have a fixation about that, old man," said Jonathan.

"Fixation! You call fixation the disappearance of five Naval Aviation Avengers on December 5, 1945 and of the special rescue hydroplane that was sent to search for them and disappeared the same day?"

"I read about that too," David interrupted him. "It's a well-known story but I think the word disappearance is too strong. It would be better to say that they lost track of them."

"But you split hairs!" said Jerry.

"Let me continue. In the general public's mind, a disappearance means total vanishing, especially since no traces have ever been found. In fact, our ship is inevitably somewhere, lying under the surface of the water in a more or less great depth."

Jerry interrupted curtly.

"I'm sorry, Mr. Klein, but you arbitrarily eliminate the possibility that it might also be found somewhere else other than the sea or anywhere on dry land."

David angrily drew on his cigar.

"Let me finish. Whatever the reasons invoked such as lack of fuel, electromagnetic storms, extra-terrestrial forces, the only real fact is that they never returned and not that they disappeared, since nobody can be one hundred per cent sure that their remains will never ever be found."

"With all due respect, I don't quite get what you're trying to say," said Jerry.

"It's very simple, Captain. For me, two plus two will always be four and it's always better to be careful and not find a mystery where there's simply a lack of explanation. For me, the only proofs are those that I can see or touch."

Jerry remained silent. To the other two he seemed to be somewhere else very far away. His mind was again wandering in time and space. In Marseilles, 30 years before, he had said more or less the same things to a character that would totally change his way of seeing life. In spite of his beliefs and certainties.

He pulled himself up.

"Just like me a long time ago, you're wearing blinkers. Your view of things is terribly narrow. These things are not what they seem to be. In fact, today we know that one thing can be itself and its opposite, all at the same time. Such as in nuclear physics, with the nature of light and that of sub-atomic particles being at the same time wavelike and corpuscular… No, my dear Mr. Klein, things are not as simple as you would like them to be. One of the greatest astronomers of our century, Haldane said that the Universe is not only stranger than we imagine but it's even stranger than we could ever imagine."

Jerry felt he was sliding into a field where David wouldn't be able to follow him and he preferred to go back to the aim of their trip.

"Are you aware of the curious archeological discoveries that have been made in the Bimini and Andros surroundings?" he finally asked.

"I don't see the connection," said David.

"You don't? Don't you think that we have a right to consider them to be manifestations of a vanished, or apparently vanished civilization?"

"You mean old rocks, vestiges, and remains of something that doesn't exist anymore?"

"No, I said manifestations. Vestiges are always dead or inactive and I'm not speaking about that."

"It seems to me that you're extrapolating a little too much."

"A few years ago, within the context of the NASA's Gemini Project, I was in charge of perfecting very sophisticated salvage equipment, conceived for the rescue of astronauts in the ocean. They had an automatic signaling system that indicated the point of the fall or distress. With my instruments, I noticed that according to the zones, there were electromagnetic interferences coming from the depths of the ocean. I took advantage of my leisure time to dive in those areas."

"And you found something, Jerry?" asked Jonathan.

Jerry nodded in agreement without saying a word. His face darkened. "I'm sorry. I've said too much."

"You brought us up to this point, now you must continue."

"No, I already told Jon. I've suffered enough with the consequences of general incredulity, not to speak of all the rest."

"The rest? What rest?" David became excited.

"It's better for you if you never know anything."

Silence fell in the cabin. Jerry had spoken in a categorical tone.

"Okay," said David after a moment.

His voice was strong as if to dissipate the slight embarrassment that had settled between them.

"Let's not talk about all these stories. Instead, let's see if our Captain is as good as Jon tells me he is. You told me that you know very well all this area around here. Well, tell me where, according to you, there are chances of us finding what we are looking for."

"I can always try. Let's see… Mona Island, between Santo Domingo and Puerto Rico, could well do. It's really a frightening place. Throughout the centuries, the island has served as a stopping place for all sorts of pirates and buccaneers, from Black Beard to Captain Kid. But I hope for your sake that you're not searching the fabulous Jennings treasure. An official expedition was organized by the Spanish government and sent there to recover the treasure, but they had to beat a hasty retreat because of the ghosts and disturbing spirits that appeared every night."

Jerry had now a wide ironic smile on his face. Apparently he had totally forgotten the subject of their first discussion. He was clearly enjoying the situation. "There's also Caicos, a hideout for French buccaneers. They say strange things happen there. And there is also — I'm really stupid — Guinchos Cay, the most mysterious island of all. It seems that strange and inexplicable apparitions haunt it. Is that enough for you? Notice that the moment you stop believing in something, that something will no longer keep you from sleeping at night."

David looked at the old man's face where the smile had become more accentuated. He decided that all that deserved some consideration.

On his side, Jonathan was wondering why his old dorm buddy hadn't mentioned Warderick Wells Cay. He could not ignore the reputation of the island. There was only one possible explanation: in fact, the old crook must be perfectly aware of their destination place.

***

Linda was getting ready to cast off the last mooring. She had insisted on accompanying David. The perspective of seeing Jonathan for the last time before they left also had some weight in her decision. Unfortunately for her, he was acting especially cold and distant.

"Cast off!" David's voice reached her ears from the top of the flying bridge.

She released the end of the rope from the mooring post and dropped it in the water with a weary and disillusioned gesture. The noise of the engines had been just a purring until that moment and now it suddenly got much louder. From the prow, Jonathan guided the anchor and its chain into place and then he ran to the stern. He bent down to pick up the mooring and pull it up. When he straightened up, Linda was displaying her most magnificent smile. She made a sign to him with her hand meaning that everything would be all right.

He threw her a kiss. A wave of emotion overwhelmed Linda. Without knowing the reason why, she felt anguished and she was almost bursting out in tears.

With her hands cupped around her mouth, she yelled, "Take good care of yourselves!"

Jonathan felt that the admonition was meant for him.

***

The coast of Florida had disappeared a long time ago and the Barracuda was going at good rate of speed toward the unknown. A smell of coffee filled the wardroom. The percolator was singing and gurgling on the gas stove top.

"Stop that! Pretty soon the coffee will taste like nothing," said David to Jon, a bad look in his eyes.

The two men were stooped over their charts spread out on the table slightly set back from the helm that was held by Jerry.

Slowly, Jonathan put three coffee mugs on the table and picked up the burning hot percolator. He filled only two of them.

"Should I pour you one too, Jerry?" he asked.

"In a little while, after you have yours… You'll replace me."

A black liquid haze spattered on the charts.

"Christ! I burned my tongue with your damn coffee!" David spat. He put the mug back on the table. "I told you to turn off the burner."

"You could have done it yourself. I'm not your coolie yet."

They confronted each other for a moment with their eyes.

"Okay… okay… this is not the moment to get all worked up," David said.

To make him forget the small incident of which he felt guilty, David directed the conversation toward the heart of the matter.

"If you both agree, we'll center our activities on two big lines of force."

"Two what?" Jonathan interrupted with a half-smile on his lips.

"Two big objectives, if you prefer."

"Can't you speak like everybody else?"

"Listen, boy, I'm beginning to get fed up. It's not my fault if your mother didn't give you the necessary education."

Jonathan jumped up and stretched over the table, seizing David by the collar with his left hand. With his right fist pulled slightly backward, he was ready to punch him.

"Never say anything about my mother or it might end up really bad for you."

"You're nuts the two of you!" Jerry had released the helm and turned on the automatic pilot. He separated the two men who were already recovering their cool.

"Christ! Christ!" repeated Jonathan with a tense jaw.

Aware that he had gone too far, he let go of David.

As white as sheet, David rearranged his polo shirt with part of the collar torn off and hanging.

"Forget that," he said curtly.

"Great Gods!" said Jerry as if he were speaking to himself. "This quarrel is an omen. This is not by chance, good or bad thoughts come when they want to. We're their puppets, it's the opposite of what one might think."

David and Jonathan calmed down, recovering their breath and both men looked at Jerry as he went on with his soliloquy. The old man really seemed to believe in what he was saying and his facial expression revealed an anxiety that disturbed them.

David was the first one to regain self-control.

"Listen Captain," he said good-naturedly, but still with a shrill in his voice. "I hired you to pilot the boat, not to philosophize."

"Nevertheless, I can feel it. They're here."

"They?" David and Jon spoke at the same time.

"Yes, those evil forms are all around us now. Better yet, they swim there, right underneath us. They know that we came after them."

The boat suddenly started to roll. Surprised, they looked at one another.

"He's going to scare me out of my wits, I swear. Jon, this old fart... I'm not giving you an order, but pour him a cup of your nectar," said David. "It's so concentrated that it will quickly snatch him out of his fantasies."

The two friends burst out in laughter.

Jerry pulled himself together.

"Deep down inside, you're right... It's better to laugh than to cry. In principle, one can never escape one's destiny."

"Bravo, Captain. I see that you've come to your senses," said David.

One more time, Jon noticed that since they had been aboard, never once had David called Jerry by his first name. He saw in that not a way of marking the superiority of employer to employee — that was absolutely not David's style. Instead, he saw it as an expression of an unconscious desire to remind the old man of his total and definitive distance from the sharing of an eventual nest egg.

"Well," grumbled David, "since peace has returned thanks to the Captain, whose intervention has momentarily warded off the evil forces, I propose that we continue with our round table or better yet our triangle, since we are three."

"And as long as the devil's not present," Jonathan added, for the joke.

"Stop, Jon, you're not going to start all over again..."

"Do you think that if we speak of the Devil's Triangle right at this moment, that it's just a coincidence?" asked Jerry with a muffled voice.

David didn't say anything for a moment.

"Listen, Captain," he finally said, "if you're acting like this to put us in the mood, I'm willing, but our first goal, Jon's and mine, is the shipwreck and its remains."

"Don't pretend you're meaner than you really are, Mr. Klein," started Jerry.

"Thank you!" said David with irony in his voice. "Finally... that's it. If you agree and since the world wants it and seems to believe in it, I'm willing to take advantage of this small cruise to film... How should I put it? As long as we don't linger too much, naturally, I intend to lay the foundations of two series. The first one, as we had initially predicted, will portray the world of coral and its richness... Jon will supervise it. The other one, which might be sensational, will be about the mysteries of the underwater world. And this is thanks to you, to what you know and what you might discover. What do you think, Captain? I'm ready to sign a contract with you immediately."

Jerry took some time to respond. He turned to Jon, who had spontaneously replaced him at the helm a while earlier.

"Make sure we're on 56, son," Jerry told him.

"Yep."

"Mr. Klein..." Jerry's voice was paused. "The fact is that we belong, you and I, to two different worlds. Your past is what one would call normal, I suppose, despite all the complications that are the usual lot of one's past. But my past is heavy with consequence. Fate has decided to involve me in certain recent events in the history of humanity that will not easily be forgotten."

His forehead and his eyebrows were tense, expressing an effort of concentration as if to bring a precise memory out of the mists of oblivion.

"Mr. Klein, there was a moment when I ran into the unbelievable and refused to believe in it for many years, despite the evidence I had in my hands, very small evidence but still evidence."

"You said you had it? Don't you have it anymore?"

"No. And the circumstances in which it disappeared are strange. I'm unable to explain them. I don't want to explain them at this moment. I've always been alert. I've always kept my eyes open."

David ensconced himself in his armchair with a slight shiver. In spite of everything, he felt that he was falling into the influence of a character that managed to create around him a disturbing and somewhat mysterious atmosphere. Doubtlessly thanks to that power he had for speaking with conviction of improbable things.

The old man continued.

"I don' t know if I have the right to drag you along... I should never have met Jon and he should never have met you."

"Come on, Captain, "David was becoming sarcastic." This goes against your philosophy... do you remember? Whatever you do, it's all written ahead of time."

The old man had already closed up into himself and, pushing Jon slightly, he recovered his place at the helm.

***

David and Jonathan passed the few hours that separated them from their first stopover establishing the broad outline of their operations. From time to time they consulted with Jerry, the old man giving them a brief grunt for response. They spent the first three or four days making a short tour. On the second day they made their first dive on the very site of the Lucayan treasure, just to get into the water.

Then, they went back to Bimini. The archeological curiosities discovered just a few breaststrokes under the surface were already making the news. From there, they would go to the big Andros Island and then, finally, they would reach their island: Warderick Wells Cay.

At sunset, shortly before 6 pm, they saw the intermittent red and green light indicating the Bell Channel Bay entrance. Soon, on the port side, they could see the massive silhouette of the Lucaya Beach Hotel. Right there, right in front of them, a mere two feet from the bathers, a fabulous treasure had been stumbled upon purely by accident. Almost 30,000 seventeenth century Spanish coins.

With the compass set to 340 degrees, they cautiously entered the canal, a floating buoy marking its entrance. On either side, the washing ripples on a calm sea suggested the presence of sharp coral outcrops. They formed a continuous reef all along the southern coast of the island. A quick turn to port and the Barracuda took its place in one of the free slips at the marina.

After passing through customs and a little bit of cleaning up, the three men rushed towards the Beach Hotel lounge. The evening was mild and the perfume of tropical flowers was heavy and enchanting. After a few drinks and a choice meal offered by David, who was overflowing with vitality and optimism, they quickly forgot the abnormally tense atmosphere of that first short crossing.

CHAPTER 11

The concert of clanging ships' bells and the banging of the halyards against the metallic masts and the shrouds finally woke Jonathan up. The wind was blowing. Through the blue shaded glass window of the front hood, daylight was already penetrating the cabin. Facing the partition wall, on the other bunk, David was sleeping deeply. Jon looked at his watch: six-thirty. Stretching himself, he let his powerful muscles play for a long time.

He always preferred to be the first one to get up. He would make coffee. To his surprise, Jerry was already in the wardroom. He was freshly shaved and a little stiff in his impeccable shirt and trousers. Jonathan thought that he looked more and more like a member of the Kriegsmarine.

"Heil!" he said jokingly.

The old man's face tensed up. His body seemed to arch a little more. Jonathan expected a volley of abuse.

"Hello," he finally responded, in a slightly strangled voice.

Jonathan patted his shoulder in a friendly way.

"Bravo, old buddy Jerry! You always surprise me. I could've sworn you were going to hit me."

"Me too, I really believed I was going to."

The two men laughed. "You know," continued Jerry, "there was a time when I had extraordinary control over my nerves."

"That's possible. Anyway, you controlled yourself very well this time. You seem to be getting back in shape terribly fast."

"I must … very soon we'll need all our resources."

"You're very enigmatic. Do you really believe everything you say? Or you do that just to make fun of Klein?"

"I already told you, Jon, you're just a young man, no offense intended. We have departed on a much more complicated cruise than you two could ever imagine…"

Jonathan fell silent. The day promised to be beautiful and he had no desire to start a pointless discussion.

***

They easily put the Zodiac in the water, thanks to the small derrick. Jonathan wanted to proceed with a general rehearsal on the very location of the fabulous discovery.

"It'll be excellent training and it will bring us luck, you'll see," he said.

His idea was simple. Men and equipment had to be tested in situ. Especially David. It would be good for him to acquire, in a calm and peaceful environment, the gestures and reflexes necessary in an environment and circumstances where speed, precision and calmness are vital qualities.

All along the trawler's transom, just above the water surface, there was an extremely handy duckboard platform used for loading and unloading the diving equipment.

Methodically and slowly, David and Jon were putting away in the inflatable boat the equipment that Jerry handed to them from aboard.

"Today we'll only be able to use the tanks," declared Jonathan. "We must be discreet from now on. There's no way we can use the compressor. It's a pity because I'd love to initiate you as quick as possible into the hookah."

"What is that?" asked David.

"I already told you about it when we were shopping at Marine Surplus. Instead of breathing compressed air from your tanks, the air is pumped to you by a compressor through a long and flexible hose. There are two advantages in that. Without the heavy tanks on your back, you're much more at ease and you can remain as long as needed underwater to work, but only if you're not below 39 feet deep, naturally. The problem is that tourists rarely use the hookah and since the air compressor that feeds it is somewhat noisy, we would attract attention immediately."

"And the water dredge?"

"Much less that... No fantasy today. But don't bother, we'll inspect the bottom and we'll do a reconnoitering for the shooting."

Once everything had been put on board and moored, they finished putting on their wetsuits.

The short distance separating the marina from the coral reef was quickly covered. The strong breeze blowing from the Northwest Providence Channel was chopping the surface of the lagoon with a short and sharp lapping that shook the inflatable.

Off shore, beyond the reef whose long and dangerous presence parallel to the coast was revealed by the white foam of the breakers, the sea was really bad. The salty sea spray whipped their faces as Jon, who was controlling the engine, twirled around searching for an appropriate place to lay anchor.

"This will do," he finally yelled, to cover the noise of the outboard. "Cast the anchor."

When he saw that the old man was making a face, he added:

"What's going on? You don't like it?"

"We'll be dragging the anchor with this wind!"

"You bet… This is just an inflatable. We're not going to stay here, there's too much movement here."

Always distrustful, David was surprised.

"Is that true?"

"Are you kidding? All novice divers begin their career here. It was not without reason that professional divers gave this place the nickname Disneyland. Nevertheless, this fact didn't stop Gary Simmons and his buddies from discovering just a few feet from the surface, hardly buried under the sand, a fantastic fortune that had been lying quietly there for three centuries. All that was within arm's reach for any stupid Sunday swimmer. They were Spanish silver pieces of eight, four and two which had the highest value for collectors."

"Now I like that," interrupted David. He was shining. "This is a story that I love hearing, even if I had to listen to it every day. That's good for the morale!"

"Yes, but listen to the rest. For a few days, they managed to bring them up without saying anything but then, aware of the importance of their discovery, they decided to inform the Bahamas government officially, so that they would provide them with a research authorization. The funniest thing is that very quickly they ended up without a dime."

"But how is it possible? Didn't you mention the treasure was worth two million dollars?"

"Yep, this was its theoretical value of course, but besides taking 25% for itself, the government notified them of the formal prohibition of selling the least doubloon before an agreement in due form had been reached between them and the authorities. The true revolution is still to take place — that of the individual against the society that oppresses him."

As Jon sat down, his eyes crossed Jerry's. The old man had just put on his hood and all that could be seen of his face were his blue eyes buried deeply behind his wrinkles.

"No, son," he said. "You don't have the right to speak of revolution. That's a word that you can't understand. The State is perfectly right. Its only mistake is that it doesn't take everything. It's not logical that only one person should keep all the riches that could otherwise be shared among all."

"Oh, no… Jerry, you're killing me."

As Jonathan was preparing to continue, David intervened. "Forget it," he said, "and continue dreaming of your millions of dollars."

"It'll be more than a dream, I guarantee. But you're right, that's enough. Let's go. Fasten your belts. Put on your fins. I'm going to take you on a pilgrimage to the sanctuary."

While Jerry was putting on the aqualung by himself, Jonathan helped David strap up his double-tank. He adjusted the length of the straps so the tank valve would not bother him by rubbing his neck. He also checked the reserve to be certain the lever was indeed closed. After buddy-checking David, Jonathan performed the same routine on himself. Before fastening the weight belt around his waistline, he pushed the lead weights to the front of his body.

"Don't forget this detail, Dave. Otherwise, with the weights on your back, you'll be constantly bothered by your tanks bumping against them. Well, we're going to make a simple exploration dive. I'll enter first, you second and Jerry will be in the back. Then we'll do a series of different exercises.

As the old man jumped right into the water holding his mask in one hand, David let himself slide carefully along the rubber fender. Loosening himself as if he were a spring, Jonathan dropped into the water backwards, his arms and legs up in the air.

The crystalline and enchanting world of the lagoon was a revelation for David. The bright whiteness of the coral sand that blanketed the bottom of the coral reef dazzled him.

Here and there throughout the thick community of aquatic vegetation, schools of small, luminescent fishes alternated moments of sudden acceleration and moments of total passivity. They seemed to be playing a game. Right in front of him, in the bluish distance through the track of Jon's bubbles, David could vaguely distinguish the tortured forms of long pinnacles; all standing in tightly packed columns poised on the bottom of sea and reaching towards the sky.

He would never be really at home in his tough urban universe again.

In his silent swimming, the commonplace sentences of his professional jargon were ringing in his ears; irritated orders barked at others, questionable jokes. He quickly chased that hubbub out of his mind and only paid attention to the very particular sound of his own respiratory rhythm underwater, deep and relaxed.

He turned back for a moment. Behind him and a little below, nearly scraping the bottom, the old man followed him, supple and fluidly. He must have noticed David looking at him because he gave him a friendly sign with a slow movement of his hand. David was surprised and almost moved by the gesture.

A swirl of thoughts was assailing Jerry. It was a long time since his last dive. He experienced a sense of intense well-being. The weight of the last years that almost destroyed him had disappeared as if by magic.

The sea was still bewitching, this sea to which he had given everything. He could feel its physical presence. The limpid water into which he slipped amorously was his magic power source and it invigorated him instantaneously. How could he have let himself fall into the trap of the streets of the big city and forget this sumptuous flowerbed that paraded itself slowly under his mask? He knew all its aspects, its slightest details.

Passing by, he greeted all that insolent life surrounding him. Facetious rainbow-colored snappers and parrotfishes, butterflyfishes casually grazing on coral polyps, surgeonfishes with their curious yellow fins, playful schools of small groupers and blue chromis, countless sea cucumbers dragging their giant tired worm-like bodies through the sand, frightened sea anemones suddenly retracting their bouquet of poisonous tentacles…

To think that all that lived in perfect symbiosis! What unbelievable and fascinating diversity! An alarmingly complex ecosystem! He considered the perfect society he had always dreamed of. Unfortunately, he would not live long enough to see it.

A sudden frustration seized him, revealing anxieties still smoldering. The final meeting was approaching, he was certain of that. The sole fact that he was swimming underwater, having miraculously recovered his physical form, was the proof — everything was unwinding as predicted. It was disturbing but predictable.

Jonathan was in excellent humor. If he were not underwater, he would have been whistling. He dreamed of the colossal fortune that had been found right there, a few feet below the surface. Who knows what had happened to Jack, Biss, Dick and Garry since then? Very soon it would be his turn. Many ideas, each one more pleasant than the last, rushed through his mind, but he refused to pay attention to them.

He looked briefly behind him. The other two men were following him wisely. David had adapted to diving with rare ease for a beginner. As to Jerry, he had not lied: he really was in his element. His calm and precise movements without waste of energy were the proof of his ease underwater.

Jon looked at his watch. They had been swimming for 20 minutes. He thought that the little outing had lasted long enough. With a movement of his hand, the thumb pointing to the surface, he ordered them to go up.

***

The reports were very good in the Zodiac. Especially from David, who was filled with wonder.

"Don't get excited, Dave. What you saw today is nothing; the place here is too full of people. To blossom fully, the coral needs the clearest and most transparent water possible… not a public' park like this."

Jonathan was speaking mechanically, paying attention to the tuning of the Pegasus, a long device shaped like a torpedo that took all the space on the bottom of the Zodiac.

"Okay, let's go, let's try our two little toys. First, we'll try the submarine wing. I'm sure it will please you!" Jon looked at David as he said that and winked at him.

After having dropped the board that was tied to the Zodiac by a rope, he adjusted the boat's speed, so that a simple inclination of the board would be enough to pull the diver gliding toward the bottom.

David was in awe. Once more, Jerry showed his mastery of everything related to the underwater world.

When Jonathan thought they were accustomed enough to the device, he decided it would be better to change places.

The wind had become slightly stronger and moving along the reef, they looked for the quietest anchoring point.

"Look over there! It looks like a buoy." David pointed ahead.

When they approached it, they saw that it was a big round floating device that most likely served as a seamark for a mooring.

Its color was a fluorescent blue and it was apparently new or had been placed there recently. It was tied to a long white nylon cord that disappeared into the crystalline water until it reached a truncated cone made of cement about 15 feet below the surface. Grabbing a mask and holding it against his face with one hand, Jonathan leaned over one side of the boat.

"That's a mooring all right," he said. "I wonder what it's doing here."

Jerry had become very pale. His face suddenly became stiff.

"Hey, Jerry, what's going on? Did you feel dizzy?"

"The color of this buoy…" Jerry finally said, as if he were speaking to himself. "No, this cannot be just a coincidence."

He was leaning over the buoy, his nose very close to it. He was examining it in close detail, but at the same time he seemed to be trying to avoid any contact with it.

"Are you afraid of being electrocuted?" asked Jonathan.

Jerry straightened up his body. He pulled the end of the rope many times to make sure it was very well tied.

"I don't like this buoy," he said simply.

David got irritated.

"Captain, you're beginning to bug me with your opinions. This mooring was placed here by people who use it. The instructors at the hotel probably use it for their dive classes."

"I'd be very surprised," said Jonathan. "This place is not safe for beginners. Well, since it's here, we'll use it, even if it displeases you, Jerry."

The old man didn't say anything to that. He came to help the other two get the Pegasus. They managed to lift it out of the boat and to put it in the water with a series of very well synchronized movements.

"I'll dive with Jerry," said Jon.

Noticing David's negative reaction, he added right away:

"Don't make that face. You'll replace me shortly after, as soon as I'm certain that this thing is working perfectly."

"Okay. But I'd rather dive too, so that I don't miss anything."

After putting on their tanks, the three men jumped into the water. After releasing the two rope ends that he coiled up and hooked onto his belt, Jonathan laid his body along the torpedo-looking device. He checked that the two fins were responding correctly to his commands. Then, he did the same with the small rudder in the back. He turned the device on. Propelled by its electric engine fed by batteries, the Pegasus started up slowly, almost silently.

David was fascinated by the maneuverability of the submarine vehicle. In Jonathan's hands, it literally flew over the bottom. It behaved exactly like a small airplane, with its glides, dives and risings. As it passed very near Jerry, the German grabbed Jon's ankles and the small convoy quickly disappeared into the sky blue lagoon.

David's immediate reaction was to try to follow them, but then, realizing the vanity of his effort, he decided to wait. As an apparition arising out of the blue all around them, they materialized in his field of vision as suddenly as they had disappeared a while before.

With childlike joy, David let himself be dragged in his turn, after Jerry gave him his place. He gripped Jon's ankles firmly, and watched the landscape streaming before his eyes.

It was a very different sensation compared to what he had experienced when, as a very young boy, he jumped from wood pontoons into the dark waters of the Hudson with the boys in his neighborhood. In that dark and hostile element, he had felt limited and disabled. Now, thanks to Jonathan and to the compressed air in the tanks, this submarine world had become fascinating and welcoming.

At the controls of the tamed torpedo, Jonathan penetrated deeply further into the spectacular and chaotic universe of coral. Every now and then, he turned his face and saw David's face shining through the glass of his mask.

When they were returning, they noticed that Jerry had preferred to wander his own way, doubtlessly tired of waiting for them. He was making a sign to them. With a stroke of the Pegasus, they quickly approached him. The old man was in front of the opening of what seemed to be a hollow in the limestone concretions. It was about four or five feet wide and it seemed to sink in vertically.

Jonathan put the Pegasus on the bottom and left David to watch it. Then, releasing the flashlight from his belt, he entered into the opening cautiously, followed by Jerry. Although they expected to reach the outside slope of the nearby reef after a bend, the well continued to sink vertically. They quickly gave up.

Jonathan lit up his depth gauge. They were 60 feet deep and already it was completely dark. The inner walls were getting wider and there was a great chance that they would reach a much bigger cave. In spite of their curiosity, they could absolutely not take the risk without more appropriate equipment.

They found David near the Pegasus. He seemed nervous. The three men came back to the surface. David was the first one to notice. He took off his mouthpiece, removed his mask and exclaimed:

"The Zodiac! It's gone!"

**

Jonathan asked Jerry to take care of the tanks. He took off his weightbelt and let it sink. Stroking with his long fins and stretching his body, he tried to keep his upper chest as high as possible out of the lapping water. He searched all around.

After many lurching attempts, he finally said:

"I think I can see it. It's drifting toward the coast, pushed by the wind."

"Is it far away?" asked Jerry.

"It's hard to say… I would say about a mile. It's going to touch land soon."

Jonathan was controlling a terrible desire to strangle the old man; he certainly had not moored it correctly. But it was not the moment for recrimination.

There was still a possibility of catching it with the Pegasus. Putting his tanks back on, he quickly found the device where they had left it. He picked up his weightbelt, which was lying next to it.

He calmly mounted the long metallic spindle and vainly tried to turn it on. He checked it over carefully: the nickel-cadmium batteries were fully charged. It should be working properly.

He came back to the surface. The other men were getting impatient.

"I don't understand anything anymore," he roared. "All this is completely impossible! Oh, well! Too bad! Leave the tanks, belts and all the rest near the Pegasus. Mark them with a buoy and stay here."

Noticing that the mysterious blue float wasn't there either, Jon entrusted the two men with the mission of finding the mooring to which it was bound.

Getting rid of his tanks and his weights once more, he added:

"I'm going to swim up to the shore and then I'll come back here to get you."

Despite the circumstances, his two companions had shown extreme self-control, Jonathan thought as he swam away from them. Even if he could not expect anything less from a seaman such as Jerry, David's calm had been a pleasant surprise.

CHAPTER 12

At the Lucaya Beach Marina's harbormaster's office, the dock master could not give them any explanation. A powerful run-about had fished Jonathan midway in the lagoon and had immediately taken him to the Zodiac, which almost hit the corals. They luckily prevented it from breaking into pieces.

"The mooring rope was hanging and looked as if it had been cut with a knife. There was just about 30 feet left of it. The blue buoy had disappeared too, just like the mooring to which it had been attached," explained Jonathan. "We searched every nook and cranny and found nothing."

Nobody in the small group had a satisfactory answer to the mystery. They clearly were believed to be rookies and what had just happened could only be attributed to a mistake on their part.

Jerry was the only one to keep silent, perfectly aware that he was logically considered to be the one to blame. For negligence or incapability. He accepted the black humor of what he considered to be a little trick — one more — of the forces that determined his destiny. He turned around. Jonathan had just tapped him affectionately on the back.

"Now I know that it wasn't you," he said, "and you know that very well too."

"Yes," grumbled Jerry. "This is exactly what worries me."

***

David offered them a general tour of the luxurious hotel lounge.

That incident and the flirtation with danger titillated him. He had never before experienced life with such intensity.

The dark musky perfume of adventure was beginning to intoxicate him. He sat deeply in his leather armchair and drew powerfully on his cigar. Jonathan was standing up, with a glass of whisky in his hand. He hadn't shaved the last two or three days and his face, hollowed out by his efforts, seemed harder than before.

'All that's missing is a little ring in his ear and he would be the perfect image of his ancestors,' David thought with sympathy. On the other hand, his feelings for Jerry were much less clear. He had already had the opportunity to appreciate his competence and his erudition, but the man was beginning to bug him with his perpetual look of suffering and his peculiar behavior.

David hated what was not clear.

They spent the evening around a hearty dinner in a most cheerful atmosphere. But in certain words, a subtle sense of embarrassment could be felt.

A little later, on board, after they had reviewed the details of their program for the following day, the three men were sitting around a bottle of aged bourbon that was already half drunk. Jonathan started coughing.

"Christ! You two stink up the air with your smoke!"

He waved his arms to chase away the bluish haze given off by David's Havana and Jerry's pipe.

"I think you're too nervous. Would you like us to reserve a non-smoking compartment just for you?" asked David with a smile.

"Very funny. No. But you could restrain yourselves a little when I'm here."

The old man opened his mouth as if to speak, but remained silent.

"Did you want to say something, Captain?" asked David.

He hesitated for a brief moment.

"Yes. Since we're going towards the south, and if there are no other suggestions, we could make a stop on Bimini or even better, off Bimini… as we had planned."

"Why don't we go back straight to Miami, in that case? I know secret places infested with beautiful sirens. We could make a sensational story. Let's be serious Captain," David giggled.

"I couldn't be more serious, Mr. Klein. But I'm not going to insist."

"Don't be offended. I said that to pull your leg. What do you have in your magic bag?"

"Have you heard about the Bimini Wall?"

"To tell you the truth, very vaguely."

"I know very well one of the men who discovered it," said Jonathan.

The old man jumped.

"And what did he think?"

"He was enthusiastic but perplexed, divided between the joy of making an archeological discovery that would bring everything into question and the fear of making a mistake. He feared it might be just a natural phenomenon."

Jerry smiled for the first time that day.

"He's right, the wall is just bait. It's of little importance if it was built by human hands or not. The mystery is all around it. It will be the enigma... exactly like the sphinx whose exact age could never be determined, and even more mysteriously, is surrounded by a deposit of seashells that reaches one-third of its height."

"Have you seen the wall?" David interrupted him.

"I've been exploring those waters for more than 30 years... and for the last 25 I've known exactly what I was looking for."

"But what is it? Good Lord, say it, instead of making all this fuss about it!"

David was exasperated. He turned toward Jonathan to take him as witness. Jon was very calmly opening a can of peanuts.

"I'm starving..."

"What sort of tramps did I bring on board! One can only think of eating and the other one can only speak through allusions and parables."

David stared at Jerry intently. Jerry emptied his glass.

"Mr. Klein, Jon," he said, "I'm going to show you something that will certainly surprise you."

Jonathan and David exchanged skeptical looks.

He got up and disappeared into the back cabin after having closed the door. The two men heard him searching for something and then he came out holding a small envelope in his hand.

Opening it cautiously, he took out a series of colored slides. He looked around. He moved to the chart table, and turned on a powerful reading lamp.

He took a magnifying glass out of a drawer.

"Come see... This is top-secret stuff."

He looked happy again. The other two men rushed together to his side. Leaning down, they looked through the thick lens of the magnifying glass at the unusual images that Jerry was holding under the lamp. It was obvious that the photos had been taken from a plane.

Jonathan understood immediately: they were photos of the bottom of the sea, taken from a certain altitude. Beyond the very well delimited outline of isles and islands, sequences of ill-defined geometrical forms appeared in the transparent water. An immense double circle… Long straight lines, also double and parallel, stretched out for hundreds of feet.

"Andros and its southwest keys. The photos were taken at 3,000 feet," whispered Jerry.

The photos followed one another, and the forms too: squares, rectangles, triangles, hexagons, a group of straight lines stretching themselves for miles, sometimes ending in perfect curves.

"Attention," said Jerry, "maybe the scale is not very clear to you. Considering the altitude from which the photos were taken, varying from 1,000 to 30,000 feet, these forms stretch themselves over many nautical miles in the case of the lines and hundreds of square feet in the case of the geometrical structures."

Against the light, they could see very clearly in the sand a very dense network of squares and rectangles grouped together.

"Looks like the outlines of a buried town," exclaimed David.

"You said that, not me. This was taken from more than 4,000 feet over Key Lobos, on the border of the Great Bank, on the verge of the abyss of the Old Bahama Channel… And this one…" Jerry's excitement grew. "This is the most impressive of them all, taken from 30,000 feet up."

The slide was divided into two parts. On the upper portion, the white mass of the shallow bank covered two-thirds of the photo; on the bottom, separated by the continuous diagonal of the very straight coast, the almost black blue of the great depths replaced it without transition. The slope of the edge, under the surface of the water, became round like a giant molding over the depths of the abyss.

"Guinchos Cay…" The old man's voice was trembling. "The door to the mystery must be here."

Jerry suddenly turned the lamp off.

"Where did you find all this?" asked David, who had picked up the slides and was examining them closely with the magnifying glass. "This is not a commercial format."

"These are top-secret Air Force documents to which I had access for the simple reason that I was the photographer who took them. I make no secret of it. They have cost me a lot already in suffering and sarcasm."

David made a long whistle. He didn't know if they would discover Jonathan's treasure, but what the old man had just shown them was worth a million times its weight in gold... provided that it was well exploited. In themselves, these photos were only hints. They had to go onsite. Who knows what they might find and film there?

"According to you, Captain, what does all this hide?" he finally asked.

Without being aware, he had put his arm around the old man's shoulder and they returned to the table together, where they took their places again. Jonathan followed them and before sitting down, he poured a glass for each one of them.

With his elbows on the table, the old man took some time to answer the question. He was holding his glass with both hands and smelling the lascivious and powerful bouquet of the bourbon.

"All this that I just showed you is located in the very core of the hottest region of the famous Triangle. The Devil's Triangle or the Bermuda Triangle, call it as you like. The pictures speak for themselves, don't they? For security reasons or so as not to create panic in the general public, these photos were never disclosed. The ones I showed you were taken more than ten years ago, at the time of the Gemini missions. Now that amateurs, divers, aviators, scholars and archeologists have started to locate these... 'traces', the people in high places pretend not to attach any importance to them. I suspect that even the media has received strict orders to minimize or ridicule all information considered to be dangerous."

"Dangerous! That's a little too strong, Captain!" exclaimed David. "Besides, we are in a free country — the press, the radio and the TV are a proof of that."

"If you believe that, too good or too bad for you. You seem to ignore what the pressure and the brainwashing can do."

"It's true that there was a time when you were in a position to know that."

Jerry grew pale but he controlled himself and took a deep breath.

"Stop, you're not going to start all that again," Jonathan intervened strongly. "I'm going to end up believing Jerry. There's an evil force stalking these waters."

David's eyes crossed the old man's. He couldn't see anything in them but empty blue. He had apparently become perfectly calm again.

"Tomorrow we'll head for Bimini. I intend to take several photos there. While we wait I'm going to bed. Everybody agrees?" asked David leaving his seat.

"That's a fine idea!" said Jonathan as he got up too.

"We'll weigh anchor at 8 am", said Jerry. He had a slight smile of satisfaction on his lips.

After the other two had left, he went to the chart table again. He took charts #11460 and #26324 out of their respective cases and studied them for a moment. Turning the lamp on again, satisfied once more, he went to the instrument panel and turned the ignition key.

The many dials lit up with red, green or blue spots: tachometer, oil pressure and temperature indicators, different warning lights. He engaged the radar and leaned his head against the edge of the cone of vision. He followed for a brief moment on the round screen the circular and silent movement of the ray of light. For a very brief moment, his position reminded him of his long, tense and focused periods of watch at the periscope in the U117. He quickly chased those images away, for he didn't want to ever evoke them again. He straightened himself up, turned the lamp off together with all its running lights. Only a diffuse light radiating through the small white tulle curtains penetrated the darkness of the wardroom. Successive waves of distant rumors, shouts and women's laughter arrived from the outside.

As he looked for his door, he stumbled over the stool. "Scheiz*," he said.

The light inundated the cabin where they had stored all the equipment. He hardly had enough room for his bunk and to get to the shower located above the engine room. He lifted the trap door and climbed down. Meticulous order prevailed. The two diesels slept side by side. He sniffed their smell of clean grease with pleasure. He petted one of them with his hand and an image of the engine room of his submarine came to mind. He started to whistle... Lily Marlene...

---

* Scheiz: crude German slang for feces.

CHAPTER 13

The Barracuda calmly cut through an absolutely flat sea. Its powerful furrow of bright white foam disappeared on the surface of the sea without ripples, in the good hot weather.

It was almost noon. David was fishing, standing up on the stern.

With his head covered by a cap with a long transparent peak, he was holding with his left hand his fiberglass tuna fishing rod, flexible and strong, while playing with the reel with his right hand. The metallic wheezing of the unwinding line filled him with pleasure.

The only thing that disturbed his peace of mind was the fact that he was extremely thirsty. Jonathan had gone down to fetch him some cold beer, but he hadn't come back yet.

A diffuse humming suddenly caught his attention. He examined the horizon. The water was deep and had an intense blue color. But there was nothing on sight, neither a hull nor a sail. That was really curious. They were certainly somewhere half way to the Northwest Providence Channel, a much used passage.

The noise was still there, never-ending. He thought about the dive the day before. Maybe that's what caused the buzzing in his ears. He blocked the reel and leaned his head on one side then on the other side, shaking his little finger inside each ear. No! It wasn't his imagination! Leaning over the handrail, he moved his face closer to the water. The humming was still there. It was much stronger and seemed to be coming from under the surface. He stood up, put his fishing rod on its stand and moved to the starboard railing. He leaned over again, trying to get as close to the water as possible. A continuous whistling vibration was superimposed over the familiar purring of the diesel engines. Jonathan's voice startled him. He leaped up again. The young man was standing in the doorway, holding a beer bottle in each hand. He looked surprised.

"Dave! What are you doing? Are you trying to catch the fishes with your teeth now?"

His ironic smile suddenly froze. With a single movement, he put the beer bottles down on the deck and leaned against the guardrail. His arm was pointing to the surface.

"Hey... Look! Quick!"

A few dozen feet from the boat, in the calm transparent water, following a course parallel to theirs and barely showing on the surface, two orange forms were floating under the water with no apparent sign of a propulsion device. They were the source of the whistling and rumbling that had called itself to David's attention.

The two men were astonished. They looked at each other, trying to understand. As much as they could see, considering the refraction, the devices must be about 20 feet long each.

The moment Jerry showed up on the deck, the objects suddenly accelerated. Then, making a 90-degree turn, they dived straight into the great depths, passing under the Barracuda. They were compact and egg-shaped, instead of long like torpedoes or rockets. They didn't have any openings or protuberances, neither fins nor rudder.

"Christ! What in the world could that be?" exclaimed Jonathan.

"I could hear them for a while... They were following us."

David regretted bitterly the fact that he didn't have his camera at hand.

"And you, Captain, what do you think?"

Jerry's eyes were shining with lively brightness. He was very agitated.

"I was certain that they would show up."

David and Jonathan looked at each other.

"Pete Petersen, a buddy of mine who's a professional fisherman, told me he sighted the same devices many times," said Jonathan. "But since he was inclined to drink too much, I always thought he was telling stories."

"That's what they'll say about you too, Frenchy, when you tell them what you've just seen."

The old man had gone into the cockpit and was returning with a big pair of binoculars.

"I set the automatic pilot," he said, as he slowly examined the surface of the water. The sea was still deserted, totally indifferent to what had just happened.

***

The conversation was getting more and more lively in the wardroom. Jerry had prepared a little snack — salami, different kinds of cheese and fruits — and he was finally answering David's questions. Jonathan was at the helm.

For a moment, inspired to eloquence by what had just happened, the old man had let them catch a glimpse of his true thoughts: the existence in that vast perimeter that included the Bahamas, the Caribbean from to the Yucatan to the Greater Antilles and the Lesser Antilles, of a secret submarine universe.

He had even spoken of a kingdom in which the modalities of existence didn't quite fit within our three dimensions.

"But why here instead of somewhere else?" David asked.

"Because of the geological structure of the subsoil and the presence of giant submarine caverns and a network of horizontal tunnels and vertical wells, such as the Blue Holes, for instance."

"And why underwater and not on dry land?"

"The races that originally formed this immense swallowed up kingdom were amphibians. The Greek mythology speaks of them. There are also echoes of them in the very ancient Indian Vedic texts, and also in the Nordic saga."

"My dear old Jerry," said Jonathan mockingly. "In all the time I've been diving here, I should have seen these amphibians. And you, wouldn't you have seen them?"

Jerry didn't say anything, but prepared himself a huge sandwich. He was thinking of the proofs that had gathered ruthlessly around him through the years, since that magic night in Marseilles. They had made him switch from the most absolute skepticism to the most total conviction.

Late in the afternoon, they could see the Great Isaac lighthouse. Its high white profile overlooked the islet and the few trees that surrounded the keeper's little pointed roofed house.

The almost black blue color of the sea had cleared somewhat and now had turquoise glints. The water was getting less deep. Very soon they were navigating on the white and shallow sands of the Great Bahama Bank and Jonathan was getting ready to give his place to Jerry, who had more experience and would guide the Barracuda in its approach to the North Bimini port, an approach littered with treacherously shallow, white sand banks.

"Dave! Jerry!" he called suddenly. The intensity of his voice was unusual.

He was leaning over the compass. The big hand was turning like a fan.

"It started turning slowly, then it suddenly accelerated."

With a sharp movement, Jerry turned off the ignition. While the boat continued to wander, the movement of the hand stopped.

"We're going back. Get ready to cast anchor!" he yelled.

While Jonathan ran out toward the front, the old man turned the engines on with a muffled rumble and David climbed onto the flying bridge. Making a wide half-turn on itself, the Barracuda entered its own wake. Jerry's voice was very excited and it reached the other two on the deck.

"It's beginning again!" Jonathan activated the windlass at the very moment the engines stopped. With a loud noise of chains, the anchor fell in the water. The trawler stopped as quickly as the hand of the compass.

"What's the depth?" asked Jonathan.

"About 20 feet", answered Jerry after taking a brief look at the sonar.

That was the depth limit for their detectors. They decided to bring them along.

As Jonathan and the old man, equipped with their scuba gear, dropped into the water, David set the tender afloat.

In the shallow water, the fine white sand stretched for as far as they could see. Taking their anchor as a starting point, the two men meticulously scanned the ground with their electromagnetic metal detectors.

The hands on the dials remained desperately quiet. Only a few sporadic jumps bore witness to the presence of some piece of metal or scrap iron. But this was completely normal in an area that saw such constant marine traffic.

They continued for quite a while. When he felt that he would have to engage the reserve, Jonathan decided that it was time to go back to the surface. He looked at Jerry, who was a few feet away. His body in an acute angle, with his nose pointing down, he was scraping the ground with his instrument, clearing out thin sand columns. He looked like a big red mullet.

Jonathan came closer to him and pulled at the end of one of his fins. He pointed his thumb up, telling the old man it was time to go back to the surface.

They slowly went up to the shimmering surface. The small dark bottom of the tender stood out against the water.

"Nothing!" said Jonathan, resting his forearms on the edge of the tender.

He had taken off his mask and was puffing loudly. Jerry came up and rested his elbows on the edge of the tender. He seemed deeply disappointed.

"I was thinking while I waited for you here alone," David said. "It would have been better if we had used the Zodiac. It's getting late, but we can still try it. I'll pull you."

With the outboard engine barely moving them along, their eyes riveted on the compass and the dials, they examined closely a large zone around their anchoring point. Nothing troubled the surface of the water.

Night was beginning to fall and they were forced to abandon the search. The barometer indicated the weather was to stay fair. It would be a full moon night. With the moon up in the sky, they would be able to see as if in broad daylight. Turning on their running lights, they decided to drop anchor right there and stay until the next morning.

***

As he verified the different mechanisms of his 16 mm camera before putting it in its long, o-ring sealed, waterproof housing, David found himself thinking of Jerry. The mystery that surrounded much of the man's life worried him. He could sense its importance and he would pay anything to discover what it really was about. By nature, he had little liking for abstractions and even less for such phenomena as those that had plagued them all day long. It was hard for him to accept them, even though he had seen them with his own eyes.

He shook his shoulders and then, with a sharp noise, he locked the camera housing. No matter what happened from now on, he would have his camera ready. That's one thing he could count on.

The two other men waited impatiently in the back. Jonathan was passing the scuba tanks through the wide-open hatch. His back was shining with sweat.

"Quick, Dave! I think you'll get value for your money. Jerry has cast anchor over his wall!" he yelled.

Through the passage frame, a white head appeared.

"Mr. Klein, I think that you'll be satisfied."

Leaning down, David took a quick look. Beyond the shimmering surface of the water, he could see a rocky bottom. The rocks were enormous!

Very close to them, on starboard, the narrow strip of flat land of North Bimini spread out its unstable white-sand bottom.

They dived and were totally surprised. Swimming in the clear water, they flew over a titanic causeway made of stone blocks fit into one another, forming a double parallel line.

They followed it for all its length. It stretched over about 1,000 feet, an incredible rock mosaic. Most of the rocks were rectangular, others square, some didn't have a well-defined form. The biggest ones were 10 to 16 feet long and covered all the width of the road. In certain places, smaller cobbles formed a finishing pavement of which the most part had disappeared, torn away by the movement of the water. In the south end, the whole thing made a wide curve and then disappeared into the sand.

On the bottom to explore its foundations, they were surprised to find very neat openings. In two precise places, the big paving stones covered all the width, resting in each corner on small vertical heaps of rocks. Clearing the cracks of the seaweed, sediments and concretions that obstructed them, the two men were astonished to see that the daylight showed at the other end. They were doubtlessly swimming in front of structures that were built by men following the same principle of the European dolmens.

They went back to the surface when they were almost at the end of their reserves. As David took the film out of the camera, he could not stop whispering:

"Fantastic... Guys, this is absolutely fantastic..."

Jonathan went down to grab a cold beer and some quick snack. When he came back up, Jerry and David were sitting down next to each other, leaning against the partition. Jerry's white hair contrasted with David's bald head. With their legs stretched out, warming up in the sun, they were having a conversation.

"I had sensed its existence a long time ago," the old man was saying. "The first time I dived here was in 1938. At that time, only a long wide and dark trail was distinguishable in the surrounding sand. Examining it with the point of my speargun, I noticed that it was hidden under a thick layer of seaweed and other marine rubbish. All that was a sign that there must be an artificial structure underneath. I never went back there again... In 1968, I heard that a team of divers had discovered it. One of them was the French diver you know, Jonathan."

That's amazing!" interrupted David. He was rubbing his hand. "This story deserves to be told, that's for sure. But for this, I'll have to go back down to do some more shooting."

He could already imagine the possibilities. He seemed so impatient that Jonathan started laughing, in which he was followed by the old man.

"Why are you laughing at me? Did I say something funny?"

"No, no. Let's rest for a while. We'll go back later."

In the next hours, David used two rolls. He used the Pegasus, for it had started working again the day after the incident, with no apparent explanation. Initially, he limited himself to taking panoramic shots and doing some photogrammetric work, using an archeological approach. Then he gave free expression to his own conceptions and indulged in a profusion of framings and angles destined to grab the audience in their couches and make them dive into this fantastic and magical world that they would otherwise never have the opportunity to know.

Jerry, on the other hand, was playing hooky. Moving away from the wall, it wasn't long before he discovered other revealing structures shaped like trenches, filled with deposits and sediments. One of them was 24 inches wide, about 24 inches deep and very straight. He followed it for more than half a mile.

As he was coming back, he had a sudden intuition. Taking off his hood, he leaned one ear against the sand. The ground was vibrating very faintly but distinctly. His body was filled with a shiver. He was right, all that was not as dead as some people thought.

CHAPTER 14

Lying on his belly in the front part of the inflatable, with the engine barely more than idling, Jonathan was telling them where to go.

"If we made a few changes, we could fasten a camera there," said David. "We could make wonderful sequences from the surface and we would not even have to get wet."

"We can always try that," answered Jonathan. "This is not my creation. I just adapted it. The fishermen have always used it."

He was examining the bottom using a very simple instrument: a bucket the bottom of which had been replaced with a piece of cut out glass firmly attached.

Jerry was looking for seamarks, mysteriously guided by information the origin of which he would have absolutely refused to reveal.

This site was even more spectacular. According to Jerry, the double, sometimes triple ring of dark and regular spots were the traces of a giant enclosure system with a diameter of about 1,000 feet.

While David was filming, the other two men were drilling at different points. Every time, the long rods would stop half way, hitting a hard mass.

Back on the inflatable, Jerry recovered his breath while taking off his dripping wetsuit. Pointing to the sea, he said:

"If I had the time and the resources, I would uncover from under the sand right there, a megalithic compound comparable to the one in Stonehenge, in England. Do you realize the implications of this? The existence of a culture, more than ten thousand years ago, in perfect continuity with the culture of the megaliths of ancient Europe."

"I have no problem with that," replied Jonathan. "But I can't do anything with that and I think we're wasting our time."

"You exaggerate, Frenchy," said David. "As far as I'm concerned, we'll keep going, as long as I can film interesting things."

"Don't tell me that you care about all that, about all this foolishness," Jonathan said.

"You speak like a landlubber, son," said Jerry coldly.

For a brief moment, only the light sound of the water lapping against the inflatable interrupted the total silence that fell over them.

"You're lucky you're 30 years older, you old son of a bitch. If it weren't the case, I'd make you swallow your words, washed down with seawater."

Jonathan was having a hard time trying to control his fury. He took David as his witness.

"When I think that I was the one who took him from his shit hole to introduce him to you."

"Calm yourself, Frenchy. This is not the moment to get worked up. Don't forget that we still have a lot of things to do and we have to do them together."

Jonathan gave Jerry an unkind look. The old man ignored him. Jonathan shrugged his shoulders.

"Okay," he muttered. "But there are words that I really don't like."

***

A little later, Jonathan would make the most disturbing discovery.

They had gone up north the following day, navigating close to the coast. They continued to find and film many forms more or less apparent in the sands of the Great Bahama Bank. According to Jerry, these forms made the bank the most extensive of all the archeological sites presently known.

After passing Andros, they headed for the Berry Islands. The afternoon was well advanced and Jon proposed a change in the evening menu. He would find and shoot with his speargun a beautiful dinner for them.

As Jerry, who stayed on board, worked on his notes, David and Jon put the inflatable on the water. Under them, the sand plain stretched its white monotony.

"Stop!" Jonathan exclaimed suddenly. "There are some rocks... or maybe it's a shipwreck."

He leaned down, with his mask underwater, while David stalled the engine.

"That's good… There are holes…"

Once in the water, he was overcome by the strangeness of the site.

There were three holes placed in such a way as to form a perfect triangle. This was in an area that lacked all traces of life, as if it had been completely destroyed by a huge explosion. He compared it to a grenade or a dynamite explosion, although it would have been incomparably more powerful.

He approached one of the holes. The opening had been carefully blocked with paving stones that prevented anybody from entering. The other two were the same.

He was running out of air. He shot his spear vertically into the sand and let the gun float up just below the surface, and then he went up.

His excitement surprised David.

"Hey, old buddy, I think I've really found something. Let's go see Jerry."

"I thought you weren't speaking with him anymore."

"Oh, yeah? Well, I changed my mind."

He went back and tied a little floating buoy to the spear gun's butt.

Very soon, the three of them were aboard the Zodiac. At the site, they dived together and tried to clear the opening of one of the holes. It seemed very much like a well. A clearly fresher current seemed to come out of it. Jerry took off his mouthpiece to taste the water. He signed to them, and the other two tried it too. It was fresh water.

They continued lifting rocks relentlessly. Jonathan signaled to them again, pointing to the bottom with a finger. They could just make out two clear lines in the sand. The lines started at the biggest of the three holes and continued absolutely straight and parallel well beyond their field of vision.

They followed the lines. After leaving the devastated area, they became perfectly visible against the coral bottom. The lines looked straight as a die. All along their path, their barrenness contrasted with the richness of the marine world they traversed and this made them stand out even sharper. They looked as if they had been traced by a giant laser beam.

At a certain point one of them traced a geometrically perfect curve away from the other, and then returned to its straight, rigorously parallel course.

On their way back, they made another discovery that surprised them even more. Jerry was swimming in the lead and he was the first one to notice the phenomenon. The fine cloud of sand that they had just lifted with their fins on the way was slowly falling back inside the limits of the line; not one particle fell to the side. They made several experiments. Always the powder returned exactly to its starting point, irresistibly recaptured by some invisible attraction.

***

In the late afternoon, they navigated around the buoy marking the Northwest Channel. When night fell they cast anchor, sheltered by the safety of Chuckpoint Cove. The sound of the backwash at the reef reached them from a respectable distance.

During the dive, Jonathan had managed to catch a beautiful bonito that had been a bit too curious. The mouth-watering aroma coming from the oven suggested his real talent for cooking.

"Tomorrow we'll enter the Northeast Providence Channel," said Jerry.

He was sitting at the table, facing David.

"We'll pass over vertiginous walls dropping more than 6,500 feet deep in one direct fall," he added.

"Well, Captain, I trusted the Barracuda, not a submarine, into your hands. I hope you'll keep it on the surface. I've acquired a taste for underwater shots, that's true, but there's a limit to everything."

David was in excellent humor. He admired the Havana he was rolling between his fingers, which he would only light after the meal.

"Well, when is the grub coming?" he asked Jonathan.

Jonathan made his entrance and put the huge plate on the table. Its strongly spiced and peppered aroma immediately filled the entire wardroom. The bonito was delicious with spicy sauce and Creole rice. They attacked it all ferociously.

"Hey guys, what would you think of a stop at Nassau?" asked David.

"Are you kidding? We didn't come here to join the tourists. After all is done, we'll see." The young man was outraged.

"I agree with you. It's better to keep going," assented Jerry.

David accepted the verdict reluctantly. He would gladly have brightened up this cruise with a beautiful Bahamian woman, preferably a black one. There was no chance that could happen in Miami. Such a thing was poorly thought of there.

Picking up his cigar, he lit it conscientiously and drew in the smoke with sensual delight.

"What do you think of that submarine current of fresh water, Captain?" he asked.

"In itself it's nothing extraordinary. Fresh water currents in the sea are commonplace, but over there, it's a bit too far from the coast. And it's also strange because a source right in this area inevitably makes one think of the Fountain of Youth." Jerry seemed to be reflecting.

"The Fountain of Youth!" exclaimed David. "I thought that was a myth!"

"Is that the fountain in which they bathed every day so that they would remain young? Is that it?" Jonathan approached the table and straddled on the chair.

"Exactly. As strange as it may seem to you, this story is a permanent dream for humanity. It's spoken of in the Vedic texts of India and Hesiod also mentions it in his texts. Not to mention the Garden of Eden in the Bible and the fact that Ponce de Leon looked for it in the seventeenth century exactly in the same Bimini that he had just discovered. The Lucayan Indians also had given him their version of the legend. He spent the rest of his life looking for it. But we should not forget that in ancient times the entire Great Bahama Bank platform was located above the present sea level, forming a vast continent. After the ice thaw, the sea level was considerably elevated and a big part of that continent is not visible anymore."

The old man spoke solemnly.

"That's probably Atlantis," observed David.

"It's not so simple," responded Jerry. He shook his head with a smile on his lips.

"But tell me," interrupted Jonathan, "if what you're saying is true, someone living in those times who bathed himself regularly in the fountain could very well still be alive, couldn't he?"

The old man froze. How could he not have thought of that before? He suddenly seemed to hear the echoes of a rich and deep voice that had said to him a long time ago, "In the old times of buccaneering and the Brotherhood of the Coast, I was another man, Kapitän Müller."

The declaration that had seemed unbelievable at the time had now become suddenly plausible.

David's voice brought him back to the present.

"Do you realize the fortune that we can make if it's really the Fountain of Youth? Captain, I hope you have noted its coordinates in your log. We could open the most fantastic thalassotherapy establishment."

"Yes, and I'd be the bathing attendant, to make sure I wouldn't miss any drop of it," affirmed Jonathan joyfully.

They laughed willingly and for a moment, like two big kids full of the joy of life, they pounded on the table with their hands.

Jerry had gone to the chart table. He lit the lamp, which threw a powerful light on the white surface of a chart he had just unrolled.

"Since we're not stopping on Nassau," he said finally, "I suggest that we pass west of the island, directly into the Tongue of the Ocean."

The resonance of that name always disturbed him.

He shivered and lifted his eyes for a moment. Beyond the outlines and the inscriptions on the chart, he could see a dreadful abyss: a gigantic Blue Hole that dived directly toward the bottom of the Bahama plateau, opening into other immense caverns many thousands of feet below. He suddenly felt as though he was leaving. The young man's voice came to him as if from very far away.

"Jerry, what's wrong?"

"Captain, you're very pale. Are you not feeling well?"

The two men rushed to help him. He came back to his senses and shook his head.

"It's nothing... I'm okay. It was a simple dizzy spell."

"You should go lie down," suggested David.

"Yes, that's true. Tomorrow we'll have a long day," confirmed Jonathan.

They helped him into his cabin. Lying on his bunk, he could distinguish vaguely through the partition the hubbub of their conversation. 'They must be talking about me,' he thought.

But he could not close his eyes. He kept seeing in front of him the Tongue of the Ocean. One thing was certain, he thought, we are very far from a simple fiction. He had personally examined the reports made by astronauts. They had seen strange white gleams with metallic reflections in that same place, well under the surface of the sea. Many airplane pilots had seen them several times too. The White Waters!!! The White Waters were more evidence of the unbelievable although real activity of the forces hiding underwater right there.

CHAPTER 15

From the flying bridge, David looked at the dark ultramarine line of the ocean on the horizon, trimmed with a turquoise fringe that stood in sharp contrast to the whiteness of the shallow sand bottom where he was navigating. The contrast was even brighter in the intense brightness of the morning sun.

"Fantastic," he whispered.

"Yes," replied Jerry, who was standing beside him. "It's really a shame that we're not going up to the very end of the Tongue of the Ocean. You'd be able to take extraordinary shots there. It's a spectacular place, a gigantic and almost closed circle with a 50-mile diameter. From a depth of about 6 or 7 feet, the bottom suddenly drops off over a phenomenal wall that's almost a mile deep. You have to see it to believe it."

"Have you been there?"

A bitter smile floated on the old man's lips, surrounded by the deep wrinkles on his face.

"Actually more than once. I had a post at AUTEC*, which is an American Navy base that performs underwater research off the Andros coast. I've witnessed some very interesting experiments and seen first hand the immense variety of fishes here. Especially sharks.

David made a growling sound.

"I'm happy that we haven't seen any sharks yet," he said.

"Not yet. Those little creatures are not very fond of shallow waters. They need a great volume of water to feel at ease."

Jonathan climbed the ladder slowly.

"The Captain was telling me about the richness of fishes in this region," said David.

* AUTEC: Atlantic Undersea Test and Evaluation Center

"That's true. I've caught great game fish around here, tarpons and beautiful barracudas. But for sport, I much prefer dealing with some monster hidden away in its den."

"At that level, this becomes a professional job," added Jerry. "Where were you?"

"Around Kemps Bay."

"Yes, I see. Me too, I've made great catches there."

"With a speargun?"

"What do you think, son? Do you think you the young people invented underwater fishing? You were not born yet and I was already hunting. I built my own speargun and even my own mask. I used to dive without fins."

"But not here obviously!"

Jerry hesitated a little before responding.

"Yes, right here, before the war. I was absolutely the only one here. But I started in the Mediterranean. There too, we were just a few."

"And you still dive?" asked David.

"Not recently, obviously. But until very recent times, yes! I consider underwater fishing the best way to approach and know the submarine universe. All those water boy scouts, young or old, who think they're divers just because they have compressed air tanks attached to their backs, they all make me laugh. For the most part, they had their initiation in a swimming pool. The submarine world is a universe that we must face as an equal — as men, not as tourists. Apnea diving sets the very limit of man's penetration into an environment that is not his anymore. The artificiality of air reserves or compressed air mixtures is the open door to the invasion and very soon the great havoc."

They let him speak, surprised by his fit of rage.

"They want to do away with underwater fishing almost everywhere now. That's one of the rare ways in which a man has to go beyond his limitations if he wants to feed himself. At the same time, they're starting to talk about aquaculture! Poor men, if they don't reduce themselves to atoms, it will not be very long before they disappear, transformed into little women, and then into devitalized worms."

"What a tirade!" exclaimed Jonathan. "You're absolutely right; the sea is a fierce jungle where there's no room for dreamers. Each species eats other species with neither pity nor a shadow of remorse. Men who have lived with the sea or for the sea have always understood that very well. Each one for himself, isn't that so, David?" He gave him a big thump on his back.

"Yes, and nothing for the others," if I understand it well.

The three men laughed.

The sun was at the zenith when they left behind the sinuous crest of Morgan's Bluff hills on the starboard side. The heavy and humid heat was beginning to take over as they lost the benefit of the fresh breeze coming from the corridor formed by the Northeast Providence Channel. They had set up the awning and were enjoying a cold beer.

Jerry had chosen to stay as long as possible in the deeper waters of the Tongue of the Ocean, instead of approaching the shallow waters too early in the day. With the· reflection all around, the temperature there must be unbearable. When they reached the White Bank, he planned to change direction and head straight for the Exumas and Warderick Wells Cay.

***

The atmosphere was getting a lot heavier. On the horizon, the clear sky was loaded with a low ceiling of cottony cumulus heavy with rain. The trade wind was blowing in their direction and the dark threatening front advanced toward them quickly.

They had taken down all that was loose on the bridge and deflated the inflatable. A brief gust of wind humid with the smell of rain came whipping at their faces. It portended nothing good.

"Speed up!" The old man's voice reached them from the bridge where he stayed for the better visibility. He had put on his oilskin and then the life jacket on top. Its yellow and orange patches contrasted sharply with the surrounding gray.

When all the openings were carefully blocked and the heavy objects firmly tied or blocked inside and outside, the two other men joined him. David was wearing his oilskin too. He was surprised to see that Jonathan was barefoot and wearing his wetsuit.

"I feel more confident like this!" said Jonathan.

It was an imposing spectacle. A gloomy vault of moving clouds completely covered the sky above their heads. Ahead of them, the horizon was still clear and shining with the intense light reflected from the surface of the water, which was crowned with a long band of translucent unreal green.

The swell was getting wild and the Barracuda was beginning to dance.

"We have one chance to pass through. It's like a long tunnel!" yelled Jerry.

"Look!" Jonathan was pointing ahead, slightly on the port side.

At a certain distance, a big circle was forming on the surface of the sea that was quivering with very small waves like the water in a teapot just before the boiling point. Suddenly the chaos transformed itself into a rotation. The swirling accelerated into a dizzying speed and a whirlwind of small drops drenched them. A column of water, a huge apocalyptic mass, slowly swelled up toward the sky.

"It's a waterspout! It's very close!" yelled Jerry.

"Is it dangerous?" asked David, with a strangled voice.

"It's catastrophic! We have to avoid it at any cost."

The ascending cone had joined with the one that was descending from the clouds and they now formed one immense swirling column made of water and air." It's coming directly toward us!" Jonathan yelled.

The sea all around them suddenly calmed. The only thing disturbing the surface of the sea was the giant spiral pumping water toward the clouds. Turning toward starboard, Jerry moved the boat away in a 90-degree angle. The waterspout seemed to move away.

"What could be its speed?" asked David.

They stood tightly packed against one another so that they could talk.

"Three times ours."

"It seems it's coming back toward us," said Jonathan who was observing it with the binoculars.

"Take the helm! Quick!" Jerry ordered David. "Keep the same direction."

He grabbed the binoculars from Jonathan's hands.

"We're not going to make it. It's too close. It's going to pass right above us. I'll pull down at the last moment to avoid it."

He went back to the helm, pushing David aside.

"Quick! Go down you two! Clear all the openings and the hoods! If it passes over us, we'll explode like an empty shell because of the depression effect. At the last moment, if I'm not able to avoid it, jump into the water without your life jackets and dive as deep as possible. Throw as many moorings as you can overboard so that you can come back up and may Neptune have pity on us!"

In the rumble of the engines in full throttle, the Barracuda turned around completely and headed directly into the huge threat. Hanging onto the wheel with his senses alert and the muscles totally strained, the old man was trying to chase away the idea that the monstrous umbilical cord that linked the sky to the earth was meant for him. He didn't believe in coincidence. Only a conscious force could have made such sudden change of course.

The waterspout was approaching at maximum speed. The howling wind and the violent sea spray whipped his face painfully. In a few seconds, the colossal wall of whirling water would hit to the right of the stem. The old man turned the helm to starboard abruptly, laying on it all the weight of his body to stop it from turning back.

"No! It's not yet the time for old Kurt!" he yelled like a maniac. His cry was lost in the roaring storm.

Engaging the engine gear lever at full tilt with a sharp movement, he tore the Barracuda off the deadly zone. With a gigantic water and ice draft tornado, the waterspout brushed against them. For a moment the trawler suffered under the impact, vibrating and oscillating dangerously and then suddenly found itself again in calm waters. David and Jon had gone down into the wardroom. Jerry was waiting for them, exhausted by the intense effort.

"I had already seen waterspouts… but always from a distance," explained Jon.

"Me too, but only in the movies."

David was trying to make fun. He was still trembling with the chill that had taken him over. He emptied his glass in one gulp and grabbing the bottle of bourbon, he poured himself a second glassful. The old man was silent, sitting deep in one of the two armchairs with a glass in his hand. The sun and the heat were returning and Jonathan took off his sweater.

"I've heard stories of 40-foot cruisers lifted up by a waterspout and thrown back down in pieces," said David.

He was staring curiously at the old man. He felt better now. He would have wanted to compliment the Captain for the skill and the calm he had demonstrated in such terrible circumstances. But he could not get rid of the idea that, in a certain way, Jerry was responsible for what had just occurred. He could have sworn that the waterspout had changed its course to come right into them, as if it had been intentionally guided.

***

"I'm telling you I'm right." David was talking to Jonathan.

They were lying on their bunks. The Barracuda was rolling quietly on a quiet sea, its running lights on. They had decided to cast anchor as soon as they left the Tongue of the Ocean, so that they could check the damage to the boat and also avoid the risk of navigating during the night over the shallow coral waters separating them from Exumas Cays. It was better to set off again at daybreak.

"You saw very well, just like I did. It changed its direction and came directly toward us."

"No, Dave… These waterspouts are unpredictable… It's the whirlpool at the base that decides."

"That's possible, but this one chose to come after us deliberately."

"You're exaggerating. In any case, we owe him the fact that we're still alive."

"Yes, but he was also saving his own skin. Do you remember the inflatable in Lucaya? Remember his face when he looked at the buoy? It was as if he had seen the devil himself."

"Listen, that's enough! What you're saying doesn't make any sense. I thought you always judged based on facts without letting yourself be influenced by superstitions."

"Precisely. For me, if we almost capsized twice in just a few days, that's not a coincidence but a fact. Listen, Frenchy. I owe what I've become to the faculty I have of reaching conclusions while everybody else is still starting to think."

Leaning on one elbow, he half-sat up on his bunk and turned toward Jon shaking his index finger at him.

"In this precise case, my conclusion is that we have to get rid of the bringer of this bad luck."

"That's impossible."

"Why?"

"Because we're going to reach the most difficult part of our trip.

Without the old man at the helm, the Barracuda will end its days on the coral heads."

"Don't you feel like piloting the Barracuda?"

"No, not where we must take it. Those places are terribly treacherous."

Now it was David's turn to keep silent. He was very agitated. He sat up completely with his two legs hanging outside his bunk.

"I'm going to the deck. I think I'll smoke a cigar before I go to sleep."

"That's a good idea. I'll go with you."

They climbed up to the flying bridge. The night was surprisingly calm. The bright circle of the moon had a slight dent on one side. It was reflected in the clear shallow waters through which they could see the wan surface of the sand below.

"Calm down," Jonathan said gently to David. "We're almost at our goal. Tomorrow we'll cast anchor at Warderick Wells Cay and the day after tomorrow will be the beginning of our fortune."

"I'd love to be as sure as you are."

They noticed the two distant lights of a boat moving very slowly.

"Okay, I'll give your German one last chance… against my will and just because we're stuck here. But at the least odd manifestation, I'll drown him without hesitation."

Jonathan was surprised by David's animosity.

"You're very ungrateful. Have you already forgotten that he made it possible for you to film many interesting and extraordinary things? You can't have anything without taking risks, David! You have to know what you want: adventure or a pair of slippers next to the fireplace?"

The cigar's ember was glowing red in the dark, illuminating their faces.

"You're right, Jon. Consider all that I've just said the result of fatigue… or emotion. Whatever you prefer."

***

The next day they could not lift anchor. Surprised when he could not find Jerry, who was an early riser, in the wardroom, Jonathan went into his cabin. The old man was still lying on his bunk and he was grumbling in his sleep. Jonathan put one hand on his forehead — the man was burning with fever.

"That's all we need now!" David muttered when Jonathan came to give him the news. "I hope he dies."

"That would certainly help! We're stuck here while we wait."

"Oh, yeah? If you don't feel capable, I'll take charge of my old Barracuda. After all, I've never needed anybody's help before."

"Maybe to make round trips in Biscayne Bay off of Coconut Grove... but it's not the same here. From where we are up to the Exumas, one has to navigate by sight. There are coral heads everywhere, especially close to the islands. There's too much risk involved. We have to wait. Tomorrow he'll be standing up. He's a tough guy, he's seen worse."

***

The fever had become very high. The old man was delirious.

"Listen... Can you understand what I'm telling you?" David approached the prostrate body.

They listened for a moment. The old man seemed to be reciting some litany. Jonathan leaned down toward him with a glass of water and a little bottle of pills.

"I think he's repeating a name."

"That's it! It's a name. It's seems to be a Greek name," confirmed David. "Let him go to hell."

They spent the day taking turns at watching the old man. They also performed many small tasks that had been postponed for a long time.

CHAPTER 16

David could not resist and they ended up weighing anchor anyway. They were navigating slowly and cautiously, taking turns in the
front and scrutinizing the bottom looking for color changes that would
indicate the presence of coral heads or a sudden shallows. Progress was
tortuously slow and the hours were long under the pitiless sun. They
cast anchor shortly before sunset at the edge of the reefs and shallow
waters they would have to negotiate in order to reach their destination.

***

The old man turned in his bunk before getting up for good. He had
slept a very bad sleep, populated by strange dreams that left a bitter
taste behind. He felt moist and realized that he had been taken by fever.
The hubbub of conversation in the wardroom reached his ears. From
the slight rolling of the boat, he could tell it was stopped. He sighed
and noticed that it was already dark. Turning on the night lamp, he
looked at his watch: it was almost 8:00 pm. How long had he been
lying there?

He had just had a terrible dream. A dominant blue still remained
from it. He had floated through a crystal universe. There was no doubt
about it, he had been somewhere in the depths of the ocean. He had
wandered along unending corridors formed by transparent walls that
almost touched one another. Abyssal creatures, real although in fuzzy
focus, slid along very close to him, indifferent to his presence. A
diaphanous bluish luminosity surrounded him, coming from everywhere as if from nowhere. He didn't feel cold or hot. He was, without
being. He circulated in the labyrinth for a long time. He felt surrounded by an immense and also perfectly invisible crowd. Finally he
returned to the surface.

"Kapitän Müller! Kapitän Müller!" A distant voice was calling him.

That forgotten name, his own name, hit him with a violent blow.

At the precise moment in which he opened his eyes, tearing himself away from the realm of dreams with frenzied effort, he thought he saw the haughty and terrible mask of the god Poseidon.

He remained stretched in bed for a moment with his eyes fixed on the ceiling. He feared the tidal wave of memory that would overwhelm his conscience should the dam his will had built over the years suddenly crack. He made the effort to get up, tottered to the door, and turned the doorknob.

The light in the wardroom dazzled him. He closed his eyes and when he opened them again, he saw two surprised faces staring at him. Jonathan's voice brought him back to earth.

"Hey, old man, are you back to the surface?"

That was exactly what he had just done. He wanted to explain it to them, but understood that it was useless.

"We managed without you, Captain," said David. "We cast anchor in front of the islands but we were waiting for you to do the last part of the trip. You must pilot the boat through the reefs."

Jerry remained silent for a long time, until the familiar reality of the voices and all that they meant had penetrated his conscience and chased away the last mists of his nightmare.

"I'd gladly eat something," he finally said.

"What about bacon and scrambled eggs?" asked Jonathan.

"Okay, with some good coffee."

"I'll have a cup too," said David.

**

The red globe of the sun was rising majestically behind the long dark outlines of the Cays and their soft hills, still hidden in the half-light. Jonathan was up very early, attacked by a whirlwind of thought. He saw the first light of the sunrise through the wardroom windows. He left the cabin without making any noise, for David was still sleeping deeply.

He opened the outside sliding door and the subtle and alluring fragrance caressed him, the gentle and intoxicating breath of the tropics that he had never forgotten. He stepped onto the wooden deck, and the moisture of the dewdrops against the soles of his bare feet was a pleasant surprise.

For Jonathan, the morning was full of the joy of life. He was standing, admiring the pale blue of the sky colored now by the thin pink and red streaks of dawn as the last mists of the night evaporated and the colors of the horizon turned to amber, ochre and yellow. With his eyes half-closed, he abandoned himself to the beauty that surrounded him. Perfectly aware of his entire being, he received a new wave of energy from this contact with nature. He knew that he felt like that because a great moment of his life was approaching.

He turned back suddenly, tearing himself away from that brief and intense moment. Through the open porthole, Jerry's face appeared dark and worried. For how long had the old man been watching him?

The sun was warming up and the trade wind breeze was lifting, still timidly. David was right. He must not trust the old man. The memory of Linda came back in his mind, fascinating and provocative and he suddenly had a crazy craving for her body. But for the moment, that was a dangerous thought, so he brushed it aside.

"We'll cast off at 8 am."

Jerry's voice sounded calm and distant and immediately brought him back from his reverie.

"Oh, yeah? Why?"

"We're anchored right in front of Norman's Cay. We'll navigate South-Southwest slowly, through the 145-degree corridor with the sun in the east for about 20 nautical miles and then we'll reach the entrance of the Warderick Wells Channel around 11 am, with the sun on the port side. We'll cast anchor and stay there until about 2 pm. Then we'll enter the pass, with the compass on 55 degrees and the sun in the west, so practically behind us. Now you understand why, son?"

"Yeah."

More than ever, they would have to navigate by sight. With the sun on their side or behind them, they would have perfect visibility of the coral outcrops and of the bottom in the shallow waters.

David had prepared a hearty snack.

"Children, I'm in exceptionally good shape. I sleep like a child on the Barracuda. By the way, Jonathan, you're a real sister to me and the Captain is like a mother to me... or maybe a grandmother."

He burst out in joyful laughter. "At least if I'm a grandmother, I'll avoid being devoured by the big bad wolf," muttered the old man.

***

They had been navigating for some time right in the quiet splendor of the Little Exumas. There was neither hull nor sail in sight. It seemed unbelievable that being so close to Nassau, a tourist center invaded every year by thousands of city people determined to take advantage of this paradise on earth, there could still be a string of small islands in such isolation. They stood out as rare jewels spread out on the immaculate white of the coral sands and the jade and turquoise of the clear lagoons bordered by the deep blue of the water in the Exuma Sound.

Jonathan was in front, watching the bottom close to the stem. David was with Jerry, watching the surroundings with binoculars. It wasn't long before they arrived at their planned anchoring point. They cast the first anchor, then a second one. The current of the rising tide was very strong. Jonathan could not stay put anymore. Warderick Wells Cay was right in front of him and it seemed to be waiting for him. The landscape was not very welcoming compared with the green goodnaturedness of the islands and islets that they had just passed by. To their left and right, in the depth of the cirque, two recesses promised little shining beaches of white fine sand.

"Your corner is very strange, Frenchy," said David. "I don't know if we'll find the Santa Isabella's cargo, but for sure the souls of her crew must be lurking around here." He laughed, but his laugh came to nothing. Surprised, David looked at the others. Jerry had a gloomy expression:

"The pass is dangerous and the currents are strong. Let's hope that the trade winds won't abandon us during our stay. With a northwest wind it would be impossible to maintain our anchorage point. The chart shows many recent wrecks, "he said. "Have you ever anchored there, son?"

"Never in the inlet. Always well off of it, on the other side of the Exuma Sound. Besides, that's where we'll do our work," answered Jonathan.

David immediately detected in Jon's attitude a trace of hesitation.

'He'll soon find himself against the wall… He had a moment of doubt,' David thought.

The three men were on the flying bridge, getting ready to cast off. In the bright light, through the clear water, they could see without difficulty the slightest details of the bottom. Schools of small, multicolored fishes were coming and going in incessant play. Following Jerry's advice, Jon and David put on their sunglasses, which allowed them to see even more clearly all the variations under the surface.

There was a slight cough and then the robust and reassuring hull of the Barracuda started vibrating. After Jerry stepped on the gas, the regular purring of the engines broke the silence of the Great Bank. Jonathan quickly finished guiding the anchors into their shafts and then he sat down at the very end of the stem with his legs dangling. He was on the lookout.

Sliding slowly on the transparent jade water, the trawler approached the entrance to the channel. Jerry avoided the many dangerous sand banks, and then he directed the boat toward the white cliff that from a distance resembled a group of little cottages. Paying close attention to David and Jon's instructions, he maintained his course in the narrow and difficult passage.

After passing three distinct islets on the starboard side and a group of rocks appearing on the surface on the port side, the inlet opened itself before their eyes. Making a wide curve again toward starboard, guided by Jonathan's calls, they advanced at extremely reduced speed toward a little sand beach, following the darker green of a long strip covered with seaweed.

"Okaaaaay!! That's perfect."

Shifting to neutral, Jerry stopped the engines. For a brief moment, in the sudden silence, the Barracuda continued moving ahead. Then the noise of the unrolling chains and the anchors reaching the water reverberated against the surrounding cliffs returning as echoes.

CHAPTER 17

The heat in the little cove was overwhelming. Typical Bahaman vegetation paraded its quiet green beauty. The coconut trees thrust their crowns toward the sky, their wide leaves swinging sluggishly in the quiet breeze coming from the open sea. They were links between the sky and the earth. All around, thick fat grass, tightly packed bushes, groves of dwarf pine trees, palmettos and mangroves spread out their intermingled carpet, descending to the beach's semi-circle of fine sparkling sand.

They eagerly assembled the inflatable, put it in the water and fastened the outboard engine. They left for their first exploration trip.

Facing the beach, even before they touched the ground, David jumped into the water, followed by Jonathan. Roaring with laughter, they knocked each other over for a while and then started a swimming course.

Jerry stayed back in the boat. He accelerated the dinghy, literally throwing it onto the beach. He jumped on the sand and turned back, as happy as a kid after a good trick, and laughed at his two companions who were just now arriving.

"Welcome to my island," he said.

The other two looked at each other ironically.

"Bravo, Captain, you're still the best!" shouted David.

Before he could say anything, they threw themselves over him. They managed to grab him under the armpits and the ankles and threw him into the lagoon. Then they joined him in the water. The water was delicious. Laughing and playing like school children, they surrendered to the joy of the moment. The tension of the last days disappeared.

When they had enough, they came back to the ground. David stayed back a little. Grabbing a handful of sand, he let the fine grinding of coral, limestone and shells slip through his fingers. The purity and the beauty of this corner of the ocean impressed him. It was so different from all the beaches covered with the garbage left behind by men, the only beaches he had ever seen until that moment.

"Are you coming?"

Jonathan's voice brought him back from his meditation. He joined the other two, who had started climbing up a narrow trail. They reached the highest point on Warderick Wells Cay very quickly. Below them, the island spread out its long and narrow strip of flat limestone land. They could see the sea on both sides. On one side, the deep sky blue of the sound and close by the foaming coral reefs showing on the surface of the water; on the other side, the immensity of the shallow waters of the Bahama Bank and its shimmering green and turquoise colors.

There was no sign of any kind of housing, no smoke, and no noise except for the squawking of the seagulls and, sometimes, the modulated song of a tropical blackbird.

"Nobody, not even a cat," declared Jonathan. "I don't know anything about cat's," said Jerry. "In any case, there are no inhabitants here except for the ghosts! You know, the Bahama Nautical Annals are very clear about this: the island is haunted."

He was trying to wipe his forehead with paper tissues, but they were all wet due to his unintended bath.

"Have we reached the summit? Captain, we didn't come here for a hike," moaned David. "I hate to walk."

"The island is not that big, Mr. Klein. Why don't we walk around it? We won't probably have any other chance to stretch our legs."

"Okay, but let's do it with the dinghy. What do you think, Frenchy?"

"Okay. On foot or in the inflatable, it's all the same to me. But we absolutely must do it. We have to be sure that we're alone here."

They went back to the Barracuda. Jerry picked up the binoculars. Jon gathered the dive gear. David got his light 16mm camera with a powerful zoom lens.

"From now on, I won't leave it behind anymore," said David. "I don't want to be surprised again. I think I'll even sleep with it," he joked.

Jonathan started the outboard engine with a sharp and precise movement. While the engine was idling, he proposed:

"First we'll go around the island. We'll check everything systematically. Then we'll take a look at my corner."

That's how they spent the last hours of the afternoon. They found some caves that opened up onto the reef just above the water and Jerry made quick notes and sketches. From time to time, David made them stop the inflatable so that he could film a sequence.

Jonathan was very happy with their enthusiasm. It was much better to have them in good humor before starting the long and tiresome work that was waiting for them! The idea that they imagined their task to be fun amused him very much.

They passed around the southern point and entered the narrow strip of shallow waters that hemmed the east coast all along its length, separating it from the dangerous coral reef. Very close to the canal that would take them to their anchoring point, Jonathan turned the boat to the port side. He aimed toward a dark vault in the hollow of a small cove that opened to their view as they approached it.

"It's there," Jonathan said simply.

He turned the engine off and grabbed one of the oars. Jerry grabbed the other one. They paddled gently. They had to lower their heads slightly so that they could enter the cave.

Their eyes became accustomed to the half-light quickly. As if prepared for a staging, the intense indirect light of the sunbeams coming from the outside illuminated the transparent water under the surface. A swarm of multicolored fishes moved about casually. They dropped the anchor and it touched the bottom, lifting a fine cloud of sand.

"I'm diving! Who's coming with me?" asked Jonathan. He was holding his waterproof flashlight.

"I'm coming," replied Jerry.

They didn't even notice that they were whispering. David decided to stay.

"Don't be fooled, guys," said Jonathan before he disappeared. "I simply want to find the place where I found the coins last time. The wreck can't be here. It must be outside, against the reefs where the ship crashed. If we find something here, it will point us in the right direction." His voice resonated curiously against the interior walls of the cave.

"Let's go, Jerry."

The old man gave him a smile. They inhaled deeply and let themselves slip into the water quietly, one at a time. Jon swam toward the internal wall without hesitation, followed by Jerry. The wall formed a recess on the right, halfway to the exit. At that spot and down to the bottom, the wall was full of ochre and mauve gorgonians and corals. During their third dive, Jerry pointed to a mass of concretions too straight and clear to be just the work of madrepores.

Jonathan went back to the inflatable to grab some tools.

"Well?" asked David. "Will this take much longer? I'm getting cold just sitting here waiting."

"I think we found a piece of the shipwreck. It's completely covered with coral. Give me the hammer."

He also took down with him a weightbelt, a plastic bag, a pair of gloves and his dive knife.

David lay on his belly in the bottom of the boat, and with his face close to the clear water, tried to watch what was going on. Jonathan seemed to be dancing an unusual dance, distorted by the refraction and the distance. He fit the point of the knife under one of the concretions and hitting the handle with the mallet a few times, he made it pop out. Then he put it in a small plastic bag that was attached to his wrist by a string. He repeated the operation several times. Before running out of air, he hit the block many times strongly. Among the pieces that were coming lose, he saw the corroded blisters of the metal.

He swam upwards, untied the bag and gave it to Jerry, who was swimming just above him. Back at the foot of the wall, he moved slowly, examining it in close detail with the underwater flashlight. Any object from a wreck becomes covered with a coating and integrates itself completely in the environment through the years and the centuries. Only well-trained eyes are capable of spotting them. He broke a magnificent coral candelabrum because its swellings caught his attention. He looked all around him one last time and then went slowly back to the surface.

***

They willingly emerged back into the hot sun. Jerry turned the engine on and Jon emptied the contents of the bag onto the floor of the raft.

"Your treasure doesn't look very promising," said David with a touch of disappointment in his voice.

Jonathan didn't say anything. Leaning over his small mound, he was sorting out the pieces. He was tempted to crack one of them open, but thought it wiser to wait and do it methodically once they were back on board. He could easily overlook a small nugget, a pearl or a precious stone…

"One must never trust appearances, and if all that shines is not gold, in our profession, the reverse is also true. If it shines, it's gold." Jon explained.

As David stretched out his hand, Jon backhanded it away.

"Don't touch it!"

"What's with you, boy? Are you giving me orders now?" asked David.

"Calm down, old buddy, I simply wanted you to know that such merchandise must be handled carefully."

A thick humid mist surrounded them. Part of the structure of the trawler, along with the whole island had disappeared, as if conjured away. The silence was complete.

"I never saw such a peasoup," said Jonathan. "Have you ever seen a thing like this, Jerry?"

The old man shook his head. In his long career as a sailor, he had seen all sorts of mists and fogs, but never such an instantaneous one. He didn't dare to tell them. He didn't want them to be alarmed.

"It's the condensation. It's been extremely hot today."

"Let's go inside," said Jonathan. "We have no time to waste."

"At least here there's no risk of collision," added David with a smile. "I'm going to turn on the running lights anyway," said Jerry.

The intimate atmosphere of the wardroom had not changed. The table seemed to be waiting for them, with the display of coral illuminated by the light.

They began to break open each piece meticulously.

"In your opinion, what is this?" David was holding a fragment in which a small mass of rust was sticking out. He gave it to Jon. Under the attentive look of the other two, he finished releasing it.

"A nail… It's a very old handmade nail," said Jon. With a smile, he showed them the rusty, one inch long, pointed piece. "This is typical. It was used to fasten the planks of the hulls on the wooden boats of the time. I've seen plenty of those. That's a good sign. Let's continue."

They resumed their work. Despite their precautions, the fragments were scattered everywhere on the floor. Very soon, a dozen other nails joined the first one.

"Uh-huh! I think I have something more interesting here!"

Jonathan slowly finished extracting a delicate small round object from its coating. He laid it flat on the tablecloth.

"It's a 2 reale silver coin," he said, holding back his joy.

"Whoa!" David screamed.

Very calm, Jerry picked up the magnifying glass and examined the coin.

"It's useless," said Jonathan. "We have to scour it. Where did you put the muriatic acid?"

"Do you want me to go get it?" asked Jerry.

"No, not yet."

Jonathan got up and went to the case above the stove. He came back with a bottle of vinegar and a glass. He poured a little bit of vinegar into the glass and dropped the coin into it.

"Dave, would you go look for a brush?"

He was shaking the glass with a circular movement. David came back quickly, holding his own toothbrush.

"From now on, you'll have to let me borrow yours," he said laughing.

"Don't worry. I'll buy you another toothbrush. A golden one."

Jonathan was exulting. He poured the vinegar into an ashtray and picked up the coin. Laying it flat on the table, he scrubbed it for a long time, first on one side then on the other. Like a negative in a tub of acid, the image on the coin began to show. Jonathan picked a clean rag and finished polishing it.

"It's beginning to show."

Stamped on the silver, they could see a T-shaped cross inside a worn off coat of arms adorned with heraldic motifs that were even less discernible. On the other hand, on the tail side the number 93 and the letters S.V.L. could be seen very clearly. Jonathan brought the coin next to his ear and, closing his eyes, he pretended to be listening.

"Do you know what this cute little one is trying to tell us? Listen. Yes, that's it... She's whispering to me that she has many little sisters as beautiful as she. For more than 250 years, they've been waiting for a Prince Charming such as we to come and release them at last."

"Are you sure that you're not mistaken, Frenchy?"

David was rubbing his hands in a quick nervous movement.

"Yes. Do you know why? Because it's impossible for this coin to have come here all alone… It cannot have dropped from the pocket of a collector right where we found it."

"Oh, well! Let's drink to that!" said David.

"Yes! Get us a bottle."

David was quick to get a bottle of bourbon and three glasses from the little bar. He filled them right away.

"Children!" said Jonathan as he lifted his glass. "All we have to do is to start working. It's not going to be easy. Tomorrow we'll thoroughly scan the bottom of the cave with the metal detector. There must be other coins like this one there, but the bulk of the loot is with the wreck. We have to find the wreck."

Once the first wave of enthusiasm had faded, they discussed the program for the following days once more. Then they cleared the table of all the promising debris.

Dinner was simple: canned chili con carne, spiced up with a concoction of red peppers. They drank many bottles of beer and still their mouths burned. As Jon quickly cleaned up the table, the old man went out to the deck. David struck a match and got ready to enjoy an excellent cigar.

"Come see!" Jerry was standing up at the doorway. He looked worried.

The fog had cleared partially and the island hills stood against the scintillating sea under the light of the waxing moon.

"What's the problem?" asked David looking all around him.

"Wait," whispered Jerry.

Suddenly, very close to the hull of the boat, a bright light as clear as a beacon pierced the darkness. Another one and then a third followed it. A whole series of lights began to flash and move quickly over the surface of the sea. Each one lit up for a brief moment here, or there, before disappearing into the thick layer of mist that was still lying stagnant over the water.

"Did you see them?" asked Jerry.

David mumbled something with an inquisitive expression on his face.

"Jerry said that those are will-o'-the-wisps," explained Jonathan. He didn't notice that he was whispering.

Jerry shook his head slowly. He was not convinced. Those lights were too bright and sudden to be the result of simple spontaneous combustion. But he couldn't find another explanation.

They went onto the deck again to see if the phenomenon would repeat itself. But nothing happened. Bright stars soon began to shine in the completely clear sky. They went back to the wardroom in silence.

***

Jonathan got up with a start. The solemn choirs of the Seville Cathedral still resonated in his ears, prolonging his dream. Impressed, he crossed his arms behind his head. Spain and the proud Andalusia were so far away! He suddenly became aware of another noise. The sound of a muttering voice seemed to come from outside.

He got up quietly and slipped into the wardroom. The door to the deck was open, but he was certain that he had closed it after the other two had gone to sleep. He went outside.

He could vaguely make out a man standing up with his back to him. He was leaning against the guardrail and talking to himself. The man turned around and he saw it was Jerry, standing under the diffuse light of the moon. He seemed to be feverish.

"What are you doing there, son?" asked Jerry.

"I was going to ask you the same question."

"I'm happy to see you. This shows that you heard it too, didn't you?"

"Heard what?"

"The voices coming from the island. They woke me up. And since you're out here, I suppose they woke you up too."

"I heard voices, but it was a dream… Just a dream."

The old man turned his head. He seemed to be still trying to listen to them, but the night was quiet.

"Maybe we had the same dream," said Jonathan. "You know, the chili was very spicy…"

"No, Jon. No, that was not a dream. The voices woke me up and I came out on the deck. They were coming from the island. It was hallucinatory… It was unreal."

He grabbed Jonathan's arm with both hands.

"Listen, Jon. You mustn't stay here… Neither you nor David. You're both at risk here."

Jonathan looked for words that could reassure the man.

"Go to bed, Jerry, you're tired. Go back to sleep... You'll feel better tomorrow, you'll see."

He went inside to avoid arguing with Jerry. He looked at the chronometer beside the barometer. It was almost 4 am. He decided to go make some coffee and after drinking the first cup, he felt better. He settled comfortably on the seat just like David loved to do, and gave free course to his thoughts. He didn't care about the old man's ghosts. Tomorrow he would be rich!

Resting his feet on the coffee table, he began to think about all they still had to do to recover the treasure. He slowly drifted into sleep. Shortly before falling asleep again, it seemed he could hear distant choirs, very beautiful and very sad.

CHAPTER 18

Raking the bottom of the cave was a long meticulous job. They used the detectors but the results were far from spectacular. The results were not totally negative either. They found many objects in the sand: hinges, nails, many of them much bigger than the ones found the day before, a small spoon and above all, a bronze dry-point for plotting charts. All those signs indicated that a ship had gone down not far from there. They finally decided to shift the search toward the reef.

Not very far from the reef, Jonathan put the submarine wing in the water and lightly equipped, he grabbed onto it. Jerry piloted the inflatable forward very slowly. Pulled by the wing, Jonathan moved without effort in the shallow waters. From time to time, he tilted the board downward and, holding his breath, he dived like an arrow toward a darker spot or an abnormal bulge in the sand that could be hiding something.

They went back and forth over an area of about half a nautical mile, slowly approaching the dark blue line indicating deeper waters. Corals, millepores, sponges and Neptune's cups were starting to replace the layers of sand. Jonathan made a sign.

"Hey!" he shouted.

Jerry stopped the inflatable. Jonathan came swimming to the boat, a big smile on his face. He pulled himself up into the boat and lay down on the floor.

"I found something," he said short of breath.

The old man turned the engine on, turned the boat around into its wake and went back slowly. Jonathan leaned against the front part of the inflatable, looking for the right place through the glass bottom bucket. He waved his arm frantically. Jerry turned the engine off and David threw the grapnel into the water.

"Let's go down all three of us. I think I found something," he repeated. "Get the mallets. I'll set up some markers."

He blew up an orange plastic buoy and tied an orange rope around it. With their double-tanks attached, straps and belts fastened, the three men jumped into the water.

Guided by Jonathan, they immediately started working on an oblong mass covered with concretions. The shell crumbled under the blows, showing a surface of uncorroded metal covered by a greenish sheen. Jonathan scraped it with his dive knife. It was bronze. He cleared the area completely and tied the other end of the buoy rope to it tightly. They went back to the surface.

"It's a bronze canon," explained Jonathan, "and there are many of those down there. They're worth at least 3,000 dollars each. Let's go back down. We'll each take a different spot and thoroughly investigate the place. We'll remain inside a perimeter of no more than 350 feet around the buoy. The first one that finds anything will tie his balloon and blow it up with his mouthpiece. We'll gather here in half an hour exactly. Okay?"

Jonathan's experienced eye soon found a heap of rocks stretching away about 60 feet on the edge of the sand. It was the galley's ballast. That was proof that the wreck should be nearby. He made a sign to David, who was moving at the very edge of his field of vision. They went down together to search the overgrowth of corals. They broke them methodically and brought out some fragments of wood.

Jerry made a sign with his arm. Jonathan swam up to him. The old man pointed to a small mound measuring 60 feet or so in diameter. That must be either the front or the back part of the ship.

They started working on it immediately. David joined them, full of excitement. A little further ahead, well in front of them, one of the arms of an anchor stood up, showing its curved end. It was taller than a man. The other arm must be buried. They had found the prow.

Leaving behind a triple wake of bubbles, they swam in the opposite direction, looking for the aftercastle or what was left of it. The ocean was very close and the number of fishes was considerably bigger. Hundreds of butterflyfishes, grunts and multicolored chromis swam by, indifferent to them. At a not very respectable distance, a school of barracudas was following them curiously, a moving curtain of silver. A big turtle suddenly rose from the sand and swam clumsily and jerkily, running away from them. They went after it but when they passed over an enormous mound, Jonathan saw what they had been looking for. He headed straight up to the surface and was followed by the other two.

The first probes produced immediate results; iron scraps and many other metal objects, wooden board stumps, a huge eroded pulley and many bits of pottery. The three men didn't notice the passage of time. Their air reserves were almost exhausted when Jonathan made them a sign to go back to the surface.

Their excitation reached its height. David was completely euphoric.

"Let's strike while the iron is still hot. We have to go back there. Let's get other tanks."

"It's too late. We've done enough for today."

Jonathan calmed down a little.

"I'm going back there to set up a marker. We'll continue tomorrow."

He took a little red buoy and dived down to attach it. He felt light and happy. They had really made it! This wreck could very well be his wreck. The ship was certainly made before 1650. The fact that the canons were made of bronze was reasonable proof of that.

Back in the Zodiac, David was still very happy and agitated. The old man had resumed his cold and distant expression. He turned the engine on and let it idle for a while.

"I think we'll have to take the Barracuda directly onto the site of the wreck. Our work will be easier like that," Jonathan said.

"I agree, but we have to find a good path of retreat. If there's a sudden tornado or even a bad northwest wind, we'll be thrown against the barrier. In that case, you'll have to say goodbye to your treasure!"

"Yes, I've been there. Let's mark out the area right away."

***

They were having a hard time carrying the big compressor to the rear deck when the mist reappeared again. As on the day before, it appeared simultaneously from the two points delineating the cove in the middle of which the Barracuda was anchored. Two big cottony masses converged toward them at great speed. They flowed down from the summits of the island and fell silently as a curtain.

"Well?" asked Jonathan.

"May I be damned," David exploded. "Captain, what might that be?"

"I was thinking of something that maybe you haven't ever seen, the smoke screens we used during the war. Of course, they were much stronger. But this is not smoke. There's no trace of any particles in it."

Jerry moved his lips quickly, as if trying to taste the air.

"This is steam, nothing but steam."

"It seems you were expecting something else, Captain!"

The old man didn't say anything. He turned back and crouched down next to the compressor to finish the tuning that had been interrupted.

***

The night passed with no more incidents. In the morning, the Barracuda made its way through the newly marked canal all the way up to the wreck, following the inflatable. They cast two anchors, one at the prow and another one at the stern, and then started the maneuverings. It was a tiresome job under a sun that was becoming hotter all the time. They jumped regularly into the water to cool themselves.

The installation of the water dredge* took a long time. Toward noon, Jonathan decided that everything was ready for a first attempt.

"Did you see your back, Dave? It's red as a lobster. It's time you come dive with me!"

The old man agreed. "In that case, I'll stay on board and take care of the water pump."

He waited until the other two had taken their positions on the surface to turn the engine on. After a few hiccups, it finally started with a deafening noise.

Ignoring a parrotfish that was a bit too curious, Jonathan grabbed the grips and directed the intake toward the sand. David nested the hose under one of his arms and held it tightly. Jonathan opened the intake valve. The long tube stiffened under the brutal flux and they had to struggle to keep it in place.

All around them, the water was becoming agitated. At the intake, a

---

* Water dredge: a big underwater vacuum cleaner

hole was being dug slowly. With a muffled rumble, debris and pieces of limestone were moving about wildly. They seemed to hesitate for a moment, and then with a sudden acceleration they disappeared, snatched up by the dredge.

On the surface, in the uproar of the coughing engine, the big flexible hose was vomiting into the basket in a constant flow. With a greasy rag in one hand and a wrench in the other, Jerry was tuning the engine, indifferent to all of it.

David made a sign to Jonathan, meaning that he had had enough. Jonathan suggested that they go back to the surface. On their way up, he gave David a friendly wink through his mask.

Back on board, the silence seemed even bigger with the water pump turned off.

"This is more tiresome than I thought," said David.

He placed his beer next to him and started massaging his ribs.

"It was very hard for me to keep the damn hose in place. And with all the vibration, I felt like I must have the St. Vitus dance!"

"I warned you it wouldn't be easy at all. You're going to lose a few pounds. Linda won't recognize you when you get back."

"I hope it'll happen soon! Something tells me that we should hurry. As you know, Jonathan, I always follow my intuition."

"Your intuition! Admit that all you want is to fuck her!"

David acted as if he hadn't heard him. He was beginning to miss Linda.

"Well, this is what we're going to do," he said. "If in three days we don't have any more results, we'll simply go. That's it."

The other two remained silent. Jonathan got up and stretched himself. He picked up an orange and burst it open with one hand.

"Today we're going to use the hookah. We have to dig deep into the mound. David will stay on board to make sure the compressor is working well. When Jerry gets tired, he'll change places with you, David."

David mumbled some incomprehensible response. The idea of resting for a while was not unpleasant at all.

***

He didn't have any more doubts; they were certainly in the rear end of the wreck. Thanks to his probe — a long stem of flexible steel with a handle in the end — Jonathan had discovered solid objects under the first layer, items that were out of place on that kind of sea bottom.

They were lucky. The galley had sunk outside of the coral proliferation zone. In 300 years, it had slowly been buried in the sand and the currents had carried the alluvia along. The site should not present any particular difficulty.

From time to time, Jonathan lifted his head and looked at Jerry. Connected to the world of the surface by the long air hose, he worked with amazing focus and regularity for an elder man. A man who, not very long ago, was himself no much more than a wreck.

An hour passed and Jonathan decided to go back up. He would rest for a while and then he would come back down. This time he would bring David. There was still a huge amount of work to be done with the water dredge. They had to choose specific spots to work on. They had already marked out many spots using small red or orange buoys. Jonathan smiled. From a distance, they were like strange sand flowers with long thin stems.

The hour spent all alone had done David good. He reflected upon his desire to go back to Miami and abandoned the idea. Despite the uncertain results, he made up a plan for the next day. When the other two reappeared on the surface, he welcomed them with joviality.

"So, everything went well?"

"Tonight you'll eat like a king."

Jonathan handed him a silver fork.

"Is this all?"

"It's not much, I agree. But this is the key to the treasure chamber."

After a couple of cups of coffee, Jonathan felt in shape again to go back down.

"Dave, do you still feel like going down?"

"More than ever. I spent an hour here doing nothing."

"Well, we'll continue working with the dredge."

He left them to look for a dry diving suit. When he came back, Jerry was teaching David how to breathe with the hookah. David was delighted. He felt he had attained the status of a professional of the sea.

When they came back up one hour later, the basket was full. Jerry had already started cracking the limestone concretions open. Jonathan poured the basket's contents on the deck.

"We'll work on this first thing tomorrow morning," he said.

***

Night fell quickly but this time with no mist. The clear sky was lit up by the rising moon and the dark outline of Warderick Wells Cay stood out against it. The other two had been sleeping for quite some time but the old man still could not sleep. He climbed onto the deck. The vault of the sky above swarmed with stars. He suddenly stop, all his senses alert: he could hear the faint voices of a choir in the distance, as if carried by a breath of air. He hesitated for an instant, and then he went into the wardroom. He opened the front cabin door and approached Jonathan's bunk in the dark.

"Jon," he whispered. "Jon."

"What is it?"

"It's me, Jerry. Come!"

The two men stood side by side on the deck.

"The choirs, I've just heard them again."

They listened carefully for a moment, but didn't hear anything.

"Listen, Jerry…" Jonathan finally said. "I'm willing to believe you. In exchange, promise me that you won't talk about that with David anymore. Each one of us is looking for something and unfortunately we need him. All that's happened around you since you've been on board makes David nervous. You heard him. He gave us three days and, believe me, he always does what he says he'll do."

Placing his hand on the old man's shoulder, he added:

"Jerry, I want to know if I can count on you. We should not, under any circumstances whatsoever, lose control of this boat. Do you see what I mean?"

Jerry made a brief affirmative sign with his head.

CHAPTER 19

They woke up before sunrise, had a quick breakfast and started working on the imposing heap of coral fragments piled up on the deck.

Almost immediately, Jonathan found a flat blackish coin, still trapped inside its dead limestone coating.

Dropped into a bowl of acid, its pattern quickly revealed itself.

"It's an eight reale coin," said Jonathan, filled with contained joy. "A piece of eight."

"Bravo, son!" said Jerry.

David grabbed it quickly and put it inside his cigar case.

"Now, dear little one, grow and multiply! We want to have many grandchildren."

In the warm morning sun, the day promised to be beautiful. Jonathan resumed his work underwater eagerly. Passing through the thick layer of silt and sand, he reached a worm-eaten wooden floor. The wood was crumbling like a wet blotter under the effect of the huge vacuum. Held with firm hands, the nozzle was widening the cavity more and more. Slightly behind him, David was filming. He had many ideas again. Many subjects and characters filled his mind. For now, he was shooting a sequence of Jonathan with the dredge.

He thought about Jon. In what measure could he be leagued with the German? They both seemed to understand each other instinctively, despite their age difference. What would happen if they really discovered a treasure? It would be easy for them to get rid of him in one of those deserted islands. What the eye doesn't see...

A shiver went up his spine. He would not be tricked. At the slightest sign, he would strike the first blow. When they least expected, he would abandon them to their own fate. Comforted by this resolution, he went back to the surface to replace Jerry.

***

Jonathan had been digging up kitchen utensils for some time now: spoons, tin plates, jugs, bowls and pottery objects in a thousand pieces. They were proof that he was in the officers and high-class passengers area. The loading wedges should be a little bit forward toward the prow. He would have to move the working site.

When Jonathan came back on board, David was polishing a piece of metal.

"What' s new? It there any hope? I saw that you found something every now and then," said David.

Jonathan disappeared through the hatch and reappeared right away with a folding basket in his hand. He tied a nylon rope to it and gave the other end to David.

"Hold it firmly. I'm going to harvest."

Jon dived with the basket in his hand and no equipment at all. Every now and then, he loved to jump into the water like the sponge or pearl fishermen of times past. Just 30 feet deep — child's play!

He gathered everything slowly and made a sign to David by pulling the rope. As the basket was going up slowly, he continued his little outing, taking his apnea up to its extreme limit. Held his breath until he reached the surface, where he emerged making a long and strident whistle. David ran to the back to help him.

"You' re nuts! I thought you had drowned."

Jonathan was blowing like a seal.

"Instead, you should have thought. Good riddance!" said Jonathan.

"You're right. But it's still a bit too early for that!"

David burst out laughing, happy with his nastiness and Jonathan laughed too.

"That's the David I know. Life is nothing but a masquerade and cynicism is the best proof of one's health. The strong man lives for himself and one day at a time. If you want these magnificent Caribbean islands to recognize you as one of them, you have to reject your petit bourgeois mentality. Never forget that pirates and buccaneers were the lords of these waters once."

David stared at Jonathan as he went away wiping himself with a towel. From now on, one thing was certain: David would have to be on his guard. The young man was certainly capable of anything.

***

The three men admired the fine blue porcelain plate with darker motifs that Jonathan picked out of the basket.

"It's Delft," said David after a moment. "It's beautiful and ancient. But it's Dutch and your galley was Spanish… a simple Batavian pirate perhaps."

Jon remained quiet and pensive. If what this idiot said was true, it meant goodbye to all his dreams!

Jerry interrupted.

"I don't believe it, Mr. Klein. The Delft came much later. This porcelain is Chinese. It's Ming. It was manufactured in the Province of Kiang-Si, in sixteenth-century China and exported all over Europe through the Philippines, Acapulco and Vera Cruz. It's quite the opposite. This tends to prove that we're on the right track. To a well-informed collector, a plate like this one would be worth around 500 dollars."

David's face lit up.

"Ha! Ha! Now it's really becoming interesting. Two bronze canons worth 3,000 dollars each, earthenware worth 500 dollars a plate… You're right, it's a vein. At least I'll recover part of my expenses while we wait for Jonathan's treasure."

Jon inwardly blessed the old man. He turned the engine on and David was overtaken by the fever to search. At Jonathan's insistence, he and David went back into the water while Jerry turned the compressor on again. During the next two hours, with the help of the dredge but also working with their bare hands, they cautiously searched the sand bottom.

A magnificent and intact teapot was extracted and also two rice bowls identical in every aspect to those in any Chinese restaurant in Miami. The only difference was that they were more than 300 years old!

They found two square bottles eroded by the sea, three spoons of different sizes and forms, and two forks identical to the one found the day before. All that was a confirmation that they should be right in the middle of what would be called the officer's mess nowadays.

They continued to work relentlessly. They reached a second layer of worm-eaten wood. Rubble and fragments of all kinds were accumulating in the inflatable while the fallout of sand and silt into the water darkened the site.

***

They had just come back on board when the sudden mist surrounded them again on all sides. The sun was not yet fully set and the pale halo of its globe could be seen intermittently through the thick cottony layer of fog. They turned on the projector and forced themselves to break open and sort out all they had accumulated since morning. The results were quite disappointing: nails of all sizes and endless corroded bits and pieces.

Despite the crevalle jack Jonathan captured during a short dive, and then prepared using his usual recipe, the atmosphere in the wardroom was sullen.

"Listen, Dave. If you really want to go, there' s nothing we can do about it. But I think this would be a big mistake. It's absurd to believe that we would put our hands on the loot on the first attempt. We already found many hints. Tomorrow or the day after tomorrow the sand will deliver its secret to us."

"Tomorrow or the day after tomorrow. Okay, Frenchy, but not one day more than that. I'm fed up! I'm wasting my time and my money here."

David's mind was made up. The days were passing, and he was beginning to see things in a new light. He had given in to an impulse. That was unusual for him. It had been a sudden, and perfectly natural folly. In every man there's a latent need to break up the monotony of everyday life. He had let himself be intoxicated by the perfume of adventure, as if by the secret charms of a disturbing unknown woman.

"Listen, Jon," he said finally. "One day either way won't make any difference now, but we need some results very quickly."

***

The following day, Jerry and Jonathan worked on the other end of the tumulus. They cleared out a few long pieces of a dark and soft metal very quickly. It was the lead sheathing of the hull. This was the method used at the time to protect the big wooden vessels against the drillings made by tropical burrowing worms, commonly known as shipworms.

That layer of sediments was much loser now, and they went

through it easily. On their way, they picked up quite a lot of domestic paraphernalia. The folding basket went back up to the surface regularly, carrying pots, tumblers, pieces of caldrons, and many different tin, iron, earthenware or fine porcelain utensils.

Sometimes the brightness of gold shone for a moment among the grayish debris of the coral coating — a signet ring on which the coat of arms could hardly be made out, three unlatched buttons, a brooch that had lost its precious stone... These finds managed to keep their enthusiasm alive.

It was late when Jonathan freed from its limestone coating a fused block of silver coins. They had been welded together by the salts and sulfates of the sea, and formed an ingot measuring about 10 inches long.

David was satisfied.

"Frenchy, as long as you can keep finding this kind of change, we'll continue."

Jonathan smiled and said nothing.

The coins were almost all different from one another. Their origin could only be the vest pocket of one of the shipwreck victims. He was beginning to be shaken by doubt: this was probably not his galley. It was very possible that this ship sunk on the way to Cadiz toward New Spain and not on its way back to Europe. That hurt. Except from some jewels and some objects of personal value belonging to the victims, there could not be any gold on board, much less a treasure.

He was fuming with rage. No, that could not be! Fate could not be playing such a trick on him! He couldn't admit that the dream he had been chasing for so many years would once again fade into nothing. He regained self-control. He would have to keep working until the tumulus was completely disemboweled. In any way, he should not show anything that might arouse any suspicion in David.

***

The thick and heavy fog was back again. Jonathan got up nervously and, searching for some air, he climbed onto the deck. A slight noise made him turn back. Jerry's long silhouette was standing in the doorway.

"You can't sleep, son?"

It was more an observation than a question.

"You're worried. There's nothing valuable in the wreck, is there?"

"Why do you say that? We haven't finished clearing up the site yet."

"I'm afraid you have."

Jonathan looked at him surprised.

"Yes," said Jerry. "The weather is going to get bad, that's for sure. This sudden rise in the temperature… Have you looked at the barometer? It's in free fall. It's probably almost 4 am. Around 6 am, we'll listen to the weather forecast and we'll get under way in double quick time. We can always come back."

He continued mockingly:

"If you believe it's really worth the trouble…"

Around 5 am, a small regular clapping gave a slow oscillation movement to the Barracuda's hull. A bottle that was left on the edge of a shelf in the lavabo slipped and crashed on the floor making a loud noise of breaking glass. It woke David from a deep sleep. He jumped up and realized that it was still dark and Jon was not there. He grabbed his pants and had hardly finished fastening his belt when the cabin's door opened, showing Jonathan with a bad day look in his face.

"Move! According to the old man, we're in for some very rough weather."

He followed the young man into the wardroom. Jerry was sitting on a turning chair with his back to them and had headphones on his ears. He was listening to radio conversations. The nasal voices could also be heard through the speaker. The old man turned to them and let the headphones drop around his neck.

"I've just joined Freeport Pilot at 2,738 kHz. That's it. They're announcing the formation of a hurricane. There'll be more detailed information in the Bahamas radio station weather forecast, at 6:30. Have you seen the barometer, Mr. Klein? We can't waste a second. We must go back to the open sea, and then to a port or better yet, to a hurricane hole*."

"Can it be really bad?" asked David.

The old man was laconic.

"It would be a good thing to find shelter somewhere."

They quickly put on their wetsuits. Outside, in the almost complete darkness, brief salty and moist blasts of wind arrived from the

---

* Hurricane hole: a small cove completely sheltered from storms.

Sound, apparently determined to shake off its lethargy. Jon lit up the spotlight, illuminating the Zodiac and the big basket.

"Dave, I think it's better that you dive with me. Jerry will stay on board to prepare everything and also to deal with any surprise."

The two men equipped themselves and jumped into the water quickly. It was the first time David found himself in the dark under the surface, but he didn't have the time or the desire to enjoy the phantasmagoric spectacle of the liquid ceiling illuminated above them. The current was getting stronger. In the light of their flashlights, the small universe suspended in the water seemed to be dancing a slow dance, coming and going.

With the pipes and the nozzle safely on board, they worked on the basket, disassembling it completely. All the equipment was lowered into the engine room through the trap door and securely fastened.

The trawler was rolling more and more. It was attached at the bow and the stern by the anchors and the oscillation stopped dangerously every now and then. Jerry lifted both rear anchors and the Barracuda placed itself in the direction of the aggressive, gusty wind.

They had a hard time passing the big compressor through the hatch cover. Tied by slings to the derrick, it was swinging out of the narrow opening moved by the rolling movement of the boat. They wasted precious time before they managed to pass it through the opening. By the time the inflatable was deflated and firmly attached onto the roof inside its bag, the sun was beginning to rise.

Jerry finally started the two engines and they moved toward the east. A yellowish line stood across the horizon in the light of the rising sun, crushed by the dark mass of the cumulus. Short choppy waves began to appear everywhere, now and then passing over a swell that was forming in the west.

At 6:30, a special weather report spoke of a hurricane depression forming in the Gulf of Mexico and moving north toward the North Bahamas and the Atlantic through the Florida Strait. "There are very good chances that this hurricane will go north around Florida but we can't predict anything," said the old man. "Anyway, we have to run in the opposite direction. The farther we are from the epicenter, the less violent the winds will be."

"No way!" David interrupted with a brittle tone in his voice. "Since we have weighed anchor, we'll return to the fold. Captain, I want you to head toward Miami."

The old man eyed him up and down.

"'I'm sorry but in these circumstances, and as the captain of the boat, I'm the one who gives the orders here. To go back would be suicide."

Without warning, David pounced on Jerry and pushed him out of his seat. The old man fell on the floor, bringing David down with him. Jonathan ran to separate the two as a muffled thump on the starboard side shook everything on the boat. The wardroom was filled with the sudden clash of objects tumbling down and breaking glass as the Barracuda listed dangerously. He stumbled over something and ended up joining the other two on the floor. The helm was spinning wildly with nobody to control it.

Jonathan heaved himself up and, with an acrobatic movement, he managed to grab the helm and stop it. Then, using all his power, he straightened the boat.

"Stop! You're crazy!"

White with anger, David got up.

"I won't allow anybody to give me orders on my own boat!"

Jerry got up. "It's for our own safety," he said. "The fact that the Barracuda belongs to you, Mr. Klein, doesn't give you any rights."

Replacing Jonathan at the helm, he said:

"Give that to me, son, if you want the three of us to pull through this alive."

Before David could try to attack him again, a new hammer of water, stronger than the first one, shook the Barracuda. A big wave broke over the stem and hit the glass panes. They each caught onto the closest thing they could find to keep their balance.

"What can we do?" David was hanging onto the chart table.

"Fasten everything that moves! You, Mr. Klein, check everything inside. You, Jon, take a look on the outside. Be careful!"

When Jonathan slid open the door, a violent gust of wind rushed in blowing about the charts, newspapers and tablecloths. For a brief moment, they looked directly into the violent onslaught of the unleashed elements against their boat.

"Close it! Close it!" said Jerry. "Too late…"

The three men were gathered on the front part of the boat, against the pilot's station. Jerry held the helm but often let Jonathan replace him, so that he could collapse into the armchair for a moment. David had the headphones on his ears, and was deeply immersed in the radio. His eyes stayed on the small radar screen.

Once the first moments of emotion passed, Jerry decided to put to flight and was struggling to keep the direction. He was worried and tired. The waves were betting bigger. He noticed that the speed of the engines fluctuated wildly whenever the two propellers came out of the water. The vibration lasted a little longer every time. Also, sometimes, a wave bigger than the others caught up with them and hit them in the rear, dangerously shaking the hull of the Barracuda.

Jerry gave his place to Jonathan, opened the bar case and grabbed the bottle of bourbon. The cork that he placed on the table rolled immediately to the floor. Bringing the neck of the bottle to his lips, he gulped the whisky. Alcohol had rarely before given him this sensation of well-being. He held out the bottle.

"Anybody else want it?"

David grabbed the bottle without a word and followed Jerry's example.

Jonathan turned back for a moment and looked at Jerry, who was apparently out of action.

"You feel bad, old man?"

"It's nothing… I'm just a little tired."

Jonathan had said 'old man' as always. But this time, it hurt Jerry. It was true; he was becoming an old man. But it was not such a natural fact as getting old that bothered him. A feeling he believed he would never experience was insidiously beginning to overcome him — fear!

He didn't want to admit it, but the anguish he felt after the dream hadn't abandoned him and the crystalline but gloomy, almost funereal singing he had heard coming from the island had definitely sealed the spiral of fright deep in his guts. It was neither physical danger nor death itself that he dreaded with all his heart — he had rubbed shoulders with them so many times! It was the secret threat of the forces he thought he had unleashed. He felt guilty for that.

Those forces had always been close by since the death of the big Cretan in Marseilles. Instead of manifesting themselves in reality, they could be sensed in the shadow of his life. Curiously, he was convinced that it was precisely these secret forces that had facilitated his arrival in the New World after the fall of the Third Reich. Juridical and political obstacles that he would never been able to overcome on his own disappeared as if by magic. He even had been given an important position at NASA.

One morning, after having spent the whole night alone in a hotel room in Nassau, with his door locked from inside, the precious orichalc disc he always wore on a chain around his neck had suddenly disappeared. He didn't know it at the time, but that had been the sign of the beginning of the fall. The forces had begun to manifest more openly, as if trying to make him panic. They had been playing with him since he left Miami. Quite slowly, through what seemed to be very natural manifestations, they were tightening their vise on him. The storm they were facing now was the last proof. It didn't have anything to do with the announced hurricane. This tempest was too far from the epicenter. But he didn't want to tell them that. They already thought he was a crank!

A new thrust, followed by a sinister cracking sound and a brutal listing of the boat tore Jerry from his numbness. He jumped up. Jonathan was leaning on the helm with all the weight of his body, and David was helping him. Jerry tried to speak, his face pale.

"The radar... It's not working anymore..." he finally said.

"Yes," said Jonathan, also very pale. "The wave must have torn off our mast."

The two men looked at Jerry as if he were their last hope. He had regained his self-control. His reflexes as an old sailor, conditioned by all his years at sea, started playing again.

"We're going to use a sea anchor. There's no other choice."

Jerry was speaking very slowly, to reassure them and also to reassure himself.

"This is not a sailboat and the maneuver is dangerous," he continued. "When we pass across its course, we'll receive all the impact of the storm. As soon as we're facing the wind, you'll throw the sea anchor. It must be in one of the front boxes."

He went back to the helm while the other two were getting ready. Following Jonathan's example and advice, David put on a wetsuit. They pulled up the long canvas cone-shaped device and its floats. Wearing safety harnesses connected by long jacklines to a big handle above the door, they got ready to come onto the deck.

Jerry reduced the speed of the engines slightly and started to change the direction of the boat slowly. Almost immediately, the Barracuda started listing and rolling from one side to the other. He could feel it being shaken by the short breaking waves that crashed into the boat more and more. A huge wave hit them transversely, and under the shock, the trawler toppled over to the starboard side and into the water. Laying all the weight of his body onto the helm, Jerry acted as a counterbalance. The moment the Barracuda was starting to come back into position, in a slow pendulum movement, amidst the creaking and moaning of the entire hull, he opened the throttle full out and in a last effort placed the boat into the wind.

"Let' s go! Now!" he roared.

A torrent of air, rain and sea spray rushed into the wardroom through the open door when Jon and David ran outside. They moved fast, crawling along the catwalk, dragging with them the floating anchor. When they reached the forecastle, they were stopped by the fury of the wind. The big waves that were passing over the stem crashed over them every time the boat went into a nose-dive. Through the glass windows, Jerry was following their efforts anxiously. They were too slow!

They disappeared for a moment, submerged by a big wave. When they were visible again, he understood that they had accomplished their task: beyond the davit, the anchor was hanging on its rope. Jonathan finished coiling it around the bollard.

Relieved, Jerry lifted his eyes toward the horizon. He was flabbergasted, shaking his head. That was not possible! In the livid light, in the distance but very clear in all its details, a Cretan trireme with its big rectangular sail fully displayed in the storm, was moving as if in a dream. Its long hull with a triple row of oars flew by with ease on the raging waves.

When Jonathan and David returned, leaving outside the gusts of wind and the sea spray, they found Jerry prostrated, pale and rigid. In a few broken words, he explained to them what he had just seen.

"But this is impossible, Captain! It's a mirage caused by fatigue."

"David is right. In any case, a galley from 4,000 years ago would not last 10 minutes in this hurricane."

The old man kept his head buried between his hands. Maybe they were right, but he was certain that it was a Cretan trireme.

CHAPTER 20

While Jerry was resting, David and Jonathan tidied up the boat.

The damage was minimal. The mast was still in place, only the boom had been torn off and was hanging overboard held by its rigging. It must have taken down the radar wires when it fell. This explained the fact that the radar wasn't working.

As the hours passed, the wind seemed to weaken and the waves were losing their aggressiveness. Well attached to its sea anchor, the Barracuda was tracking perfectly. They talked about the old man and his latest vision.

"I tell you Jon," said David, "you know me, I have my feet on the ground, but your kraut will end up making me believe in the supernatural. All these odd things that are always happening around him... Look, even this storm, which is already calming down... This cannot be a simple hurricane! I'm not trying to understand, I don't want to understand, I loathe anything complicated. I'm only interested in results. And by the way, what I'm interested in is staying alive. And for that to happen, I have to get back to Miami as soon as possible."

Jon was laughing at the ease with which David let himself be impressed, but he was also crashing head-on into the wall of his refusal. He was inwardly cursing the tropical storm that had produced much more damage than a real hurricane. It had broken David's momentum and now he seemed to be going back on his decision.

They were terribly shaken once again by the passage of strong gusts of wind. The old man got up each time and each time went back to his bunk.

"Nothing serious now... Anyway, there's nothing else to do but wait. It won't be long before the lull now," he said.

Despite everything, they decided that one of them would always be on watch. So, at 10 pm, Jonathan found himself alone with the howling wind, the creaking of the hull and his thoughts, which were darker than the clouds above him.

He had been mistaken; there was not a shadow of a doubt anymore. The shipwreck was not the right one and Jerry himself knew it too. What should he do now? Go back to Warderick Wells Cay with or without David's permission and look for another wreck along the same reef line? That could take weeks, even months.

He went in to get his small file folder and opened it. One thing struck him immediately. The drawing he had made of the island according to the Spanish Admiral's description was round and not oblong like a cigar as their island had been. How could he have made such mistake? He had let himself become obsessed by the fantastic reputation of that island... But that was not the only one!

With an ill-tempered movement, he pulled down the folder's cover. Tony would really laugh at him... He would probably propose that they raise alligators together. He got up and paced the wardroom.

Should he force David to go back to Warderick? Just the two of them wouldn't be able to keep an eye on David all the time and also, in a few days, they would start running out of supplies. No, not again! He had failed once more. But wasn't that almost always the rule in the difficult path of treasure hunting that he had chosen for himself?

When shortly before midnight, Jerry came to relieve him, he found Jonathan amazingly quiet and relaxed. He had regained control of himself and was even smiling.

"Everything all right, son?" asked the old man.

He must have noticed his own change of humor even if unconsciously.

"Yes, but I'm going to bed. I need to sleep."

"You look very disillusioned, Jon."

"That's hardly surprising, but I always accept what fate gives me."

The old man stared at him. In his own way, the young man was a living replica of the Greek hero of Antiquity — young, handsome and powerful, but also vulnerable. Cutting sword and expiatory victim at the same time.

"Our fate sometimes has strange turn-arounds in store for us," he said.

Jonathan stopped with one hand on the doorknob and turned his head back.

"What do you mean?"

"Your fate is attached to mine, Jon, and as far as I'm concerned, the bell announcing the last round has just rung."

Jonathan didn't say anything. He went into the dark cabin. Groping around in the darkness, he undressed and lay on his bunk. Overcome by fatigue, he sank into sleep.

***

It was almost 4 am when David came to relieve Jerry.

"It's calming down," Jerry said. "I listened to the weather report. The hurricane, which is just a tropical storm with less devastating winds, is going up toward the north, as I predicted. We'll be able to get under way as soon as the sun rises."

The old man marked time for a moment, writing in the logbook and studying his charts. Since David answered the few questions he asked with grunts and growls, Jerry assumed he wanted to be alone, so he decided to go to bed and get some sleep.

And for David, the moment had come to relax a little and smoke a good cigar, something he hadn't been able to do for two days. He opened the case looking for the bourbon, but all he found was an empty bottle. He got up to go get another one. Through the glass panes, he could see a pale light low on the horizon, announcing the dawn. He sat deeply in his favorite seat, noticing that the boat was moving very little now. His thoughts scampered about his two companions.

He didn't like the old man. That was a fact. His presence made him uncomfortable, but he didn't know exactly why. On the other hand, he was very happy to have met Jonathan. Thanks to him, he had faced physical danger for the first time. Also thanks to him, he had experienced a new kind of life, made of unexpected events and adventure, which was very different from the pettiness of his habitual routine. He would certainly try some other project with him later on.

His thoughts brought him to their present situation. He had a sudden chill in his spine as he considered all the money he had wasted. Grabbing a hold of himself, he decided that it was better to go back to Warderick Wells and get the two cannons and all they could bring aboard in two or three days. Happy with his decision, he drank his bourbon in a gulp. He smiled, thinking of the face that the other two would make when he gave them the news.

***

Noises and shouts coming from outside tore David from his train of thought. He jumped up.

In the grayness of dawn, approaching the Barracuda, he saw a mast from which hung the rags of a torn up sail. Surprised, he hesitated for a fraction of a second, as Jon and Jerry suddenly burst into the ward-room. All three of them rushed outside.

"A Bahamian sloop," said Jerry.

"Yes, shellfish or turtle fishermen," confirmed Jonathan, who had a coiled up rope in his hands and was getting ready to throw it.

"It seems to be in very bad shape," said David.

He had grabbed a hitch and was walking toward the front of the boat. He stopped.

"Oh! Now I see, Captain!" David exclaimed cheerfully. "That's your trireme! In the distance, the rain, the hollow of the waves, and with the help of your imagination, you were confused…"

The old man didn't say anything and shrugged his shoulders.

The boat had a finely shaped stem, and a well-formed body. Its big mast was clearly swerving on the fore end of the vessel and the long boom was overflowing onto its stern. The boat's Bermudan sail was in rags. That sail was typical of the sailboats of the islands, built to be able to use the slightest of trade winds and also to resist the brutal assaults of tropical hurricanes. All this was possible because of the width of its foundation and the solidity of its planks.

Big smiles lit up the dark faces aboard the Bahamian sloop as they waved their arms happily when the two boats touched alongside each other.

In the blink of an eye, the men invaded the wardroom and explod-ed with cries of happiness as Jonathan announced that he was prepar-ing a round of coffee for them all.

Just like them, those guys had been surprised by the hurricane. They had also tried to escape it initially, and then also moved very slowly to avoid further damage to the boat.

Their leader was a man with a few frizzy gray hairs. He explained that they were fishing conch along the reef. They had also managed to get a big supply of turtles, abundant at that time of the year.

"Man! We were surprised when the bad weather came on so quickly. The night was magnificent and the stars were shining and then, all of a sudden, the devil and all its creatures were set loose."

David interrupted him.

"Are you saying that the weather was clear? We were surrounded by mist, like all the other evenings…"

"Mist?" The old man was looking at him with his eyes wide open in amazement.

He thought for a while, and then he seemed to hesitate.

"Were you maybe near Warderick Wells Cay? Mister!"

"Yes, exactly!"

The man shrugged his shoulders and shook his head, then called the others as witnesses.

"Did you hear that, guys? These Americans! You don't know anything about the things of the devil. That island is full of them; you're very lucky to be still alive."

Those words triggered a general commotion in the room. Each had his own little frightening story to tell. They were all relaxing now, after hours of tension and struggle against the raging elements. David got up and brought two bottles from the bar: one bottle of rum and another of bourbon. Again, this triggered a general commotion. The atmosphere was beginning to warm up and the old black man thought it was prudent to order the men back to the sloop. He remained aboard, accompanied by his lieutenant, a big string beanpole covered with scars.

Then, over a last cup of coffee, sitting around the coffee table, he offered them a share of turtle shells.

"This is a unique opportunity, mister! I need the money immediately, so I can have the boat repaired. Otherwise I would have wait to for the annual market."

David really wanted to let himself be tempted. With no information about current prices, he thought the old man was asking a reasonable price for them. He looked at Jonathan and Jerry. And also, it all felt very much like another adventure. Pretty soon, he would place them in his studios and his cozy apartment!

"Okay! We'll take them," he said.

They all went into the sailboat. Jerry admired its curve, accentuated by the hollow vault of the stern. Passing over the roof of the noisy cabin they went directly to the main cargo hold. The black man and his lieutenant cleared two hatches and they went down. The stench of dried fish and shellfish caught them by the throat. They approached two lots with a dozen turtle shells piled up one on top of the other. The old fisherman showed them one by one. The shells were very beautiful and the arches were perfectly shaped. It was a very beautiful selection and first hand… evidently!

For form's sake, David started discussing the price. He could already see himself showing them to his friends and acquaintances and telling them about how he had bought them. The negotiation was finally concluded to the apparent satisfaction of both parties, when Jerry reappeared, after having walked away from the group for a while. He looked very excited and David, as well as Jon, understood that something very important had just happened, at least in the old man's eyes. He talked directly to the old fisherman and David noticed that he was literally grabbing the man's arm.

"Where did you find those metal bars that you use as ballast in the bottom of the cargo hold?"

"Do you mean those lead bars, Captain?"

"Yes, yes… That's it…lead bars… Where?"

The black man cleared his throat and spat on the deck. Then, looking at his lieutenant and the others one by one, he finally said:

"Well… Do we agree on the price?"

David made a positive sign with his head and then he added:

"I'll pay you cash, in dollars, right now."

Jerry interrupted nervously.

"Give him some extra dollars. Those lead bars will be useful to us."

David looked at his skipper. Jerry must have a major reason for proposing that barter. He turned to the old Bahaman man.

"What do you think of 50 dollars more?"

"Okay, mister."

He ordered his lieutenant to transfer the whole thing to the other boat. Then, followed by Jon, David and Jerry, he went onto the deck and then aboard the Barracuda.

Finally with the bundle of bills in his hands, the old fisherman didn't stop flipping through them without even counting, just for the pleasure of touching them. He accepted a last glassful of rum.

"Now I'm going to tell you where we found them," he said. "There is an island, mister, where zombies are the masters. They appear almost every evening and unfortunate are those who find themselves alone there. They never come back. One day, it will soon be five years ago, right Bill?" he called his lieutenant to witness. "We were completely lost in the fog and in the morning, when we lifted out nets, we found those lead bars. We lost several of them because they made holes in our net. A really bad job! When the fog had lifted completely, we saw the island. We were very close, when we should have been dozens of miles from there. How was it possible and why? Only the sinister chickshawnees that started flying all around us would have been able to explain. No doubt they had attracted us to make us disappear into their hell."

The old fisherman was getting more and more frightened as he spoke. He stopped suddenly and then continued, speaking directly to Jerry.

"Captain, be careful with those bars. They must be bewitched!!"

Jerry forced himself to smile and reassured the man.

"I need them for my work. Chief, could you at least let us know the name of that bewitched island?"

"Guinchos Cay! But don't get too close to it!" He laughed cheerfully and then got up.

He now seemed to be in a hurry to leave. They shook hands vigorously and the three men accompanied him back to his boat. They cast off the moorings and against the rising sun in the radiant sky, the sloop moved away slowly, elegant and solid, until it was out if sight.

"Fifty dollars! What do those bars have that is so special, Captain?"

Jerry had placed one bar on the table in front of Jonathan and David. He had the proof now and he postponed the moment of revealing its truth. Jonathan lifted it and turned it in all directions. Under the naked light of the light bulb, it looked dark, almost black. Nevertheless, it shimmered with the colors of the rainbow just like a puddle of domestic oil or gasoline shines in the water or on a wet ground.

"This is really curious," said David. "Are you going to tell us what it is?"

"Yes, started Jerry with an almost solemn voice. "This that you see here, my friends…"

He seemed really moved as he said the word 'friends'.

"No man has ever seen it, no matter how unbelievable that might seem."

He hesitated for a moment before he continued.

"This... This is orichalc, the sacred metal of the people of Atlantis."

Surprised, they looked at him. He was trembling; his eyes welled up with tears.

Together, they had grabbed the bar again and were turning it around in all directions, examining it closely. Jonathan got up to look for a magnifying glass.

"The metal of Atlantis? This is unbelievable!"

"Is it worth anything?" asked David cautiously.

"I repeat, nobody has ever seen this before. This is priceless. There's no market value for it. It's rarer than the biggest of diamonds!"

There was a long moment of silence. David picked up the magnifying glass and studied the block even closer.

"Do you know where is Guinchos Cay, Captain?" David finally asked, with a strangled voice.

"Yes."

"Well, if we all agree, we'll go there immediately!"

CHAPTER 21

They regained the sea quickly, in the direction of the Old Bahama Channel toward their new destination.

The good weather had come back. They soon passed by Green Cay and regained the deep royal blue waters of the Tongue of the Ocean. A school of playful dolphins escorted them for hours, joyfully leaping very close to the stem, as if they too were happy for the return of the good weather.

The turquoise line delimiting the shallow waters of the Great Bank appeared on the horizon, as the reddish globe of the sun was getting ready to disappear. They navigated for a few more hours until it was dark. Because of the danger of the surfacing coral outcrops, they decided to drop anchor in those quiet waters. After a quick meal, they went to bed exhausted.

The three men got up before sunrise. The good-humored atmosphere around the morning cup of coffee contrasted with the heavy hours of the previous days.

"I know Guinchos Cay from its reputation," said Jerry, as he poured himself a third cup full of coffee. "It is indeed a strange place. According to some, it might be a Blue Hole, dug in ancient times through the underwater limestone plateau of the Great Bank, and inexplicably filled in. Together with its distant neighbor, Key Lobos, they are like two advanced sentinels on the edge of the Old Bahaman Channel. I've already told you, in my opinion, that's where lie the doors to the mystery."

"Captain, please, don't start that again!"

"He's right, Jerry, stop telling us your stories, will you?"

The old man looked at them; too bad for them. He was just trying to warn them about the danger, and give them a chance to come through it safely.

From the flying bridge, where he could oversee the shallow transparent waters, Jerry was at the helm. He could distinguish through the bulges in the sand, long darker strips and sections cut in angles. They were like buried vestiges of a powerful civilization whose cities and monuments must have been spread all over that shallow limestone plateau, just about 10 or 12 thousand years ago. It was the probable origin of the great Aztec and Mayan cultures, much later.

Toward noon, a small islet appeared in the distance.

"Guinchos Cay!" shouted Jonathan.

"Guinchos Cay!" repeated the old man in a muffled voice.

The perfectly round islet, covered by a tight scrub, stood out lonely and green, on the immensity of the Bank. Immediately behind it, just like at Warderick Wells Cay, the long dark blue line of the deep waters could be seen all along the horizon.

They dropped anchor close to a slight headland on the starboard side, which marked a little sand beach opening to the north and protected by three coral outcrops.

***

David was the first to discover a sign of the treasure.

They had swum the distance of about 300 feet separating them from the inlet. Now they were walking on the beach, enjoying the pleasure of the softness and the warmth of the fine sand on their feet. David felt something caught between two of his toes. He leaned down to pick it up…

It was bright yellow in the sun. Speechless, David handed his discovery to the others. It was a gold coin!

Jon grabbed it, with an abrupt movement.

"It's a doubloon! I tell you, we finally found our treasure!"

"Hey! This coin is mine! I found it!"

Laughing, David tried to take it from him.

For a moment the excitation reached its peak. The old man tried to calm them down.

"Wait! One coin doesn't mean anything."

"Yes, it does! I'm sure! That's how Kip Wagner found his treasure. He found a coin on a beach in Florida, and he was not even looking for it."

Jonathan stopped for a moment and looked at the sea, in the direction of the boat.

"If you want to hear what I say… The wreck is right there… I can feel it. It's lying against the coral outcroppings."

"How is it possible that nobody has found it before us, it being so close?" asked David, who was always prudent.

"First, nobody ever comes here. Then the storm has done us a favor. Something in the wreck must have been loosened. And then, you know… We're too close to Cuba and too far from everything else."

Without wasting any time, they went back aboard. In the wardroom, they examined the coin with the magnifying glass. It was exceptionally well preserved. In fact, it seemed as if it had just come out of a modern coining press. When David placed it solemnly inside his cigar case, next to the other coins, he was surprised by its perfection.

"It looks like a brand new Cadillac next to some old rattletraps," said Jonathan.

Moved by their enthusiasm, they equipped themselves without any waste of time. The last three full tanks were thrown on board the Zodiac. They were soon ready to get down to the job right at the three masses of coral that Jonathan had seen.

With the two magnetic detectors, they started searching all the faults on the coral wall, the façade of which stood surrounded by sand, complex and tormented as a gothic cathedral.

Near a long furrow filled with pieces of branchy acrapora, the arm of the magnetometer suddenly stopped. Putting the instrument on the ground, Jonathan started clearing up the coral deposit. He found sand. He scraped the sand and then, suddenly, he found countless coins. He picked up one and brought it close to his mask. It was a piece of eight, an eight reale coin. He was beginning to know them! He released the little floating buoy, filled it with air using his mouthpiece and managed to attach it to the spot.

With a strong stroke of his fins, he started looking for the other two, who were searching together. Jerry and David understood quickly. They came toward him. For them, the little orange buoy floating in the distance in the coral, looked like the victory flag.

David and Jon remained there to scrape the sand and collect the coins, and Jerry went back to the Zodiac, to anchor it right above them.

Then, it was a coming and going of baskets full of coins until their tanks were out of air.

In the evening, there was only total jubilation on board the Barracuda.

They had poured the contents of the baskets higgledy-piggledy on the table. The streaming sound of colliding coinage was very pleasant to them. They were exclusively silver pieces of eight that had never been used, originated directly in a Peruvian or Mexican mint. Jerry had brought up pieces of pottery, which in his opinion proved that it was an original transportation. Contrary to what one might believe, for the crossing of the ocean, the coins were stored in pottery pots or wooden boxes instead of bags. All of them had the same date: 1633. That was the year of the Santa Isabella's last trip.

Outside, the backfiring of the small compressor filling up the air tanks was the only sound disturbing the quiet of the night. From time to time, Jerry and Jonathan got up to watch the process or to replace one of the tanks.

"We won't be able to keep all that aboard," said the old man, as he polished the coins after soaking them.

"I hope we'll continue to amass them. Why do you say that, Jerry?"

"Yes, Captain, why?"

"Have you wondered what might happen to us if we were surprised by a Coast Guard or Bahaman police patrol boat as we're working here? Or even worse — the Cubans, who might very well come here on the quiet."

"I hadn't thought of that. It's true," said David, as he looked at his cigar. "They would confiscate everything, including the Barracuda. We would be in a right fix."

"Not to say anything about the fine!" added Jonathan. "It would take us all our lives to pay it."

"What can we do then?" David was beginning to worry.

"Very simple, we'll have to stash them away in a good spot, somewhere on the ground."

"I don't like that idea very much, Captain. Is there really no other solution?"

"I can't see any other."

Jerry thought for a moment and then added:

"I think we'll have to take turns of duty during the night. Two men in a bivouac on the ground and the third one on board."

They started working in the very first hours of the morning. The derrick was out of service. They wouldn't be able to lift the water pump onto the deck anymore to use the dredge. Jonathan got around the difficulty. Instead of vacuuming, they would employ the water jet principle to clear up the sand. The portable auto-pump in the engine room would serve the purpose perfectly. The old man quickly fixed up the tubes and links of the right sizes.

They worked all day without stopping and the baskets were always full. The first vein was quickly exhausted but under the air jet, the sand and the debris revealed new discoveries.

Jonathan was right. After the tornado, a whole section of the coral overgrowth must have given in. They had been incredibly lucky. One day more or less, and they would have passed by their fortune.

The coins were accumulating by hundreds now. At the end of the day, they reached a first assessment: 2,347 four and eight reale coins. They piled them up in beer cartons, after emptying these of their contents. They reinforced the cartons with several turns of string. Then they put them in the Zodiac and steered toward the island to look for a good hiding place.

It didn't take long for them to find one. Slightly set back from the little beach where they had landed the day before and behind the first curtain of vegetation, they found a crevice on the limestone rock. It was easy to get into it on all fours. They all agreed that they wouldn't find a better place anywhere else.

That evening, dinner was sumptuous. Jonathan had picked up several huge crayfishes, as easily as if they had been shells on the sand, and prepared them with a whisky and red pepper sauce. Three bottles of excellent Californian claret added the final touch.

Coffee and bourbon followed the meal, and their conversation reached a paroxysm of enthusiasm and exaggeration in celebration of such an event.

After they had calmed down, Jonathan and David got on the Zodiac to go to the little beach.

The night was deep. The thin crescent of the moon was rising, barely lighting the darkness of the night. With the wood they had prepared the day before, they quickly set up a good fire and, wrapped up warmly in their covers, they lay down on the ground, each on one side of the fire.

There was a long period of deep silence, interrupted only by the discreet rhythm of the water, washing the sand right at their feet, the chirping of the countless grasshoppers and other insects and, every now and then, a night bird's song.

"Frenchy…" David's words stood out in the darkness. "All my part of the treasure would not be enough to thank you for allowing me to live moments like this."

The answer was a grunt. Jonathan was already deeply asleep. He was dreaming of Linda.

***

Jonathan woke up with a start. It was still dark and he was certain he had heard voices. He kept on his guard, conscious and strained. The memory of the long watch periods during the war, in the Vietnamese jungle came back to his mind.

He could hear a diffuse, indefinable sound coming from a little mound. He could see its top standing out against the starry sky. He could not really make out the words, but it seemed like a whispering to him. And then, no more.

He was annoyed with himself. He never thought of exploring the island, although it was the first thing they should have done. Not for an instant, it never seemed possible to them that the island could be inhabited.

At sunrise, the three men armed themselves with Winchesters started searching the island. They didn't find anything. Not the slightest sign that there was or had been somebody there recently. For three hours, they went over the island with a fine-tooth comb. Every inlet deserved a meticulous investigation. They found nothing to indicate that somebody had been there recently. They had to bow before the evidence. Jonathan must have dreamed or at least he must have taken the sound of a nocturnal animal for the sound of human voices.

A good player, Jonathan said:

"We'll see that tonight."

Once they were back on the water, they forgot all about the incident. David's almost immediate discovery of a pre-Colombian statuette in solid gold marked the beginning of an unbelievable series of finds.

Sacred objects adorned with precious stones, torques, necklaces, and bracelets. A chain measuring almost six feet, stylized characters and fantastic animals molded flat according to a technique long lost, according to the old man. All of them made of gold and finely chiseled. Altogether, it was exceptionally rich loot.

In the wardroom, David couldn't stop rubbing his hands and Jonathan kept patting his back. Only Jerry seemed more and more worried.

That evening, after a crayfish barbecue on the beach, Jerry stayed with David, and Jonathan went back to the boat.

Toward midnight, the old man was torn from his sleep by the sound of distant voices. The young man had not lied. He picked up his Winchester and loaded a round in the chamber. For a moment, he thought of waking up David. But what for? He got up and walked toward the copse.

The sound of distant, muffled sobs stopped him on his tracks. 'Must be the blackbirds of the islands, they're great with that kind of song…' he thought.

Nevertheless, a chill ran up his spine. He kept on walking. A branch caught him on his way. As he tried to free himself, he heard laughs and then murmurings and whispers nearby. He could feel he was sweating, but he kept his calm.

He remembered his first stay in the Amazonian jungle. He couldn't close his eyes because of the fantastic concert of the creatures of the night.

He walked for a while, surrounded by indefinable noises, and then decided to go back to the camp. Whatever happens, all he wanted was to see it and understand. On his way back — was that an impression? — he was sure that he was being followed.

He only turned back when he had reached the fire. Nothing! He crouched down, stoked the fire and then sat down facing the hill with his back to the sea. An owl hooted and then, there was not a sound until dawn. That was strange too.

"I didn't sleep well, but I didn't hear anything," Jerry told Jonathan when he came to join them.

Jonathan looked at him. The old man was lying, that was evident, but he thought he must have his reasons.

"Me, I slept so well that somebody could have strangled me and I wouldn't have noticed a thing," said David, still wrapped in covers.

He stretched himself, yawning.

"I wonder if I wasn't made for this kind of life!"

"You would soon be fed up with celibacy!" Jonathan was kicking him with his foot, to make him get up.

"You know, if we searched really well, I'm sure we would end up fishing up some sirens! Really, maybe it was the sirens that were making all that noise the other night. They can probably smell a male..."

He jumped up.

"Besides, I thought a lot about it and I finally understood our skipper's secret. He had a secret rendezvous with them. Isn't that so, Captain?"

The old man became pale. In a certain way, not really realizing the scope of his words, David was warning him about what would happen. He tried to keep his composure and stammered a few words of protest, while the other two laughed.

They quickly resumed the work in the water. And also very quickly, they ran into another vein of coins. This time, they were golden coins. They spent the whole morning bringing up baskets full of doubloons and escudos.

During the afternoon, as he probed the terrain with his steel rod, Jonathan felt that it was sinking almost completely in a crevice of dead corals. He cleared it up feverishly and then started digging with his dive dagger. Suddenly, he heard the screech of metal under his blade. He finished clearing it out with his hands. His fingers grabbed the edge of an object. He moved it in all directions and finally managed to bring it out. It was a disc measuring about 12 inches in diameter. Puzzled, he brought it closer to his mask. The dark shining metal was covered with engraved motifs. He made a sign to David, who was nearby. Together, they worked on the small site. They enlarged the hole and discovered eight more discs. Once they were absolutely sure that they wouldn't find any more discs, they went back to the surface.

***

Onboard, David had lit up the spotlight. In the powerful glare, the disc became iridescent with the colors of the rainbow.

There was no doubt; it was made of orichalc.

On one side, a stylized flower with twelve petals stood out in the center. Starting at the flower, 360 compartments each one containing a different motif, a drawing or an unknown hieroglyph, unwound themselves in spirals like snakes and ladders. Some of the motifs were repeated — a small circle containing seven points, a head with a flowing mane and dolphins.

On the other side, a double inverse spiral covered all the surface of the disc.

"What a fantastic continuity," murmured Jerry.

He quickly explained to the others that the magnificent symbol had been found engraved on objects since the earliest Antiquity along the entire European shoreline.

"From the Gravinis Neolithic tumulus in Brittany, built 5,000 years B.C., to King Minos' Cretan palace, passing by the great temples on Malta, that were built at the same time the Cheops' Great Pyramid was conceived!"

In certain aspects, the disc reminded him of Phaistos Disc, which at the time hadn't been deciphered yet. He had the opportunity to study it at the Archaeological Museum of Herakleion, on Crete. And above all, there was the medallion, a sad heritage of the tragic evening of January 1943 in Marseilles.

"Have you noticed," he asked, speaking more to himself than to the two men, "that the motifs alternate in a different manner on each disc? There is certainly a connection with the Zodiac. I think that each one of them could represent the theme of a different character."

He looked at Jonathan as he reflected upon that.

"We have found nine discs, but I think there should be ten. Ten! Like the Ten Kings of the Sea!"

"But we only have nine," repeated David.

"Because there's one missing," said the old man, with a worried look on his face. "That's really curious."

"This could then really be the Santa Isabella's wreck — Jonathan's galley and the treasure listed in the Seville Archives?"

"I would say it is, Mr. Klein."

"But how can you be so sure, Captain?"

"Because of the signs and indications that don't leave any room for doubt. Besides, do you remember the plaque I have often told you about, that I used to carry around my neck on a chain, until it disappeared in that hotel in Nassau? It's undeniable that it has the same origin."

"If I understand you well, these discs don't look like anything known by man."

"Yes, son, yes, and they could well take us to the summit of glory and reknown."

"That's what I feared."

"What you feared? What do you mean, Jonathan?" asked David.

"They're not convertible into cash."

"It's not a matter of selling them," Jerry interrupted with a calm voice.

"No? Do you think I'm going to give them away?"

"Jon, this belongs to the universal heritage. You might have in your hands the answer to questions that have been asked by generations of historians and researchers... and by me too..."

Overexcited, the young man interrupted him roughly.

"I don't give a damn. I think I've already said this: glory, heroism, that's not for me. I decided that a long time ago, during that dirty Vietnam War. To have holes pierced on your belly, to be cut into slices, to have your eyes gouged out, I could do without that! All that so that others could keep on living in opulence and indifference! So that a government of bastards could sacrifice the victory of its own army to politics! No. Never more. There'll always be suckers. But not me!"

He let explode a long rage that he had managed to control until then. Hammering on the coffee table with his fist, his face contorted by resentment, he continued:

"Jerry, I've chosen a life without concessions. I don't ask anybody for anything and in return, I don't want to owe anything to anybody. I live in the present."

He grabbed a disc and brandished it.

"For me, this is a relic. For me, it doesn't have any quality other than that of belonging to me. Fuck your universal heritage!"

The old man looked hard at him and then turned to David.

"Do you agree with him?"

David hesitated for a moment before responding:

"In certain respects... yes."

He grabbed Jonathan's arm.

"Frenchy, you must not get carried away. There is certainly a solution, there's always a solution."

"Yes, you might lose all the profit of our efforts if you shout from the rooftops: we discovered the treasure of the Kings of Atlantis! I would have thought you were smarter than that… I'm going to have these discs melted down and we'll resell them for the price of the metal. No one will be any the wiser. Just like the Spaniards did long before us. Besides, that's a service that we render to their gods. Religious objects belong in a temple with believers, not in a museum, exposed to a parade of morons and non-believers."

"You're not in a position to speak of morons and non-believers, son."

Jonathan turned to the old man furiously and grabbed him by the throat. He started to clench his hand, and then threw him onto the seat. David rushed in to set them apart.

"You're crazy! Jon, let him go. He's not completely wrong, whether you like it or not. We don't have the right to conjure away such a discovery. It's enough to leave the discs and all that belongs to that unknown civilization. We'll stash them away in the hiding place. We'll go and then we'll come back some time later, all three of us, and we'll be able to reveal them to the world. After the dough, glory! Come on, Frenchy, be reasonable!"

"And who's going to cover the loss of profit? You don't care David, because you're already loaded!"

"I'll cover it!" Jerry got up and was rubbing his neck.

"You? According to our deal, we don't owe you anything."

"According to our deal, no… But morally, yes."

Jonathan calmed down and looked at Jerry with amusement. 'The old man has a lot of guts,' he thought.

"Okay, grandpa, but only because it's you."

Conscious that he had found the only possible solution, David tried to calm down the tension in the room.

"Come on, let's regain our self-control," he said. "We have almost everything. This is not the moment to argue."

He offered Jerry a cigar. The old man seemed to be recovered and was starting to relax.

The smoke of the tobacco was rising into the light of the electric lamp.

All of a sudden, David felt the need to know more.

Addressing Jonathan on purpose, he said:

"You know, Frenchy, when I think of all those phenomena, sometimes I wonder if there wouldn't be a hidden empire under the earth's crust or maybe under the sea. An empire made of superior beings, completely different from us, or maybe even extra-terrestrials, who are watching us humans, the little hoodlums of creation!"

His eyes were shining, he was happy with his stroke of inspiration.

The old man took his cigar out of his mouth and shook the ashes into the ashtray meticulously.

"You're saying that to me, aren't you, Mr. Klein? Well, you're a good loser, but I know that you play dumb to find out what you want to know."

For a moment, he stared at David in silence, as if he was still hesitating.

"It's very hard, if not impossible, for a man of the 20th century to conceive of a world that is not strictly material. Even less a society whose beings and things are not... how can I say it... completely solidified. For that man and for me in the past — before I 'understood' this — as well as for you today, matter is a fact of the senses, an irrefutable reality. As a matter of fact, matter is just sensation, like all the other sensations: it's a pure creation of mind. In fact, it's no more 'solid' than its own reflection in a mirror. Science, as well as all our contemporaries, is plagued by the dogma that our perfect industrial society is the result of a long adaptation to a hostile environment. That's absurd! As if any environment would be hostile to its own components!

"In fact, it's exactly the opposite that happens; each new species appears with its genes perfectly programmed to function in the new environment. The species succeed one another, in an implacable process of degradation, from light towards matter.

"To say it briefly, there's no doubt the future is behind us. The Golden Age precedes all others: degradation and degeneration are the only great rules of the cosmic play. Compared to the original societies of light from whence it stemmed, our own technological and industrial civilization is just the distant and fatal outcome of a long deterioration... defecation... a big shit!"

In the middle of the laughter and protests from the other two, Jerry went into his cabin. He closed the door in a rage.

CHAPTER 22

As planned, Jonathan and David had taken the Zodiac to guard the treasure. Lying on his bunk on the Barracuda, Jerry was unable to sleep. The flow of thoughts and memories was chaotic, but he nevertheless took some pleasure in watching them. The hours ticked away slowly on the chronometer.

The unexpected sound of an approaching boat broke the monotonously soothing rhythm of the water gently slapping the hull. He came suddenly awake and got up slowly. His right hand grabbed the Colt he always kept under his mattress.

The cabin door opened suddenly. "Markantakis!"

"You're not going to play the same trick on me that you played in Marseilles, Kapitän Müller. It's of no use now."

The impressive mass of the big Cretan stood like an apparition against the doorframe.

With his habitual self-control, Jerry was ready to face the Cretan the same way he had faced him many years before in Marseilles.

"This time, it is I who have come looking for you. I made an offer and a promise. I have continued to follow your long journey during all these last years. I saw your struggles, your fight for survival, your successes, your disillusionment, your fall and now your final attempt.

"In times past, our paths have often crossed. I was an enigma to you. But I managed to eradicate your materialistic concepts. Our world is nothing but illusion. It is Maya. It exists only as the interpretation of our senses, our intelligence and our consciousness. Modern particle physics has itself recognized the 'dead-end'. Without the observer, there is no object. This world of form does not exist outside of the Consciousness that creates it, maintains it and supports it. All is possible insofar as it is conceivable.

"The universe that I come from, this that you call Atlantis, is as real as this realm of relative space in which you exist. Before it disappeared beneath the waters of the Atlantic, it was a direct offspring of the Golden Age and the Primordial Tradition, just as was the continent of Mu in the Pacific Ocean.

"Beyond their vestiges and ruins, both of these worlds live in a subtle realm well outside the reach of your scholarly archeologists and other pre-historians."

Jerry burst out laughing.

Markantakis hadn't changed at all. Jerry found him as cynical and self-assured as during those dark years of the war. It had taken him some time to admit the Cretan was of a different essence. He was beyond Time and Space. Without truly acknowledging it, Jerry had been aware of the absolute truth of the nature of the Cretan, his true identity — he was one of the Ten Kings of the Sea!

Could it be that the ancient Greeks were right? Did demigods really exist? The proof stood before him.

Jerry, aka Kapitän Müller, got up. He was astonished at how fast he had made up his mind.

"I'm going to follow you now. I've wanted to do this for many years."

"All right, but we cannot waste a minute now. Let's go to the islet where I hid my yacht. The first thing we should do is get rid of the Barracuda. We have to make it disappear. Then I'll take you to Florida. In Miami, you'll vanish into thin air and you'll join me in Crete."

***

The incessant cries of seagulls woke David and Jon, who had spent the night on watch on the island.

A light breeze was blowing. The weather was going to change. Jonathan turned toward David, who was just opening his eyes. Between the two men, two spirals of bluish smoke were rising from the ambers of the barely smoldering fire. He lifted his body and looked at the sea. With a quick jump, he was up on his feet. The Barracuda was gone!

"David! Quick!"

He climbed onto a knoll. The sea was deserted. There were only a few white cumulus clouds perched low on the horizon.

"Maybe he thought it would be better to anchor somewhere else."

David joined Jonathan, his anxiety showing on his face.

"Do you think so? Without letting us know? The bastard beat it!"

They put on their shoes and climbed onto the highest point on the island, which was just a few feet high. From there, they could see all the immense nothingness of the Bank. Their eyes simply crossed and they climbed down without saying a word.

David was fulminating. He was convinced that the old man had made his decision after the discussion with Jon the night before.

"You should have kept your mouth shut!"

"And you'd better shut your own mouth, right away! We're stuck here. We have to face things as they are. I'm not the least worried about your boat, as long as we can manage to get out of here. Your declaration to the Coast Guard will trigger the search and even if you don't find your boat later on, the insurance company will pay for it. You don't need to be so worried. Anyway, we still have the treasure."

Jon was right; the situation was critical, but not desperate. Crying wouldn't help. For reasons that only he knew, the old man had disappeared and left them behind.

They made a quick assessment. Nothing in the hiding place had been moved. They still had the Zodiac and two full jerry cans. On the other hand, they didn't have much left in terms of food supplies: a big box of crackers, coffee, a few cans of condensed milk and beer, and a half empty honey jar.

Jonathan had all his dive gear, including his speargun. As for drinking water, they only had the plastic gallon left, plus the remainder of the last rains accumulated in the crevices on the rocks.

They would have to leave as soon as possible and look for another boat. They would have to bring it back with provisions, so they could recover the treasure. Then, they would have to reorganize the whole operation for another time.

Obviously, they could not take the loot with them now; much less leave it in its hiding place unprotected. The closest spot, excepting Cuba, was Key Lobos, about 40 miles to the East. It was inhabited only by the lighthouse keepers.

"I think one of us will have to wait here until the other one returns," said Jonathan. "The old man is undoubtedly just waiting for us to leave so that he can come and collect the treasure."

"Yes, but who?"

"Me, if you agree," proposed Jonathan.

As David took some time to respond, Jonathan added:

"Or we can toss up a coin. Do you have one?"

David gave a faint smile and took a piece of eight out of his pocket.

"Best two out of three. You throw it," said Jonathan.

"Heads, the T-shaped cross, I win and tails, the coat of arms, you win."

David threw up the coin three times. It came down twice on tails.

"You won," David said. He picked up the coin with a weary, disillusioned gesture.

They didn't waste any time and loaded the Zodiac. The moment he was going to step into it, a dazzling idea rushed into David's mind. Jonathan could very well be in cahoots with the old man.

He went back to the beach and stood up right in front of Jonathan, who looked at him surprised.

"Frenchy, I hope you and your German are not planning a rip-off on me!"

"Are you kidding?"

In fact, he had often fabricated all kinds of possible combinations that might make him the only owner of the treasure, but he never thought of including Jerry in his schemes.

"If you doubt it, you can stay in my place."

David seemed to hesitate, but he didn't have a choice anymore.

"Don't forget, I'll always find you no matter how cunning you may be," said David. "I have the means."

"Go on… go and be careful. I don't feel like starving to death here on this island," Jonathan replied.

Jonathan pushed the Zodiac into the water, holding it while David jumped in. When David started the engine, Jon remained where he was, looking at the boat as it went away.

After making a long turn to the left, the small boat disappeared behind the small headland. When its wake had been reabsorbed into the clapping water, Jon slowly went back to the camp.

***

The Zodiac was floating on the surface of the water, barely touching the crest of the waves. The continuous purring of the engine and its

vibration that was retransmitted by the tiller filled David with a pleasant feeling of safety.

The sun was at the zenith and, with only a slight wind from the
movement of the boat, the sun was becoming more and more scalding.

David checked his direction constantly on the compass. It had
been a wonderful idea to leave it on the Zodiac when they were at
Warderick Wells Cay. He felt optimistic. If all continued to go well, he
would be able to see the lighthouse at sunset.

He opened a can of beer and moved it quickly to his mouth, lest
he might waste one drop. It was certainly not as refreshing as the
cold beers aboard the Barracuda, but at least it was something to
drink.

He tried not to think about the old man anymore. He still could
not understand the reasons that might have made him play such a trick
on them. But it was not the moment to be overwhelmed by the muted
anger that was bubbling inside.

When David was finally getting quiet and relaxed, the engine suddenly choked. It started again, coughed once more and then stopped completely.

David, in panic, tried frantically for a few minutes to restart the
engine with a series of violent pulls that left him breathless and in a
sweat. He breathed a sign of relief when he realized that his brave
engine was okay. It just needed some gas. He was surprised and filled
up the tank with the content of the second jerry can. The vapors of the
gas gave a trembling and unreal aspect to what he saw.

He was alone, absolutely alone. Lost in that immensity, he became
aware of his smallness.

The engine started again with his first attempt and resumed its regular and reassuring rhythm.

David glanced at the compass and drank one more beer. He was
telling himself that it was even warmer than the first one, when the
engine started choking again and then stopped for good.

This time, despite all his efforts, it was final.

David struggled to keep calm. Around him, there was nothing but
water. The sea was slowly becoming darker as clouds covered the sky.

Key Lobos could not be very far now. He stood up, holding onto
the edge of the boat. Once the night fell, he would certainly be able to
see the lighthouse. He would then try to paddle up to it. And there was

always the possibility that he would see a boat. He would then fire a rocket.

He tried to lie down more comfortably and for a brief moment, a light breeze appeared out of the blue.

That was short respite. The wind became stronger and the inflatable started to move, but in the wrong direction.

After two hours, the sun was low in the horizon, and David was yielding to despair. During all that time, the boat had been moving with constant speed. He didn't have any idea anymore of how far he had drifted.

He scrutinized the immensity desperately. He massaged his tired eyes. Everywhere he looked, there was only the sea. Always the sea.

***

The day was spent in a very pleasant way for Jonathan. He dived without equipment and went back to the wreck. Relaxed, he continued the exploration.

Countless fauna, now confident because of the absence of noise, kept him company. After all the tension of the last days, he finally found himself in his real element — the water.

When the night fell, he looked at the big orange disc of the setting sun as it disappeared slowly behind the blue line of the horizon. All of a sudden, he felt he was part of that universe that he could not explain, and in no way was interested in worrying about. To live with total lucidity, with no complications and no regrets. He didn't owe anything to anybody.

In such excellent disposition, he lit the fire and waited until it was big enough for him to grill his now daily meal — two magnificent crayfishes. He had also managed to gather some wild berries that looked like the ones he had often bought in the markets. He had also seen Indians chewing them. With the berries and the abundant fishes, his mind was at rest.

He was thinking about Jerry. What had really happened to the old man? He couldn't possibly have run away because of their discussion the night before. The discs were in their hiding place with the rest of the treasure. Therefore, he hadn't left to save them from their promised destruction. He smiled for a moment, thinking of that. Jerry wasn't the kind of man that reacts suddenly. All that time since they left Coconut Grove, he had acted as if he was always expecting something to happen.

Maybe it had really happened and they never even noticed. One fact prevailed over all else. The old man was deeply, sincerely, a man of the sea. He would never have abandoned his friends without giving them a better chance to survive. No. As time passed, Jonathan became convinced that the old man had acted against his will. A distant giggling startled him. He got up slowly from the crouching position he was in, and listened. Nothing disturbed the silence of the night, except the usual, ubiquitous night noises.

He was leaning down over the fire again, when the air he was breathing seemed suddenly different. It had become heavy and poor, just like when he dived with scuba tanks and had to shift to the reserve.

The smoke from the fire made him cough. A series of shivers ran through his body, followed by cold sweats. He decided he was really tired and that it would be better to try to sleep right away.

He got up and gathered a pile of branches. He set them aside next to the fire, stoked the fire and then, pulling up the cover, he coiled up and lay down as close as possible to the heat.

Even lying down on the bare sand, he felt a little better. His eyes embraced the sky above him directly. A long ray of light crossed the night vault. Another one followed it, parallel to the first one. All his body started trembling as the sky was set ablaze with fireworks.

Suddenly aware of danger, he tried to stand up. His eyes were burning. He tried to grab the rifle lying on the ground right next to him. The sand yielded under his feet and he collapsed.

Before he collapsed, the entire space seemed to resonate with the choirs he so detested.

***

David was feeling terribly alone. The inflatable continued to drift on the endless sea. There was nothing left of the sun, except for a pale streak of light low in the dark sky.

He had given up searching the surface of the water. He realized that often times he would take a shadow or the crest of a nearby wave for a rescue ship.

As he lay on the bottom of the raft, his hand touched the smooth metallic surface of his last bottle of beer. He decided that he would not drink it right away. At least tomorrow, in the early hours of the day, it would be cooler. He burst out in nervous laughter at that idea.

No, he would not abandon the game. He could not die in such a grotesque, embarrassing fashion. He tried constantly to think about his work, in an attempt to chase away the thoughts of his present situation, but it didn't help. His mind always came back to the previous days and above all, to the old man.

He had indeed played a dirty trick on them. Who could know why?

Patience. All he had brought were problems, but one day the old man would certainly pay for all that.

He thought he heard the purring of an engine approaching. He kneeled down on the boat. He feared it might be another hallucination. Absolutely not. Leaving a double wake of white foam behind, a big cabin cruiser was coming directly toward the Zodiac. The hull had a bizarre blue color. On the prow, painted with big letters, David read, 'Poseidon'. He stood up and started laughing and waving his arms frenetically.

***

The heat of the sun on the back of his neck finally woke Jonathan up. He had slept on his belly, with one side of his face on the ground, something that he usually never did. He turned around and sat down. The sea in front of him was blue, flat and beautiful and the sun was already way up in the sky.

He remembered the events of the night. It had not been a dream, but he couldn't find any explanation. He thought of the berries he had eaten. They had certainly seemed identical to those that the local fishermen ate, but he could have made a mistake. Those berries must be harmful; they must contain some hallucinogenic substance, just like certain mushrooms. Reassured, he decided to go back to diving. He felt in perfect physical shape again. He spent all that second day in the water.

The sea bottom seemed very ordinary, except for a long and deep rift in the south part of the reef, which sank deep into the great depths. He promised himself he would explore it using the last air tanks he had.

One more time, he had two huge crayfishes for dinner and smiled at the idea that he should end up hating that white flesh if he kept that diet for much longer. Again the same shivering and trembling took him. The suddenness of the attack surprised him and he tried with all his forces to resist the invasion of the delirium. With his eyes racked by the dazzling streaks in the sky and his ears tortured by the clamors and howls, he slumped down.

***

To his great surprise, he woke up the next morning in good shape, as if nothing had happened. Again, he went over the circumstances of the previous night, thinking about what he might have eaten, drunk, touched or breathed. There must be a microbe or a virus on that island that provoked those sudden fits of fever, somewhat like malaria or maybe even worse.

He decided he wouldn't eat anything more other than the rest of the provisions from the Barracuda. There was certainly nothing there that could give him indigestion, and at least he would eat safely.

To keep his mind busy, he resumed his searches around the island. He visited the hiding place. Nothing had been moved and he felt reassured.

Back to the camp, looking at his double-tank outfit, he thought of the rift he had found on the reef the day before.

He put on his neoprene wetsuit, attached his dive knife to his calf, fastened his belt and then, grabbing his speargun, more to protect himself than to fish, he carried his tanks to the edge of the water, where he sat down. He spat on the glass of his mask, adjusted the fins to his feet, checked his regulator one last time and then put on the tanks. He let himself glide into the wonderful crystalline waters, and forgot all his troubles. To save air, he swam on the surface, breathing through his snorkel.

As always, the contact with the water stung him, bringing him an intense joy of life nothing on the ground could hold a candle to.

He spent some time observing the sand along the way, before he arrived at the place he had found. He was looking for traces of a recent anchoring. Except for the furrows made by the Barracuda and the tracks left behind by passing sea stars and holothurians, he didn't see anything special.

Once he arrived at the spot, he was impressed with the clear-cut sharp opening through the exterior slope of the coral wall that disappeared into the Big Blue*. He entered it.

With their pointed teeth, violently colored snappers and grunts were grazing amidst the immense ochre or mauve gorgonians that covered the flanks of that corridor. At his approach, hundreds of little orange groupers sought refuge in the arms of acrapora colonies or the long velvety tentacles of the hydroids along the corridor's internal walls.

Disturbed actinia and tubicolous worms retracted with a sudden movement, just to spread out again, once the calm returned.

With a furtive and powerful stroke of its fins, the enormous mass of a grouper dashed in front of him.

Jonathan followed the fish as it went deeper into the tunnel. He hesitated for a brief moment, because he didn't have his depth gauge. He lifted his head toward the surface. Way up there, his frosted mirror was shining. He estimated that he was already about 100 feet deep.

He kept going deeper. The passage was too perfect, too regular. That vertical canyon didn't seem natural. Nevertheless, the thickness of the coral layer witnessed to its antiquity.

Its internal walls were pierced by a multitude of holes and crevices. Countless hosts such as crayfishes and spotted moray eels huddled up in them. Almost invisible and feigning indifference, scorpionfishes, their bodies spiked with poisonous stingers and bulging eyes, watched Jonathan as he passed by.

He finally reached the sand, stretching out in its impressive solitude. For the first time since he started diving, Jonathan experienced an unusual sensation of hostility. In the distance, dark spindles swam away and disappeared into the indigo blue — sharks. It would have been better to stay alongside the walls as he went back up, instead of in the middle of the water. But he yielded to his curiosity and decided to explore the bottom, as he had initially intended to do. When he approached the sand, he saw the perfectly shaped arch of a gapping entrance to an imposing submarine cave a little further ahead. As he was moving toward it, he heard a sound. Astonished, he stopped on his

* Big Blue: an imprecise zone in which the light of the sun confounds itself with the blue of the great depths.

tracks. A continuous whistling seemed to coming from inside the cave. The memory of the two orange devices they had seen after leaving Lucaya came back to his mind. The sound was identical. All of a sudden, it increased in scale. It filled up his head and everything became distorted in front of his eyes. The curtain of small richly colored fishes, which had been floating quietly, suddenly seemed to be caught in a crazy and wild fandango. In a desperate reaction, Jonathan struggled with all his might to escape the whirlpool in which he felt caught. With an instinctive movement, he released his weight belt and realized that it had freed him from the grip. He swam upward, kicking his fins with all his strength. A few feet from the surface, his reflexes told him that he should make a stop.

The minutes passed by with Jonathan in a state of half torpor. The moment the air began to fail him, he moved on to the reserve. It was empty. Without panicking, he waited until the last breath and released his tanks. After having completely emptied his lungs, he pushed himself up like an arrow. Piercing the surface, he cried out in relief.

The sight of the bright sun and the blue sky gave him the strength to swim to the shore. He crawled onto the sand and, leaning against a rock, he tried to get up, as his whole universe collapsed.

CHAPTER 23

In the thick mist, the Santa Isabella was agonizing on a slack sea becalmed for several days. On the prow, the bowsprit stretched out its wooden stump. After the fall of the foremast, the upper deck was nothing but a tangle of broken yards, torn up sails and mingled shrouds.

Since the terrible and sudden storm of the hurricane, the heavy galley was dying slowly, stricken by a strange and pernicious fever.

Furtive shadows were still circulating on the deck, among the rotting bodies of passengers, members of the crew and slaves, all stricken by the epidemic. The potbellied hull was taking on water everywhere and the last sailors sent down to maneuver the heavy pumps in the bilge had long since collapsed. Carried by the currents, the ship was drifting toward the reefs and shallow waters. From the barrel at the end of the stem, the watchman had detected them with his sounding pole and threw himself into the water with a last cry.

Unable to explain it, lucid and with all his senses alive, Jonathan watched the scene from the past that was taking place in the present, right there in front of his eyes.

With a series of cracking noises and sinister bursting sounds, the ship hit the coral outcrop. In the roaring sound of planks being torn off and desperate screams and prayers, voices yelled orders in Spanish. Giggles and incomprehensible singing dominated the racket. The same singing he had heard on the island.

A whirlpool of enraged water opened in front of the wrecked ship, taking into it pieces of wood and, corpses, and wreckage, and all kinds of debris. The Santa Isabella was being inexorably drained and then dragged down into the abyss of the swirling currents.

Jonathan felt that it caught hold of him. He struggled to free himself. The movement was accelerating insidiously. Desperately, he tried to swim and run away from that deadly spiral. He was beginning to suffo-

cate. He was going to drown and disappear with all those damned people. Far away, very far away in his memory, he saw again Jerry's face.
David had guessed it. He should have listened to him — the old man
was damned.

***

"Hey, Jon!"

Jonathan lifted his torso with difficulty, leaning onto one elbow. He
passed one hand on his forehead.

David was right there and he was smiling at him.

"David… Dave… You came back."

"Of course. And I'm not alone."

The strong and a slightly strident voice hurt his ears. He lifted up
slightly. Linda! She was really there, standing in front of him. He instantly noticed her ultra short shorts. The sudden appearance of her long
legs naked up to the top of the thighs awakened him completely.

"Jon… Poor Jon!"

She still had that throaty, warm and sensuous voice. He struggled
against the dizziness and managed to get back on his feet.

Slightly behind them, a huge bearded guy was staring at him. He
stood solidly on his feet with his legs slightly apart, resting his hands on
his thighs. A hint of a smile appeared between the deep wrinkles on his
face.

"This is Mark. He fished me out and he also brought us here."

David's voice reached him in a fog of sounds and impressions. The
man made a slight movement with his head and Jon returned it.

"I had fever, a very high fever and I was delirious."

"Poor Jon," repeated Linda, as she held him by one arm. "I… we'll
get you back in shape." She pressed her body against his to better sup-
port him. Instead of suffocating him as usual, her perfume gave him a
new energy.

He tried to take a few steps, but staggered. The other two rushed
to hold him. It was then that he suddenly became aware of the powerful mass and the strength of the newcomer. The man had grabbed him
by the wrist and he could feel the stranglehold of his hand.

"It's okay."

Jonathan looked at his dive watch. It had stopped.

"What day is it?" he asked.

"It's the 24th," answered David. "I left you on the 16th."

Jonathan shook his head slowly. He had been in that comatose state for at least five days. He started to tell them what had happened to him, but David interrupted him immediately.

"Don't get excited, Frenchy. We're going onboard. A good cup of coffee will be good for you."

***

"Welcome to the Poseidon, Mr. Larue."

Jonathan was startled. That giant knew his name! In itself, that might not be anything surprising, since the others must have told him. But in that ceremonious manner! He didn't like that. And, thinking about it, he didn't like the guy either. He sized the man up. At least 6 and a half feet tall! The short-sleeved polo shirt revealed biceps that suggested strength dangerously above the average. He seemed self-confident and rich, judging by the way he was dressed. Anyway, he was a disturbing character. All of a sudden, Jonathan wondered if the man wouldn't be the final obstacle that he always feared, the test that was reserved for him by a malignant fate that had never until now made him the slightest concession.

***

Aboard the yacht, fully equipped for no-kill fishing zones, everything suggested richness and affluence. In the lounge, richly decorated with leather and mahogany, Jonathan was eating a hearty breakfast Linda had prepared for him. He was enjoying his bacon and eggs and buttered toast, while they exchanged details about their mutual adventures.

David explained how he had lost all hope of escaping a terrible death by starvation, when the Poseidon appeared all of a sudden, as if by magic. Jonathan glanced at the giant, who was faintly smiling.

"I had already seen you a long time before that," the man said.

"But I had noticed absolutely nothing."

David turned toward Jon and continued.

"Mark is originally from Greece."

"Crete."

"Yes. That's what I meant. He is a ship-owner and he is now living in Miami. He has two passions: fishing in no-kill fishing zones and his collection of marine antiquities. By the way, do you see this?" David pointed to a polychrome fresco representing two playful dolphins. "That's real, it's not fake!"

Some trigger in his subconscious alerted Jonathan.

He stopped chewing.

"Are you a shipwreck hunter, by any chance?"

"Shipwrecks? No."

"A treasure hunter, if you prefer."

"I don't know what you're trying to say. All the objects of the sea are valuable to me. They can be made of gold or made of lead."

The giant was openly taunting him.

Aware of the spontaneous hostility between the two men, Linda intervened.

"Come on, Mark… Jon's still too tired. This is not the time to tease him with your subtleties."

She leaned toward the Cretan and Jonathan thought he saw a look of complicity between them. She must be sleeping with him. He was certain of that. He could read a girl's eyes as from a book and he knew Linda's eyes by heart.

David's voice pulled him out of his animosity.

"What about you, Frenchy? Give us some more detail."

Jonathan shook himself. He must regain control of his nerves. He told them about the circumstances that preceded his fever and elaborated on the noises and sensations that had assailed him for two consecutive nights. When he started telling them about his last dive to the cave, and about how he saw the catastrophe happening all over again, he noticed the condescending smile on the Cretan's face.

"You were imprudent, Mr. Larue. That's a classic case of nitrogen narcosis."

He turned to David and then Linda, who was drinking in his words.

"Or the 'rapture of the deep' if you prefer. You should never have gone that deep in such a state!"

Jonathan interrupted him.

"That deep! How do you know about that?"

"It was a simple supposition."

Jonathan shut up, but he didn't stop staring at the man. He was certain he had noticed a glint of amused scorn in his eyes. 'This is really a dangerous man...' he thought.

An idea germinated in his mind. It was certainly not by chance that the man and his boat were in those same waters at such a favorable time.

CHAPTER 24

The dinghy was moving toward the island, leaving behind the Poseidon.

"Do you really like that guy?" asked Jonathan.

"Why not? He is very well known in Miami. He's very rich. He is a ship-owner and he also builds boats. They say he has more money than Onassis himself."

"He doesn't impress me."

"You've always been distrustful, haven't you, Frenchy?"

"If you like… Do you leave him alone with Linda?"

David smiled in a strange way.

"No, nothing… I was just thinking…" Jonathan said.

"You think the wrong way, old friend. It was either this or nothing at all. Besides, I don't see how we would have managed, you and me, to make it back to the hiding place alone. The missus must serve for something every now and then. He would never have let go of us if I hadn't left Lindy behind."

Jonathan looked at his friend.

"You've changed a lot, David."

"Yeah. I've learned a lot from you. And not the best things!"

They burst out in laughter. They felt united by their complicity. They ran the distance that separated them from their hiding place and entered the dark hole hastily.

This time, the blow was too hard; the treasure was gone!

The two men came out livid, despite their tanned skin. Petrified, without saying a word, they looked for some trace that might enlighten them. They had to yield to the facts — it was unbelievable. They had been taken in.

The fabulous richness that they had gathered had vanished. Under the flashlights, the ground in their hiding place looked exactly the same as it did before they had dug a hole. It had all its little stones, shells, and twigs and leaves blown in by the wind.

"This is witchcraft! This is an evil spell!" David was stammering.

They looked at each other without understanding it. They didn't dare to understand it. David moved back, trying to approach a rifle that was jutting out above the piece of canvas that had served them as a tent.

"Jon! You're a true son of a bitch! I already suspected that. I've always suspected that you were scheming with your dirty kraut friend!"

Jonathan got up and stood in his way.

"Don't be a fool, David. You're crazy! I have nothing to do with this. How could I have done it in the state I was in? Besides, I could say the same thing about you."

They searched the whole island thoroughly, but it was in vain. Either the job had been done with unbelievable refinement or it was something unnatural. After having made a complete tour of the island, they found themselves back on the little beach, feeling ridiculous and helpless.

"Christ! Christ!" Jonathan repeated in a low voice.

He was opening and closing his fists, playing with his muscles under the white T-shirt.

"If it was Jerry, I'll find him sooner or later and I'll bump him off."

Nevertheless, he was convinced it had not been him. Just like them, the old man had been a victim of that immense and inexplicable farce.

As their last resource, they decided to dive into the site of their discovery. Nothing there showed any signs of their recent and feverish activity. All the holes and trenches dug with the hose had disappeared. Even the coral was intact. It was as if nothing had ever happened! As if they had just had a bad dream. The same bad dream, all three of them!

***

Waiting for them on the gangway, Linda saw their faces and she understood right away that something was very wrong. In their cabin, David gave her a quick update and she stormed at him with sarcasm and insults. Jonathan's arrival put a stop to the storm. He encouraged them to calm down, begging them to consider only the facts. The loot had disappeared. Although that was completely inexplicable, considering the perfection of the camouflage, he refused to see it as anything other than human intervention. Seething with anger, they agreed on the attitude to adopt so as to not betray themselves in front of their host.

"Let's go back to Miami," said Jonathan. "It's not over yet. We can come back and continue our search. There's certainly still a lot to be brought out. Besides, one disc is still missing. By itself, it represents a fortune. You must remember, Dave, Jerry affirmed that there must be still another one somewhere."

David interrupted him brutally.

"How can you speak about that bastard? Don't you see that he is the source of all our problems?"

With a forced smile on his lips, Jonathan turned to Linda to call her as a witness. Before he could say a word, she turned her back on him.

"Shut up! I feel sorry for you!" she spat.

He grew pale with the insult and brutally grabbed her by the arm, intending to slap her in the face. Somebody knocked on the cabin door. The door opened and the impressive mass of the Poseidon's owner appeared in the doorway. He was smiling.

"If everybody is ready, we're going to weigh anchor," he said nonchalantly.

***

The day promised to be blazing. The radiant sun penetrated the turquoise waters. Very soon, the green crown of Guinchos Cay would become a blurred spot behind them on the port side.

The three men were gathered together on the bridge.

Linda retired to the back of the boat. Moved by who knows what feminine intuition, she preferred to isolate herself on the quarterdeck, where she was perfecting her tan.

David lit up a cigar. He was sitting in the best armchair. Leaning over the chart table, Jonathan was studying the route back. The Cretan was at the helm. His bass voice broke the silence that had dominated the bridge for a while.

"I'm setting the automatic pilot. Would you mind taking a look every now and then?"

Jonathan muttered a vague word of acquiescence. The lever was engaged with a sharp cracking sound.

The tall silhouette of their host had almost disappeared down the three steps leading to the cabins, when Jonathan's voice stopped him on his tracks.

"Mark. I'm sorry… But I have a question I want to ask you."

David lifted his eyes. Jonathan's glacial tone, which he had learned to know so well, didn't portend anything good."

"Yes… Please?"

"That object over there. Where did you find it?"

"Oh, that!""

In a stride, he climbed up the stairs again and joined Jonathan. David got up hastily.

Jonathan was holding a small pendant in his hand. He was shaking it and the metal shimmered with the colors of the rainbow.

On the flat varnished wooden edge that ran along the windowsills on the bridge, the little case where Jonathan had found it was open. Inside the lid, a plaque had a name engraved on it: Giorgios Markan-takis.

"Yes, that, as you say it!"

Jonathan handed the jewel to David.

"Look well, Dave, doesn't it ring a bell?"

David grabbed it. He noticed right away the double spiral finely engraved on one side and the curious motif formed by two dolphins head to tail. That was exactly the pendant the old man had so often told them about.

"It looks exactly like our orichalc piece," he said. His voice was trembling slightly. He turned to his rescuer.

"Mark, this is really curious. Our skipper, the one that disappeared with my boat, he described to us a pendant exactly like this one. Not just once, he spoke of it at least fifty times. He always wore it on a chain around his neck. But it was somehow stolen from him neverthe-less. He was sleeping in a hotel room with his door locked from inside. When he woke up in the morning, he didn't have it anymore."

"Yes! Exactly!" Jonathan made a big step to move away from the partition. The two men were staring right into each other's eyes now.

"And according to him, it was an exceptional piece. Unique even."

"Exactly!"

"Exactly! What do you know about it?"

Jonathan glanced briefly at David, who responded by coming closer to him.

The big Cretan man straightened up his torso. He crossed his arms, highlighting even more his gnarled biceps. Behind his thick beard and the thick arches of his eyebrows, a glint of amusement shone deep in his eyes.

"I'm going to surprise you," he said. "I know this piece in its slightest detail. For the good reason that it belongs to me. In fact, your friend stole it from me."

"Really? So it is the same pendant!" said Jonathan.

The young man made a short sign to David, telling him to be alert.

"Everything has become clear now, don't you think, David? Jerry and your chance rescuer know each other. And they have known each other for a long time! Isn't that so, Mr. Markantakis?"

"If you are speaking of Kapitänleutnant Kurt Müller, aka Herman Schmidt, aka Peter Braun, aka Jerry, of course I know him. And much better than he could ever suspect."

He was laughing boldly now, as if he'd heard a really good joke.

"Unfortunately, he always had a very serious flaw that cost him a lot. He was too curious!"

Jonathan interrupted him with spiteful anger.

"What do you mean? What's this game you're playing? Is Captain Müller dead or alive?"

Silently, with all his impressive mass, their host made a few steps away from Jonathan and toward the wide open door. He seemed to be thinking for a moment, looking far away at the sea. Then he did an abrupt about face. With his hands in his pockets, he looked at them calmly.

"You'd very much like to know. Well, let's say he's somewhere else."

"He thinks we're idiots."

Jonathan was furious. Either Jerry was still alive and those two were playing some trick on him or this bastard killed Jerry and kept everything for himself. In either case, he wouldn't get by just like that. He must speak! And right away! As if he had read his mind, the man started speaking again.

"Luckily, there are levels of knowledge that are forbidden to you, the uninitiated. Destructive curiosity and cupidity rule your small world. I had warned Müller many years ago, just as I'm warning you now."

"Don't waste your energy on sermons. You remind me of Jerry. I recognize a crook when I see one. Dave! We don't have to look any further! He's our robber!"

Jonathan didn't stop staring at his opponent's eyes. Tight and vigilant, the man had lost all signs of his good-naturedness.

The young man moved forward imperceptibly. He would be the first to attack, before the giant had any chance to prepare.

He could not accomplish his plan. With a quick movement, the man took a short barrel revolver out of his pocket. He aimed it toward the two men.

"Slow, don't make any stupid movements. In any case, you would not be a match for me."

He stepped back to better cover both of them.

"It's you who have to give me some explanation. You came here to loot shamelessly, to grab ancient riches with impunity. You are bold and audacious, just like all the other ones! But I was there, all the time. In Müller's shadow and then in yours."

He shifted the aim of the Smith and Wesson between David and Jonathan.

"The Sea will remain intact. Woe to those who touch it! To all the wretched wreck looters, woe to all the technocrats and scientists who are ready to sacrifice it in the name of a pseudo-conquest of its riches and its resources! The sea is our last sacred space. It's the original matrix of us all. The end of such vermin is near, very near…"

He could not continue.

Jonathan made a dazzling spin, kicking his leg with all the strength he could muster. He hit the giant with a powerful blow direct to the solar plexus. Markantakis was thrown against the rail, the seasoned wood splintering under his weight.

Both Jonathan and David threw themselves onto the man. Their momentum was so great that they broke the railing and all three men tumbled into the ocean.

David was the first to go. As he fell, his head caught the edge of a shrouded spar. Within instants, the ocean, cold or warm, no longer mattered to him.

Jonathan was fighting desperately on the surface, trying to free himself from Markantakis' powerful grip. He was strangling. A dark veil descended upon his consciousness. Moments before his death, he whispered faintly:

"Who are you?"

"I am the last of the Ten Kings of the Sea."

These words reached him clearly, although they seemed to come from a distance...

Markantakis watched the Poseidon as it continued its way toward the horizon. He was not at all concerned. Neither Dave nor Jonathan ever returned to the surface.

***

Linda was wondering why none of the men had come back on deck yet. Two hours had passed since she had lain down in the sun.

She decided that it was time to reappear on the bridge. With a gracious movement, she stood back up on her feet. In front of the cockpit, she put her head through one of the portholes. The cockpit was empty.

Astonished, looking at the helm, she called David.

With no answer after many attempts, Linda became impatient. This joke was really stupid. If they wanted to scare her, she would not give them the pleasure. She went back onto the deck and leaned over the guardrail. The wind was playing with the long locks of her blazing mane.

Her initial amazement finally turned into irritation. It was really ridiculous to see three adult men playing like kids.

Ten minutes later, she was taken by a panicky fear. Linda had looked everywhere. She had searched every nook and cranny, including the engine room.

Back in the cockpit, feverish, she was overcome by a sudden idea. With a sharp movement, she closed the throttle. As the engine stopped so suddenly, the Poseidon took a nosedive into the water. The trembling that took over the entire boat forced Linda to grab onto the helm. If it were really a joke, they would rush into the cockpit to turn the engine on again.

But nobody came. Panic-stricken, she started a second frantic search of the boat, which didn't bring any further results. Linda went back to the big lounge. Her lips were trembling and she was crying.

She started yelling the names of the three men. Dozens of times. Her voice became more and more piercing.

In the grip of a nervous attack, laughing and crying hysterically, she finally collapsed outside, on the teak deck, definitely unconscious.

EPILOGUE

Crete, Fall 1973

It was still hot on a beautiful day in mid-November, and the generous sun soaked the walls of the old Venetian fortress and the ancient picturesque port of Herakleion with its burning rays.

All the rustic and modest tables, chairs and stools spread out in pleasant disorder facing the wharf were occupied by the gesticulating and noisy usual midday customers.

Rocking himself nonchalantly on one of the chairs with his hands behind his head, a huge man was stretching himself. His eyes seemed to be floating beyond the agitation and the idle onlookers. For a moment, he contemplated his shoes and then, stretching his long legs, he put one foot on top of the other. Almost without moving, he turned his bearded face toward the back of the establishment.

"Will you find me a shoeshine boy, Zé?"

A man came out from behind the counter, a clean dishtowel on one shoulder. Short and stocky, age had already made its mark on him. His face was covered with deep wrinkles and showed the signs of many long years spent out on the sea.

"I have your mail, Giorgios. It's all from the U.S."

"I imagine they don't call you Zé very often around here. By the way, how long has it been since you came back to Crete?"

"It will soon be 30 years since I left Marseilles… I thought I had already told you that. And you, Giorgios, where did you go after that unforgettable night? All this time and you haven't changed at all! That's extraordinary! You seem to be still the same age. Have you made a pact with the Devil by any chance?"

A note of deference and, at the same time, of slight concern pierced the man's voice.

"With the Devil? No!"

The giant stared at the man. Despite his thick beard and his tough features, Giorgios' face showed deep affection.

"Zé... It is not time that passes — it's men. And not always in the same manner."

Giorgios focused deeply on reading the newspapers he had just received, as a shoeshine boy was just beginning to work on his shoes.

He went through the headlines quickly, until his attention was caught by one of them, spread out on three columns in the Miami Herald.

He started reading and a glint of amusement shone in his eyes.

New mysterious disappearances in the Bermuda Triangle

On October 28, a Coast Guard patrol boat found the yacht Poseidon drifting in the Gulf Stream. There was only one person aboard. At a Miami hospital where she had been taken in a serious state of shock, Mrs. Linda Klein told a very strange story.

According to her, there should have been three other passengers on board: the boat's owner, Mr. Mark Antakis, an enigmatic Greek shipbuilder residing temporarily in Florida and searched for by Interpol, Mr. David Klein, her husband, a famous TV producer in Miami, and the Louisianian Jonathan Larue, an underwater dive specialist.

None of them have been found yet, but a preliminary investigation has revealed certain facts. Mr. Larue and Mr. Klein had left the month before on Mr. Klein's boat, piloted by a certain Captain Kurt Müller, for a cruise to the Bahamas.

In Mrs. Klein's own words, Mr. Müller allegedly took hold of the boat and abandoned his two travel companions on an islet north of Cuba.

It was decided that only one of the two castaways, Mr. Klein, would leave the islet in the dinghy to go look for help.

Two days later, adrift at sea, he was rescued by Mr. Antakis, who brought him onto his yacht. Mr. Antakis was actually on his way to Miami, where he was going to get provisions for his yacht. There, Mrs. Klein joined the group and they left immediately to rescue Mr. Larue. They found him alone and in a critical state on the islet.

The group lifted anchor toward Florida and it was during the trip back that, waking from a long siesta, Mrs. Klein realized that the three men were no longer on board.

Meanwhile, we become lost in conjecture regarding the circumstances and the reasons for this quadruple disappearance in two chapters.

"Sic transit," whispered the giant.

His face became serious.

"Zé," he called with a strong voice. "Bring us a bottle of retsina! The best one you have. We'll toast with Kurt."

Faithful to the appointment made on Guinchos Cay, the former Kapitän Müller was standing there. A little stiff in his shirt and khakis, an approving smile illuminated the old sea wolf's craggy face.

His eyes fell on Giorgio and the little shoeshine boy.

"How much do I owe you, son?" asked Giorgio.

He took a handful of coins out of his pocket. In this huge cupped hand, amidst the small change, there was a little shimmering object. The boy grabbed it.

"What's this, mister?"

Looking at the dolphins on the medal, the boy asked:

"Is this a souvenir? Can I keep it?"

Lifting one foot and then the other to appreciate the boy's work, the impressive customer remained silent for a moment. Then he got up very slowly. The boy was squatting next to his box, anxiously waiting for an answer.

"Take it!" said the giant. "May it bring you good luck!"

He laughed for a moment and winked at Kurt.

"It's not worth anything anyway. It's only made of orichalc."

APPENDIX

Preface to the Japanese edition

We would like to share with our readers our passion for what seems to us to be the true History of Man — that is to say, authentic man — *homo sapiens sapiens.*

It is our opinion that the world of "civilization" is much older than historians would have us believe. The classic conception of Pre-History is a web of nonsense that arises from the irrational postulate that the evolution of Life from a single cell produced the incredible complexity of the brain of Modern Man in a ridiculously brief time. This theory professes that the History of Man — the history of *homo sapiens sapiens* with all its intelligence, the history of people just like you and me — begins no more than 50,000 or 60,000 years ago, at which time he would have made a sudden, unexplained and inexplicable appearance on the face of the planet. It places the first civilizations no more than six or seven thousand years ago after a very long period of faltering steps and an endless Stone Age.

According to the Traditions, sacred texts and teachings of all the sages East and West, and all the religions, the History of Humanity covers an immense length of time. For these ancient Traditions, the Golden Age preceded all other ages and a primordial common Sacred Science was the true origin of all human knowledge. This is the only rational explanation for the enigmatic and timeless ruins and artifacts scattered all over the Earth, the antiquity and perfection of which our strictly materialistic scientists strive at all cost to diminish.

All the religions refer to a cataclysmic deluge, and the entire scientific community admits to a sudden global warming ten to twenty thousand years ago, which melted the ice sheets and the polar glaciers, and submerged considerable stretches of land. As the sea level rose inexorably, all that had been established and built until then disappeared under the sea leaving only enigmas.

Enigmas such as the colossal walls in the Peruvian Andes, and the three pyramids of Giza, to mention two classical examples of impossibly sophisticated ancient engineering, the nature of which remains inexplicable. According to the teachings of our Classic Pre-Historians, it would have been completely impossible for their supposed builders to build them given the rudimentary level of knowledge available to them in the Classical model.

Beyond all the unsuccessful attempts to explain it away, and despite the wear and tear of thousands of years, there remains the Myth, indestructible in its legend: Atlantis.

In the summer of 1968, Jacques found himself in the middle of the Atlantis "environment". He joined Dr. Manson Valentine and his team of divers and researchers in Florida. With them, he would be responsible for a multitude of discoveries, most notably the very controversial Wall of Bimini on the Bahamas plateau. Today, more than 20 years later, there is no more doubt in his mind that the Bahamas plateau, submerged dozens of thousands of years ago, was the link between Atlantis and the future and opulent pre-Colombian civilizations which would explode in Central and South America, the origins of which History has had a very hard time determining.

Pierre's conviction is based on dry ground, or better yet, on the "underground". It joins perfectly with Jacques's argument, giving evidence of the very distant past of human civilization. Pierre presents fantastic and irrefutable evidence of the intellectual activity of our distant and sole direct ancestors, with whom nobody in our scientific intelligentsia had ever thought of establishing a connection!

Pierre speaks of the Parietal Art — the so-called, with a bit of condescendence, Art of the Caves — which is in fact absolute evidence of the presence in very remote antiquity of the intelligence and technical skills of the Ancients.

The recent discovery of the underwater Cosquer Cave and the extraordinary Chauvet Cave in the Cevennes mountains in France are still more proof that the beauty and precision of that Animal Art, which is more than 30 thousand years old, could not have appeared in an ecosystem as hostile to intellectual expression as the European tundra in the middle of the Würms glaciation.

Well before these two discoveries, Pierre had conducted some daring research on the famous Lascaux Caves, especially on the marvelous Hall of the Bulls. Those grandiose animal frescoes, painted with morphological precision (without a visible model, since they're located in the bottom of a cave, and in the dark) and remarkable esthetic sense, are the evidence of a genius (the word here is not too strong) and above all a true artistic tradition. They are clearly the work of extremely talented men who inevitably came from elsewhere.

Those Paleolithic artists, the Cro-Magnon men, were very tall, averaging a little over 6 feet tall, and their bone structure, their muscles and their cranial capacity were bigger than those of modern man (Museum of Man, in Paris). They completely shook off the "status" of cavemen into which our classical Pre-Historians still take so much pleasure in confining them!

There is no doubt that following a cataclysm, some forty or fifty thousand years ago, they were forced to leave their own ecosystem and take refuge on the European continent, still mostly covered by glaciers, and to adapt to it with all their sense of survival and the knowledge developed under more lenient skies.

There is also no doubt that the concentration of those caves in Southwestern France, Atlantic Spain, the Atlantic coast of Europe and, later on, the enigmatic megalithic civilization — Carnac and Stonehenge — would tend to corroborate the Atlantic origin of the European civilization.

JACQUES AND PIERRE MAYOL

INDEX

FINITO DI STAMPARE NEL MESE DI GENNAIO MMIII
NELLO STABILIMENTO «ARTE TIPOGRAFICA» S.A.S.
S. BIAGIO DEI LIBRAI - NAPOLI
PER CONTO DELLA IDELSON-GNOCCHI S.R.L.

NEW PROVIDENCE

East

Nassau

Old Fort Point
Simms Point
Clifton Point
Clifton Bluff
Goulding Cay
WATER TANK
AERO R Bn
Southwest Bay
Fleeming Point
Cay Point
Conch Rocks

Wd
Wd
Southwest Reef
Conch Spit
Wd
Wd
Wd

Wax Cut
Bat Cay
Saddleback Cay
Calabash Cay
(5) Pigeon Cays
Staniard Rock
Fl 4s 5m 6M
FR 8m 6M
Staniard Creek

VAR 4°33'W (1985)
ANNUAL CHANGE 9'W

OS ISLAND

Haines Channel
Hard Bargain
Coakley Town
Andros Town
AERO
Al Fl WGY
Iso 5s 10m

Plum Cays
High Cay
Fl 4s 21m 5M
Mastic Cay
Pear Cay
Green Cay
Kits Cay
Sugar Rock
Bristol Galley
Cargill Creek
Salvador Point
Behring Point

Swamp

Northern Bight
Red Shank Cay
Wooded
Pot Cay
Big Wood Cay
Pine Cay
Gibson Cay
Fl 4s
Fl 5s 5m 7M
(1) Middle Bight Cay
Reids Cay
Moxey Town
Bight
Mangrove Cay

TONGUE OF THE

SEE PLAN

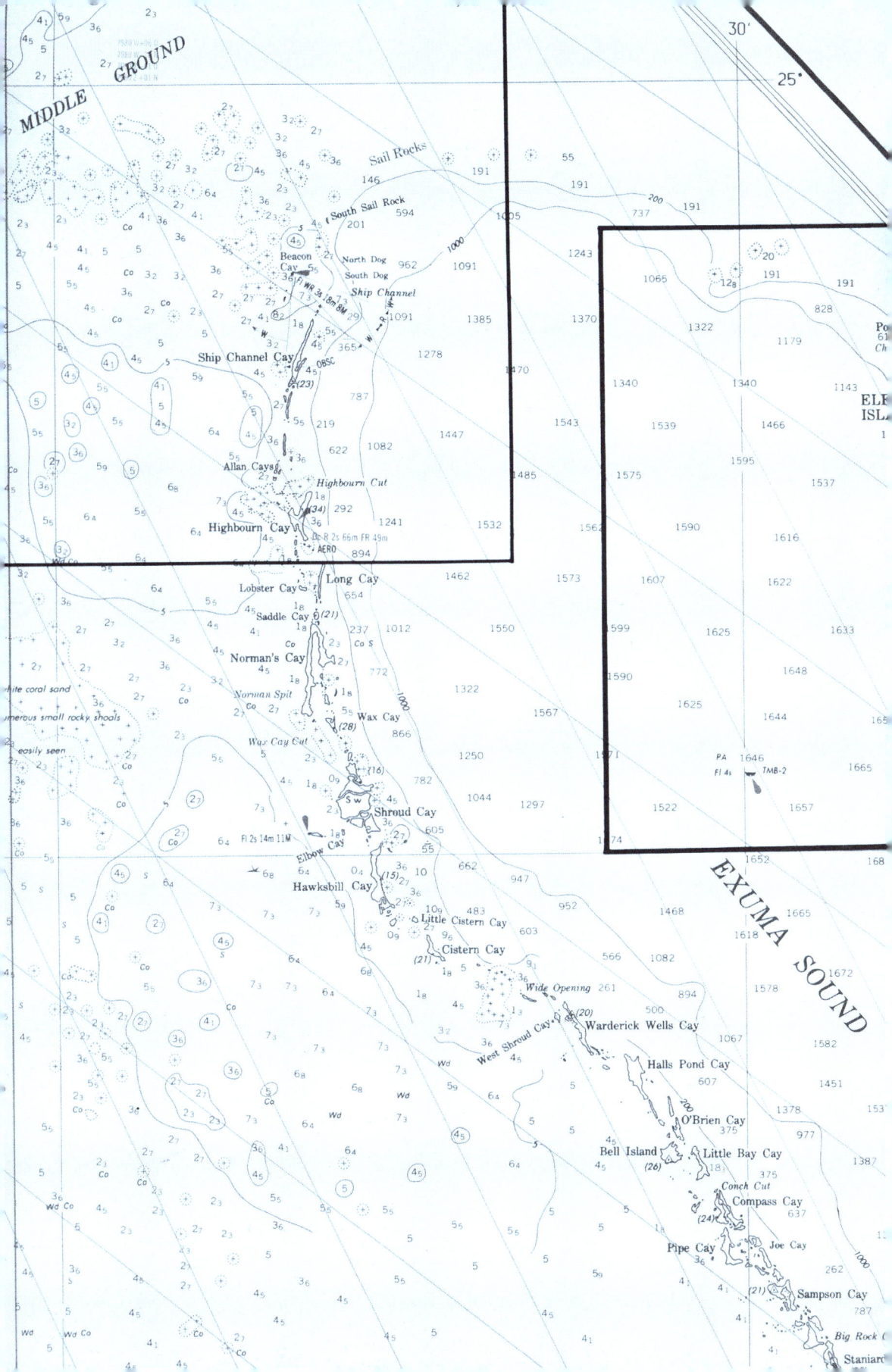

MIDDLE GROUND

Sail Rocks

South Sail Rock

North Dog
South Dog
Ship Channel

Beacon Cay

Ship Channel Cay

OBSC (23)

Allan Cays

Highbourn Cut
(34) 292

Highbourn Cay
Oc 8 2s 66m FR 49m
AERO

Lobster Cay
Long Cay
Saddle Cay (21)
Co S
Norman's Cay

Norman Spit
Co
Wax Cay
(28)
Wax Cay Cut

(16)
S W
Shroud Cay
Elbow Cay
Fl 2s 14m 11M
Hawksbill Cay
(15)
Little Cistern Cay
Cistern Cay
(21)
Wide Opening 261
West Shroud Cay (20)
Warderick Wells Cay
Halls Pond Cay
O'Brien Cay
Bell Island
(26)
Little Bay Cay
Conch Cut
Compass Cay
(24)
Pipe Cay
Joe Cay
(21)
Sampson Cay
Big Rock
Staniard

EXUMA SOUND

ELEUTHERA
ISLAND

white coral sand
numerous small rocky shoals
easily seen

PA 1646
Fl 4s   TMB-2